HAMMER OF THE DOGS

A NOVEL

JARRET KEENE

UNIVERSITY OF NEVADA PRESS | *Reno & Las Vegas*

University of Nevada Press | Reno, Nevada 89557 USA
www.unpress.nevada.edu
Copyright © 2023 by University of Nevada Press
All rights reserved
Manufactured in the United States of America

FIRST PRINTING

Cover design by David Ter-Avanesyan/Ter33Design
Cover illustration by Claudio Bergamin
Map illustration © Tiffany Pereira

LIBRARY OF CONGRESS CATALOGING-IN-PUBLICATION DATA
Names: Keene, Jarret, 1973– author.
Title: Hammer of the dogs : a novel / Jarret Keene.
Description: Reno : University of Nevada Press, [2023] |
Summary: "Set in the wasteland of post-apocalyptic Las Vegas, *Hammer of the Dogs* is a literary
    dystopian adventure starring 21-year-old Lash. With her high-tech skill set and warrior mentality,
    Lash helps to shield the Las Vegas valley's survivors and protect her younger classmates at a
    paramilitary school holed up in Luxor on the Las Vegas Strip. After graduation, she'll be alone
    in fending off the deadly intentions/desires of the school's most powerful opponents. When
    she's captured by the enemy warlord, she's surprised by two revelations: He's not the monster her
    headmaster wants her to believe he is and the one thing she can't safeguard is her own heart."—
    Provided by publisher.
Identifiers: LCCN 2023004280 | ISBN 9781647791278 (paperback) | ISBN 9781647791285 (ebook)
Subjects: LCGFT: Dystopian fiction. | Novels.
Classification: LCC PS3611.E34 H36 2023 | DDC 813/.6—dc23/eng/20230414
LC record available at https://lccn.loc.gov/2023004280

The paper used in this book meets the requirements of American National Standard for Information
Sciences—Permanence of Paper for Printed Library Materials, ANSI/NISO Z39.48–1992 (R2002).

for Jack Kirby

HAMMER OF THE DOGS

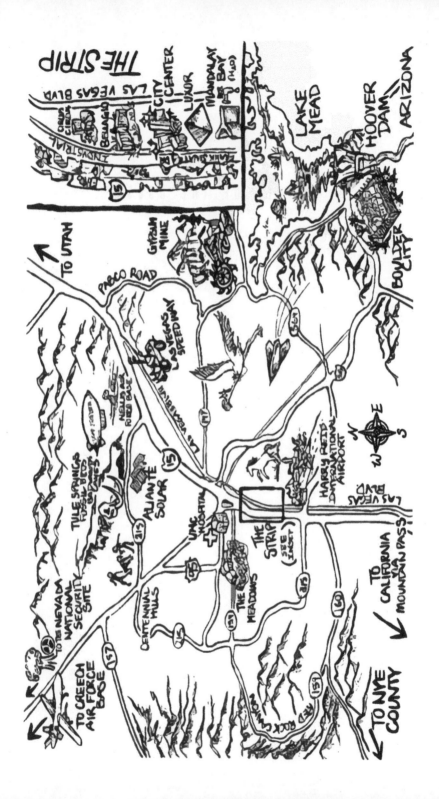

1

Lash used a rock to smash the window of a vacant tract home. Before climbing in, she looked to see if the microdrone had followed. It careened from the front of the house, the pilot overcorrecting, the machine glancing off the brick facade. It was a nasty homebrew with a thermal-imaging camera and what looked like an SRS A-2, the world's smallest sniper rifle. The four brushless motors had no gears, making it a quiet, efficient, nearly inescapable killer. She knew the hushed rotor wash would be imperceptible, even inches from her face. But Lash didn't hear drones; she intuited them. Drones changed the atmosphere around her. She was drawn to them, repulsed by them. For the briefest moment, her adversary had her mesmerized.

Then the bucket of bits and chips steadied itself to draw a deadly bead.

She jumped through the window. A shard of glass sliced her forearm. A bullet ripped through the window inches from her face. She yelped, fell backward onto a floor of broken dishes and garbage, then scampered out of the kitchen and got up to sprint for the door. In the tiled living room, she slipped on something greasy and landed on her tailbone. Shockwaves of pain racking her spine, she got up and ran again.

Still, she felt her stalker ghosting the air, growing closer.

She was outside now. The longer she avoided death, the sooner the drone would exhaust its power supply and have to return to base station or risk crashing. But she had no idea where that station might be. The pilot, Richter, could be anywhere, orchestrating her demise with a suitcase downlink powered by an old car battery. He could be across the street right now, ready to blow her brains out with an AK, SKS, or even an old Remington.

She took the chance. Lungs burning, legs throbbing, she made for the narrow space between two houses. She hoped to find a skateboard or kick scooter—anything to get her downhill fast and out of this suburban maze. She'd been searching for paint thinner. She was building a flamethrower and needed fuel that stayed liquid as it burned. She'd fantasized all year about incinerating Richter's cruel and handsome face.

Gunfire cracked, shattering a garden gnome. She bounded a wooden backyard fence and spotted shears beside a drained swimming pool. She grabbed the landscaping tool just as the microdrone whirred up behind her. Swinging the shears, she pinched the machine by its landing skid, using its momentum to bounce it once, twice, off the sliding-glass door. The drone sputtered free, bobbing like a storm-tossed fishing cork, and fired.

A giant spiderweb fracture erupted behind Lash. With her black Bedford lace-up combat boots, she kicked her way in and headed for the garage. She whimpered a prayer to Saint Joseph of Cupertino, patron of pilots, for help against her assailant. But Richter was relentless. Nothing could save her now. If only she had a GPS jammer, something to spoof the drone into autopilot mode. All she had were fields of dead grass, dust, and abandoned homes.

The overhead garage door was locked. She ducked into the laundry room and, noticing a can of lighter fluid, smiled with pyromaniacal intent. She opened a refrigerator, got in, and closed the door, fumbling in her cargo shorts for the Zippo. She listened for the drone, sensed it nearby. It was searching for a heat signal.

She would give it one.

She swung open the fridge door. It clipped one of the drone's rotors, which sent it spinning out into the hallway. As it thrashed, fighting to achieve liftoff, she drenched it with lighter fluid, then flicked her Zippo, tossed it, and squirted more fluid onto the flaming bot.

Desperate to kill, the drone fired. Melting carbon caused the bullet to miss and ricochet into a box of cat litter. Lash took the opportunity to whack the machine with a broom handle. Billowing smoke inside the cramped space made it hard to breathe. She slid open the lone window, leaped into the backyard again, and hauled, never looking back.

She ran down the hill until she reached the gated entrance, wrought iron warped, where her bike was waiting. Hanging from the handlebars was her backpack, which contained her command tablet.

She unzipped the backpack first and checked the tablet, hoping to snag a nearby Academy drone. But Richter's pulse waves blocked her signal.

She hopped on the Trek, pedaling furiously along crumbling, pothole-pocked Valley View Boulevard. Richter loved using multiple drones to play with and prey upon his victims. Right now, the skies were bright, cloudless, empty of marauders. She let herself believe she'd escaped the crosshairs, a rare feat. Only one other Academy student, cut off from his classmates, had ever survived an ambush by Richter. And that kid had a GPS jammer.

Having relied on her wits, instinct, an animal-like desire to live, Lash would fight another day. She wouldn't admit it to her classmates. She would tell them God had saved her. Not because it was true, but being caught out in the open without tech was looked down on at the Academy. At the Academy, students were asked to bond with the machine.

Even at the risk of dying.

Lash boosted off the inclined edge of a storm drain, landing neatly at the mouth of a tunnel. A dangerous no-man's land, but she'd stashed a couple of toaster-size, set-and-forget, autonomous, kamikaze bombots. They kept close and exploded shrapnel within ten feet of anything not wearing an Academy RFID chip. Before plunging in, she skidded to a stop and from her pocket fished night-vision goggles. They would improve her sight enough to spot a drone a split second before getting blown away. Better than nothing.

She kissed the modest RFID-tagged crucifix around her neck and pedaled into the drain.

It was hot. Night vision revealed vermin and spiders, too small to trigger a bombot. She passed the first wheeled drone as it zipped in the opposite direction, searching for something to rip apart. Minutes later, she noticed phosphorescent markings on the wall and braked. Straddling the bike frame, she pushed up her goggles and took in the wall's unfamiliar graffiti:

ONLY GODLESS MACHINES SURVIVE

A famous quote by Robert Duncan, pre-Collapse British evolutionary biologist. Hero in the eyes of Richter. One of his mercs must have crawled through here with a can of green Krylon. She knew this section of flood channels well and hadn't seen messages before. Richter was getting bolder, stalking Academy students in neutral territory and throwing up Duncan on the drain walls. Richter's philosophy was that *man* was the ultimate mechanism and that contraptions merely did his bidding. To see a man-machine connection, or the cyborg, as divine was bunk. The knives and fire of war were *not* gifted to us by gods, Richter insisted on his website. Drones weren't evidence of our status as chosen people. They were implements with which we carved out our hungers and ignited our lusts. They were machines that enabled men to become gods.

Sometimes Lash worried Richter might be right.

A detonation rocked the darkness behind her, the bombot shredding whatever Richter had sent to pursue her. Worried about more drones, she fumbled in her bag for a flashlight, but saw nothing back there except cordite and black shadow. The silence was eerie. Her slashed arm burned and bled. She pushed on.

Soon Lash was moving under Caesars Palace. More than three hundred miles of drains crisscrossed the city. The system offered temporary shelter and a quick getaway during drone battles. But setting foot inside was Russian roulette. One of Richter's drones might be waiting to exterminate you.

Now her adrenaline high was fading and she began to feel exhausted. The tunnel widened to form a chamber. She stopped, looked up at a metal grate, saw a sliver of blue sky then checked her command tablet for a signal. Still blocked by a jamming pulse. Not good. She was near the Academy, however. Luxor was minutes away. She could make it.

Her heart skipped when the other bombot went flying past, racing toward something on her trail. All this time it had remained well in front, but now it zeroed in. Something had tracked her this far inside the tunnels.

Seconds later, an explosion. Very close. Lash was surprised that the shrapnel hadn't clipped her. She pumped her legs, hurtling deeper into the void that led to the safety of a mock Egyptian tomb. Hopefully, her best friend and classmate, Dio, would be waiting for her with a warbot. She glanced back several times, but her goggles registered zilch. There was a definite noise, like metal scraping the concrete walls. What the hell had Richter set loose down here?

She steered along a steep side channel, ducking her head as the ceiling got lower and lower, resting her chin on the handlebars to keep from being decapitated. Something hanging nicked the top of her skull. She ignored the pain and let gravity increase her speed. Blood flowed down her face and over her goggles. She tasted it.

Finally, she dumped out into a larger channel. Before she could discern the passage leading to the Academy gates, a floodlight blinded her.

"Dio!" she shouted, hands raised to block the beam. "Richter's on my butt!"

"Ground!" the tin voice behind the light called out.

She jumped off the bike, dropped flat on her stomach, and covered her ears. The M249 was deafening, white muzzle flash spasming like a star eating itself alive. Dio had tracked her signal and dispatched a full-on warbot. It was an old treaded ordnance remover that Lash had enhanced with a belt-fed machine gun.

Rolling left to avoid getting hit with debris, she caught a glimpse of her pursuer, a sneaky carbon-fibered tri-bladed unirotor, no bigger than a hubcap, a screaming gas-powered chainsaw wedged between its T-Rex manipulator arms. The drone drifted out of Dio's ferocious barrage for a fleeting moment. But the devastating firepower swiftly smithereened the microdrone. The saw's motor sputtered to a halt.

Lash rushed the warbot, intending to grab a rifle from off its frame. She was eager to greet whatever else Richter had coming with a volley of flying lead.

"North tunnel is clear and sealed," said Dio via speaker.

Lash removed her goggles, picked up and kickstanded her bike, inspecting it for damage. Finding none, she brushed off the seat. Then she walked over to the shattered unirotor and stomped its plastic chips into smaller splinters. She felt her face contorting into a mask of fury. She didn't care. Her back was to the bot's HD camera.

"Lash?"

When she was done, she turned toward the warbot. She wiped her bloodied arm and face with the bottom of her black, sweat-drenched Slayer shirt. "Richter came after me in the Meadows."

Dio was quiet for a time, but Lash could hear the bot's camera lens whirring. Then her classmate said, "He won't hurt you. I won't let him."

For a moment, she thought he meant Prof. But he was speaking, of course, of Richter.

2

Lash led the slow-treading warbot into the gloomy womb of the Academy. Being out in the sunlight recharged her, unlike the younger students. Sunshine had felt better on her skin when she was a little girl. In ruined Las Vegas, however, rays made Academy kids anxious, irritated, vulnerable. Light offered the repellent sensation of existing in rifle sights, of standing before a firing squad. When you were outside, drones were inevitable, omnipresent. If you didn't hear propellers, you were dead or underground. Thanks to sunlamps and vitamin D pills and treadmills, students didn't need to leave Luxor's substructure to stay relatively healthy. But it didn't matter how fit and lobster-burned by UV you were when Richter's drones had you.

They'd almost snuffed Lash today. Back at Meadows Mall, she failed to detect the first drone's nearing presence. She put down her bike to inspect what she thought was the corpse of a child in brown weeds. Turned out to be a scorched dog carcass. By the time she figured it out, the drone was on her. It blasted the rifle from her hands, splintering its wood stock, misaligning the bolt, rendering it useless.

From that point on, she'd been prey.

This meant Lash was now old enough and sufficiently skilled to warrant being near or at the top of Richter's kill list. She didn't have long to live. Richter stalked the Academy's best students if they didn't leave the valley. Prof's kids rarely turned tail. They could hide for months, years, inside Luxor. But stir-craziness inevitably won out. They grew overconfident. Careless. Until the day they conducted a mission beyond Luxor and Richter's drones sighted them alone and Prof, busy watching over the entire city, couldn't help them. So older students tended to die, Richter posting their deaths on the threadbare internet for Lash to watch. And watch again. Prof presided over elegiac yet hopeful funerals, insisting the dead youth had graduated and ascended to join the Cyborg-Christ. Then Prof enrolled more kids. There were always more.

Lash could try to flee, but where? Without Academy resources, she was a mere citizen, unprotected. In Las Vegas, there were no basements, just drywall and matchstick designs, homes erected overnight in the hopes of making a quick buck before the real estate bubble popped. After the Collapse, toxic bombs had fallen. Lash didn't want to die in the skeleton of someone's stupid moneymaking scheme. The worst part was knowing that, even if she left the Academy, Richter might find her and taunt her classmates with images of her being shot to death, her red-orange-yellow thermo signal collapsing to the ground and slowly turning green, fading away, like she'd never existed. Richter was a sadist. It angered her to think he got off on killing students. The Academy wasn't perfect. But it was the singular force, as far as Lash knew, that protected Las Vegas from monsters.

Luxor's cavernous bowels teemed now with primitive student robotics. Many glowed in the dark via chemiluminescence or glued-on glow sticks. The Academy's youngest created these unarmed bots with 3-D printers, laser slicing machines that fabricated plastic and metal. They learned how to build entire drones in layers. Printers churned out powdery nylon cakes. Students retrieved the parts like pulling buried toys from a sandpit. In minutes, the still-warm results boasted everything—moving parts, microchips. By age twelve, the average Academy pup could assemble a fleet of surveillance UAVs in less than an hour.

Arming them was another matter and Lash's specialty. Sure, the cactus milk-dribblers could out-CAD her. But Lash was old-school. These pasty tunnel brats would never experience what she had growing up. They'd never know the feeling of the sun on their faces while bungee-blasting a fixed-wing into the sky. They'd never savor the rush of gripping a joystick with live airborne video. They'd never bask in the glory of a successful parachute landing. Everything they yanked from their magic dust was prefab, built on the sweat of others long dead. Lash was tired of adding weapons to McMa-chines. She mulled the irony of attaching guns to formulaic drones designed years ago for peacetime roles. She appreciated this about her friend Dio: Even if Prof's Cyborg-Christ bullshit oozed between his ears, Dio favored original designs. She loved arming his deadly bots.

When she'd been the size of these nerdlings, her father took her out into the desert. He popped the trunk of his cruiser and removed a rifle case. Inside was a modular, aluminum public-safety drone. Wearing aviators, his black uniform dry-cleaner crisp, he watched her assemble the three-piece structure and V-tail section. In no time, she hand-launched the nonmilitary drone. With a solar-powered touchscreen tablet, she zoomed the infrareds and checked for weather updates. She pushed the drone to its limit: two thousand feet, thirty-five knots.

"Hey, Icarus Girl," her father half-scolded, a smile on his thin white-guy lips, arms crossed, leaning against the hood. "Don't lose your wings."

That's what she missed most about him—the way he gently reprimanded, yet still communicated his confidence in her. The easy manner in which he loved her. How, after she'd nailed the belly landing of an expensive piece of Metro property, he picked her up, held her thin body tight against his muscled chest, and laughed.

She never wanted him to let go.

As the warbot grinded toward the Academy entrance, Lash pushed away this memory. She resented him for leaving when the bombs hit. For driving into a poison cloud to save strangers.

At least she knew her father. Prof's bed-wetting brainiacs had few if any memories of their parents. Students were plucked from desperate homes across the valley and brought here as infants. They were raised by other students and silent robo-sitters that dispensed formula and food and little else. At the Academy, kids had a chance of surviving for at least fifteen years. They had a brief opportunity to be gods, surveying Earth, choosing who lived and died, their view from Olympus through a subterranean computer screen, their lightning bolts GPS-driven. Divine, aggressive, little worms. Lash often stifled the urge to squash one.

An especially excitable bot with an absurd scorpion-tail appendage scooted over Lash's boot. She flipped it into the air and punted it like a ball, smashing it.

"What *is* your problem?" scolded Dio from the warbot speaker.

Lash grunted and made for Prof's chambers. She heard Dio's electronic sigh.

Her frequency-tagged crucifix kept her safe from the warbots standing sentry. She'd armed these autonomous, Prof-designed, metal stoics herself.

The warbots remained still, letting her pass. She strained to pull open the blast-proof doors.

Prof was dressed in a combat vestment and sat in his command chair. The ultimate push-button warrior searching for targets, checking them against his kill list. He stared intently at a wall stacked with dozens of screens. A few had broken links, broadcasting static. Most displayed aerial reconnaissance. Academy drones covered the lawless valley day and night. Prof and his more advanced students skimmed for trouble. Riots. Robbery. Rape. Richter. Index finger on his chin, Prof appeared intellectual, effete. It was surface. Even though he preached a love of God and technology and urged a fusing of them in the minds of his students, Prof had a brain for violence.

Lash cleared her throat.

Prof slowly turned his bald head, eyes wide open. He resembled a skinned and emaciated owl. Only in his early thirties, he bore the composure of a Crusades-scarred sage. "What happened?"

"Richter nearly got me," she said. "I was in the Meadows. For turpentine."

He stood up and drifted toward Lash, long wine-red robe flowing behind him. He noticed her sliced arm and the dried blood on her face. He looked concerned but knew better than to touch her. "You're wounded? Dio!"

"Here." Dio entered the chambers, a pudgy, brown-skinned man of nineteen. Jet-black bangs. Bifocals. Jeans and a DON'T DRONE ME, BRO

T-shirt. "I have the dressing," said Dio, approaching with gauze and anti-septic. Lash didn't let people or drones touch her, not even medical bots. Only Dio.

"Lash, you're not to leave the Academy walls without my permission again," Prof said. "As a student, you must follow the rules."

Lash held her tongue. In truth, she agreed with Prof's overt policies. The Academy was a force for good. Thanks to Prof and his young guns, the people had wrested control of Hoover Dam from the Feds and from desperate cities such as Los Angeles. Academy drones protected power and water, keeping them safe from griefers and thieves. Thanks to patchworked server banks shielded from the US government's online blackout switch, along with deregulation and the cyber-infiltration of America's unregistered ISP companies, the web was alive in reduced form. Likewise, Las Vegas had been diminished. People lived here despite the challenges, mainly because hordes of murderous nomads stalked the valley's edge. In return for relative safety and online access, primarily crop price updates to plan food budgets, all the remaining inhabitants who had any paid with their children.

Barely beyond childhood herself, that part bugged Lash.

Prof conscripted kids to fight with drones, patrolling the valley in search of evil. He encouraged hormone-addled teenagers to serve as judges, jurors, executioners. They presided, decided, and snuffed with the press of a button. If Lash stood in Prof's way, they would, without qualm, hunt her down. Dio might protect her for a while.

Until he couldn't.

"I understand," she said, jaw and fists clenched. Waiting for the tension to dissolve, Dio had yet to apply salve to her wounds.

Prof examined her for a prolonged moment but drew no closer. He exhaled sharply and turned away, facing the surveillance wall, what he called God's Eye.

"Lash, I provide you latitude, because at age twenty-one, you're the oldest student, the most experienced. I realize a great deal of your weapons-making depends on unlawful behavior. Sneaking. Stealing. Hoarding, even. But I need you to abide by *some* rules. I can't shield you from the mob—or from Richter—if I don't know where you are."

Lash opened her mouth to say something, thought better of it. Instead, she slipped from her cargo shorts a piece of cactus gum and gnawed it ferociously, teeth turning dark orange. Derived from red barrel cacti, the gum doubled as bot adhesive.

"I understand," she repeated through the chewing. "Am I excused?"

Prof stood silent.

Cocking her hip impatiently, Lash looked at Dio, who shrugged and continued to hold the first aid kit. He wouldn't touch her until she was ready. She popped a bubble with irritated flair. Not an easy task with cactus gum.

"Forget the Meadows," Prof said finally. He walked closer to God's Eye and squinted at a lone, dark figure scurrying across a ravaged stretch of Boulder Highway.

"No." Lash couldn't help herself. "The Meadows is neutral ground. By trying to kill me, Richter broke the treaty." Of course, she knew treaties were broken all the time. Richter's aim had been to stalk her for his sick amusement. She just couldn't bring herself to say it.

"Immaterial," Prof said. He turned to her, giving a hard stare. "I'm relieved you're safe, Lash. But we've made plans to handle Richter. Permanently. He seems to have forged an alliance with CityCenter. His Red Angels hover there now. But not for long. I'm assigning you to help Koons with his latest project."

"Koons?" Lash scoffed. "What's he got now, a tornado-thrower?" This was an allusion to the younger student's earlier concept for an acid-rainmaker, a dudbot meant to elevate sulfur levels in storm clouds, thereby corroding Richter's drones. The project backfired, smelling up and damaging the Academy's already minimal steelworks operations. Lash had to admit Koons was gifted. But he wasn't *effective*. He lacked a killer's instinct.

Prof had to smirk at Lash's crack. "I think you'll find what he has constructed—or I should say *adapted*—deeply interesting. It appeals to your epic sensibilities."

Dio finally approached, pulling a chair right up to Lash and sitting down in it. She remained standing.

"Yeah, like the rotten-egg odor he unleashed down here," she said, extending her arm for Dio to consider. "Truly epic. Took, what, a year to air out?"

Before Lash could be disinfected, Prof said, smile gone, "It's the bucket-wheel excavator."

Lash swallowed her gum. Dio paused mid-dab, taking in her reaction. The prospect of arming a battleship-size piece of surface-mining heavy equipment made her woozy.

"You know," she said, "*I* was the one who found that monster years ago in the mines."

"Yes," Prof said. "Koons has been tinkering with it onsite for months. He believes it's ready. With it, we can finally get rid of Richter and bring the Academy aboveground."

Lash didn't hear the last part. She was already going over her mental inventory checklist. She had four-dozen heat-seeking RPGs that would fasten nicely along the boom arm of the excavator. The machine was a massive desert-grinding, earth-moving blade on treads. The blade comprised a large wheel ringed with a continuous pattern of giant cast-iron buckets. As the wheel turned on the boom, the buckets scooped material, slicing away rock and steel like cotton candy. Once Koons sicced the excavator on Richter's new home in CityCenter, ripping it wide open, Lash would pick off his warbots, underlings, Richter himself.

That appealed to Lash's epic sensibilities.

"I like it," she said. "When do we launch? I say right now."

Prof shook his head. "First, you and Dio must complete the inventory. We have an important shipment arriving. Then take in a meal. Gathering's at 1900. After that, you can go. Only the three of us in this room know Koons is out there."

"Fine. Given that it's Koons, he'll need extra time."

"Don't be tough on him, Lash. He has a warrior's heart."

Lash wanted to tell him that, on the contrary, Koons was just an unlikable kiss-ass who'd been brainwashed by Prof's mumbo jumbo.

Prof waved his hand, shooing them out of his chamber. "Do that elsewhere."

The warbots were motionless as the two walked past them and into a conference room. Butt-bruised by the bike, Lash carefully sat down in a frayed chair before swiveling excitedly. Dio moistened a shred of cloth with grain alcohol.

"Can't believe Koons hacked the excavator," she said. "Upsetting."

"Why?" asked Dio, pinning her arm down on the table so he could dab it. In past first aid episodes, she'd punched him.

"Ouch! Because I nearly died just now for a flamethrower. Meanwhile, Koons was thinking grand-scale. It's risky, working in the open like that. Richter *has* to know the beast is out there. He just can't figure out how to hack it. We can do this."

Dio listened, quietly applying a bandage, then gently cleaned the abrasion on her hairline.

"I will cut Richter's palace in half," she went on, "and put his head on a pike. Ouch!"

"I'm sure you will," said Dio, "if he doesn't do it to you first."

3

Arm burning, head throbbing, armpits sweating, but tidily bandaged, Lash sighed, waiting at the docks for a semitrailer full of toys to pull up. It was a Las Vegas summer, the atmosphere heat-deadened and dry. Still, Wednesdays were her favorite, a regular midweek Christmas and a chance for the Academy to replenish arms, ammo, and drone parts. She wore headphones, her Sony Walkman blasting a sun-warped tape of Alice Cooper's *Constrictor*. Lash and Dio loved '80s heavy metal. The music felt real, visceral. Metal matched the intensity with which Lash and Dio handled drones.

"Balls out," Lash often said about a particularly blistering guitar solo.

In turn, Dio smiled, nodded, and gave Lash the sign of the devil, a metalhead hand gesture. Holding his middle and ring fingers down with his thumb, he intoned, "Hail Ozzy!"

Shades donned now, Lash smacked gum and waited for the bikers. The docks offered a sunken view of Frank Sinatra Drive and the bombed-out interstate, once a thoroughfare between Los Angeles and Las Vegas. Now, heavily armored, gun-nested RVs rumbled along I-15. The Chinese themselves didn't transport shipments to Nevada. They relied on merchant vessels, Long Beach ports, and a meth-dealing biker gang from California. The Huns didn't bother piloting drones, thanks to frequency jammers and electromagnetic pulsers from Beijing. They rode wherever they wanted with impunity, neither fearing the skies nor caring enough to upend the power structure. Too stoned and rape-happy to go to all the trouble of taking control, the Huns had it made.

Prof was a major customer of theirs. Richter, too.

Last year, the then-Huns leader—Lash couldn't recall his name, just his ugly face mapped with gin blossoms and white cancer spots—had pinched her ass. Lash beat him with a freshly delivered fire extinguisher until he lost consciousness, suffered a blood clot in his brain, and died in the Academy's infirmary. Dio kept the Huns at bay with gun-garnished warbots, while Prof sealed the docks. She was placed in an isolation pit for two weeks, partly to appease the Huns and save face with the Chinese, but also to make it abundantly clear she wasn't allowed to pummel anyone she pleased.

Down in the hole, Lash had preserved her sanity thanks to Dio. He'd dropped her Walkman into her abandoned sewer pipe beneath Luxor, along with a few thrash-metal cassettes. She was grateful to Dio and unbowed by Prof's punishment. She didn't care how many days she had to spend in isolation. She would straight-up waste anyone who tried to fondle her—power-hungry officials, biker chieftains, the frickin' angel Gabriel.

Lash heard the motorcycle engines roaring closer. Dio was ready, maneuvering two warbots into position, one on either side of her. Strangely enough, she'd earned the Huns' silent respect. They rarely engaged her in conversation or showed any expression. But now, as they turned the corner of Sinatra Drive—with their beards, bandanas, denim vests, and sunglasses—Lash noticed their unusual smiles. As the cannon came into view, sitting on a lowboy trailer pulled by a sleek and shiny semi straight from Shanghai, she pulled out her headphones and fought the instinct to bring her hand to her mouth.

It was 280 mm, an Atomic Annie, capable of launching nuclear projectiles. Developed in the early 1950s, it was fired up once at the Nevada Test Site. Of the twenty ever made, half were dismantled, the other half mothballed in military museums across the country.

The new lead Hun perfunctorily revved his bike a few times before bringing it to a halt. He dismounted, kickstanded, and removed his aviators and black-leather gloves, face beaming with pride. Like his fellow Huns, a bolt-action shotgun was strapped across his back.

Before he could explain anything, Lash popped a cactus-gum bubble, jumped down on the concrete parking surface, and said, "Where. In. *Hell.*"

"Yuma, actually. Sitting under a tarp on the airfield. But that's not all."

"For the same low price, you'll throw in some atomic shells?"

The Hun shook his head, yucked in Southwest-hick fashion, and squirted a stream of what looked like actual tobacco juice onto the ground. "No, but our buddies also sent a dozen bullets made at a plant of theirs in Shenyang. Talkin' eleven-inch bore, half-ton each. Enough to flatten any tower on the Strip. Even fancy-ass CityCenter."

"Heavy-metal thunder," Lash agreed. Warbots, having cranked down the ramp, joined her. "And the price?"

"Free."

Lash looked at him. "Forge, is it?"

"Yes, ma'am."

"Well, Forge, nothing's free."

"Love," he insisted and to Lash's surprise, he didn't sound all that rapey. His hazel eyes were bright, ardent. Chew drool in his stubble, he looked almost childlike. "Love is free."

She assessed his twentysomething physique. Shirtless under his vest, he had a washboard stomach. Tight jeans suggested endowment. Beneath road grime and appalling hygiene, an attractive specimen lurked. After a shower and prolonged toothbrushing, Forge might even be fun to fool around with in a sleeping bag next to the hot springs at Hoover Dam. But Lash knew this muscular young brigand was evil.

"I would cost you everything," she said, staring through him to admire the artillery. "This it?"

"This should hold you for now." He smacked his handlebars with one of his gloves. "Like it?"

"Yes," said Lash, as Dio remotely guided a military tractor down a dock ramp. In a minute, he would hitch Annie to the heavy-equipment transporter. Then he would drag the casino-crushing cannon off the trailer and into Luxor's loading area.

"Listen," said the biker, putting forward a prudently unaggressive foot. "My brothers and you had an unfortunate . . . *misunderstanding* awhile back. I want you to know—"

"Forge," she interrupted. She knew what was coming. She'd been leered at by enough guys to head it off. Still, she had to play it carefully. "This gun you towed here all the way from Arizona makes me happy."

"That's great. That makes *me* happy."

She couldn't encourage his King and Queen of the Huns fantasy, the two of them riding side by side into the western sunset, killer gang behind them, too transparently; she might need him and them at some critical upcoming juncture. So she smiled and said, "Good. Now I need to ask you. Where are the projectiles?"

He grinned back at her, crookedly, for a moment. Then he finger-whistled. A U-Haul truck, its aluminum panels pocked and dented from multiple impacts, strained forward with what sounded like a knotty transmission. A biker yanked the parking brake, stepped out of the vehicle, and clambered into a sidecar attached to another Hun's chopper.

Forge said, "Shells are inside. Along with the standard Ritalin and Ambien bricks and drone parts. Keep the wheels." He took a piece of folded paper from his vest and handed it to her.

"Cool," she said, accepting the inventory slip. "I need another drone target."

"I've seen your work," he said. "Scary business."

"Thanks," she said. She noticed Dio had finished lugging the massive cannon, with its thirty-foot barrel, onto the docks and was about to manually steer the U-Haul up the ramp.

"Not really a compliment," Forge said. He put on his shades and pulled up his gloves.

Lash folded her arms and stepped back, warbots sticking close. She sensed Dio watching, getting tense. She knew he was hurrying the transaction in case Forge set her off.

"Somebody did something terrible to you," Forge said. "Your heart's been gutshot and left to die." He straddled his bike, adjusting the shotgun. "I just want you to know. Me and the Huns—we've got the right meds." He boot-kicked the ignition, and the engine frapped to life.

"See ya," she said, raising her arm to wave goodbye.

Dio lurched the truck up the ramp. Lash, meanwhile, walked past the lip of the dock and tapped a control panel on the interior wall. Reinforced blast-proof doors began to drop.

4

Lash took a deep breath, exhaled, and put her ear to the doors. She was listening to the motorcycles rev away when Dio spoke up. "This siege gun is incredible."

"Range?"

"Miles," said Dio, picking up a tablet. "Let me access the archive." Prof owned a database of US weapons schematics that he'd taken from the Test Site, useful for operating Cold War equipment.

"Tell you right now we need a powder charge," she said. "See the hydraulic rammer?"

Dio chuckled, peering at the screen. "*Mija,* I know you can fire it. Just let me find the specs."

"I wonder if it made Richter nervous. Watching the Huns drag this antique here."

"Richter doesn't get nervous."

"Why did Prof order it?"

Dio shrugged. "Prof has a plan."

"But he tells us zilch. That's what worries me. We're just pawns."

"Need-to-know basis and all that."

"Prof wants to break me. Mold me into something else entirely. I don't care to crouch before a compromised leader."

"We're *all* compromised. Prof changes so much in Las Vegas for the better," said Dio, not looking at Lash. His tablet-lit eyes scanned for information. "He saves lives. Gives people hope."

"He cuts deals with psychopaths."

"So?"

"So . . ." She stopped. Dio was right. In the post-Collapse scheme of things, Prof was the least of all the evils.

He tap-summoned a trio of forklift-bots, put the tablet on top of a crate, and looked at Lash. "Twenty miles, by the way."

Lash considered this. "We could smash Koons from here."

Dio closed his eyes and playfully covered his ears.

Lash grinned, too. She donned her headphones again and pressed PLAY on her Walkman. Alice Cooper's "Teenage Frankenstein" blasted her ears.

Dio opened the U-Haul door, pulled down the loading ramp, scanned the cargo with a solar flashlight, and whistled. "Grab the forearm straps?"

Lash didn't hear, didn't need to. She'd already picked up the adjustable straps next to Dio's tablet and tossed them at him. He laid them on either side of a crate. She hopped in to help.

Together they tipped the crate and kicked the straps underneath it. They crossed the straps, then simultaneously squatted and inserted their forearms into the strap hooks, making their limbs a fulcrum. Backs straight, they stood up and moved the first container to the cargo hold's edge. A bot zipped up the ramp, forked the crate, and raised it so that Lash and Dio could remove the straps. The crate-laden bot then zoomed down the ramp and puttered off to the drone parts warehouse.

The process repeated until the truck was empty, the bots transporting everything into storage. Lash used the box cutter to open the Ritalin supply, locking it in the medical closet for Prof to dispense at Gathering. The Ambien would be processed into the food, allowing students to sleep after long, boring, Ritalin-fueled shifts spent watching the Las Vegas wasteland for signs of trouble, for evidence of Richter's mercenaries.

Ambien was why Lash killed her REM neurons with black coffee—to avoid falling into a nightmarescape. Her dreams were specter-laden, a minefield of ghosts. People she'd killed never went away.

As for the cannon and shells, Dio would take them down to his weapons lab in Luxor's basement. Right now, he was tablet-relaying instructions to the tractor. It pulled up, hitched itself to the gun, and started moving. Dio followed it to the industrial elevator, which wasn't large enough to carry the cannon. Lash knew he'd take it apart and reassemble it. It felt good to work in tandem with him and his machines, an uncommon instance when she was in sync with both classmates and bots. After a few minutes, though, her stomach growled. A headache began boring into her temples.

"Would love to dismantle it with you," she said, turning down her Walkman volume. "But I need to take care of some things."

"I'm good," Dio said.

"Promise not to fire it?"

"That's *your* job."

"See you at Gathering," she said.

"See you."

Lash made her way to the mess hall, the odor of borderline-rancid food and compost-trash growing stronger. The smell at once made her hungry and demoralized. When she entered the cafeteria, a handful of teen drone pilots were dining, each sitting alone at a table, staring into their tablets as they chewed. Years ago, this place had dished Luxor employees cheeseburgers, fried chicken, roasted vegetables. Now it was a depressing, sedative-laced trough, a beige-walled pit stop between combat drills and religious services.

The steam table feebly steamed, offering grim sustenance. Today it was frybread with cactus-fig spread—again. How was she supposed to protect the people of Las Vegas from Richter and other madmen while subsisting on gruel? At least there was something resembling coffee, the sour Arabic beans harvested in Yunnan, a province in the People's Republic.

Now that she thought about it, there were no coffee beans in Forge's last shipment. Prof's superiors were getting stingy.

She took a ceramic plate and silverware, placed them on a yellow plastic tray, then spoon-slung a hardened chunk of cactus fig on top of a slice of stale crust. She didn't bother to find a table. While folding the bread around the paste and forcing it down, she pushed her tray along the metal rails until she reached the coffee station and filled a plastic mug. The coffee was tepid, so she downed it like a shot. She did it again, belching with dissatisfaction.

Above her, Prof's face filled a dusty monitor. His latest video sermon promised students that the arrival of a digital messiah was imminent. The techno-savior would bring with him an explosion of computing superintelligence. The result would be the augmentation of human bodies, followed by the unification of souls with the mind of the Cyborg-Christ.

"Word made Flesh," Prof said. "Flesh made Information."

Lash touched the bandage on her scalp. Her head continued to throb, a seizure blooming. She thought of her own bruised flesh and its potential for digital transfiguration. She thought of Forge and his unspoken proposal. She thought of Prof and his impossible rules that had resulted in her spending two weeks in a chasm. She laughed at the irony. The assurance of an organic-cybernetic nexus came from someone who couldn't brew a decent cup of coffee.

Suddenly enraged, Lash grabbed the dispenser and smashed it against a tiled wall. Black fluid poured slowly onto the floor as if from a mortal wound. A student-designed autonomous janitorbot—like a shrunken ice-resurfacing Zamboni, lights blinking goofily—hurried over to clean the mess. Lash gave it a swift kick, knocking it over with a loud clang.

Helpless, yet still trying to reach the spill, the bot continued spinning its wheels.

A male student seated at the table nearest to Lash looked up at her. He shook his head and turned away. Two years younger than Lash, he was a Reaper pilot who'd never left Luxor. He believed he knew everything, trusted that Prof would provide. The pilot was a coward who killed people from great distances as if they were figures in a video game.

Lash slowly approached the kid. He was sweating now, eyes wide with concern. His kind always became anxious when confronted with analog violence. His kind couldn't care less about collateral damage, since it was done in the name of safety and to ensure the coming of a sci-fi savior. He didn't stand up.

A smart decision that spared him a broken nose.

She said, "The Roman god Vulcan made robot slave-girls of gold for himself."

Then she left the mess hall, leaving behind her tray of half-eaten mush. She didn't look back.

She pushed past an oncoming horde. Shift over, students shuffled toward food. It offered sustenance and sedation after hours spent staring at monitors—and killing.

5

Inventory done, stomach full of gunk, anger tentacling her chest, Lash tromped to her study. She passed the armory, which she longed to enter, but that would have to wait until after a head-clearing bath and tonight's Gathering. The armory belonged to the Academy, of course, but Lash considered it hers. She'd built it, stocked it, stayed up late organizing it, and insulated it, making it impervious to chip-wrecking nukes.

Her path toward lethal proficiency began during a single summer spent working for minimum wage at a survivalist theme park on the butt crack of the Strip, Battleborn Vegas. There she'd piloted remote-control faux-drones and assisted safety-goggled young boys in pulling triggers on mounted-for-kids M249 SAWs. That job was similar to the one she currently held. At Battleborn, she'd reloaded guns, replaced paper-silhouette targets, and explained the theaters in which each killing implement had appeared. Those boys were probably dead now. Their tourist folks had been weekend libertarians, believing they could survive the world's end with guns, gold, and dehydrated eggs.

Lash pushed deeper into Luxor, past a combat-drone hangar, formerly a convention space, where reserve Hellfire-armed MQ-1 Predators and MQ-9 Reapers stood silently, covered in their black-canvas shrouds like sleeping monsters waiting to be stirred into action. The Academy had anywhere from fifty to a hundred drones in the air at any moment of the day and night, depending on how many of Richter's UAVs were plaguing the valley. Only Prof and his oldest students such as Lash and Dio were allowed to pilot combat drones.

With the help of his associates, Prof had ripped dozens of stations from Creech Air Force Base and installed them in Luxor. From these cyber-thrones, students monitored and protected the citizenry of Las Vegas, making sure people tended their own bucket gardens and eschewed sensitive areas such as Hoover Dam. Each station surrounded a pilot with seven monitors—3-D map, forward-camera footage, heads-down displays, online relay chatrooms with intel from Prof's supporters on the ground, many of them on the Academy payroll. Which meant these snitches received additional food and water for alerting Prof to unusual activity, mainly Richter's comings and goings.

The rest of the drones were for surveillance missions, autonomous or remotely piloted with command tablets. These UAVs weren't armed or combat-ready, but they could still ruin things for the enemy. They carried powerful high-def video cameras, infrared sensors for nighttime runs, and special sensors that sniffed chemicals in the air—explosives, gasoline. Drones were why smartphones were now useless in combat, since drones could track cell signals. Prof's military UAVs could also detect guns, but in a flattened Las Vegas, everyone was automatically considered armed and dangerous.

Lash had piloted combat drones. At first, she'd enjoyed using, say, a Reaper to rain death on Richter's mercenaries from the safety of a mission-intelligence station. But after two years of killing remotely, she'd grown bored and apprehensive. She created, with Prof's cautious consent, a position for herself: Academy Weaponsmistress. These days, she focused on her armory, but she still relished steering microdrones via line-of-sight and stalking quarry with binocs, a sniper, and a cheap-ass tablet. She savored unleashing a drone of her own design, the Bride, on a pack of arrogant mercenaries and watching them die.

She entered her room and turned on the elements for the water to boil. She collapsed on her bed for a moment and gazed at her shelves. She needed poetry to subdue her brain-riot. She reached for an old standby, Christopher Logue's *War Music,* the last great translation of Homer. She flipped through the pages but found it hard to concentrate. She found herself examining her face in the cheval mirror.

Lash pulled up her shirt to gaze at the Harvesters knife scars that now ornamented her perfectly proportioned breasts. She thought she resembled a *Lowrider* magazine model, a half-Latina lass with a figure that would look great bending over the hood of a restored, candy-green, hydraulics-enhanced, 1959 Chevy Impala.

She laughed at having missed her calling.

The water scalding, she poured it into her clawfoot tub and undressed. It was a fantastic bath. She tried reading again. This time the poet's intense language allayed her mind—the gods on Olympus shocked, outraged even, by Achilles' mutilation of dead Hector.

Prof preached a monolithic, lone deity that Academy students were expected to know. Lash's father had taught her the pantheon of ancient Greece, starting to explain the narrative arc of *The Iliad* when she was just a toddler. Lash admired the immolating petulance and peculiar code of Achilles. She wondered about his concubine-princess Briseis. When Achilles died, it was said Briseis grieved, throwing dirt on her own fair skin and tearing her long blond hair. She washed his bleeding body in the shoals. Set it ablaze on a pyre. Mixed, in an urn, his ashes with those of his friend Patroclus. Buried Achilles's bones under rocks. Sometimes Lash dreamed of her corpse being treated with such ritualistic affection. Other times she pondered the pleasure of falling in love with a captor as grand as Achilles.

Instead, she felt imprisoned in a yawning realm of aggressive adolescents. Sure, Dio loved her. But she could reciprocate only with a sisterlike affection. She would do anything for him and he for her. She had the advantage, though. Even a child knows power lies in the hands of the one who cares less about the other. Dio cared too much.

Everyone else rightly feared her.

She threw the book against the wall. She closed her eyes and rubbed her temples.

Students before her, mostly eighteen-year-olds, had left the hard way, taken out by Richter's drone attacks. A few, a mere handful, had finally eaten enough of Prof's crap to realize, *Hey, I'm in a cult. Time to escape and live for myself.* The same realization agitated Lash's heart. But she hadn't run away. Part of it was Dio. The other part was Achillean. She wanted the glory of killing Richter and parading his dog-chewed carcass through cracked-neon streets. And even if she busted out, where would she go? Women didn't fare well in the city. They ended up in brothels or had babies by hardened men, violent masters of living off the wasteland.

She dried herself with a towel, put on a black-velvet worship robe, and looking at the clock, saw that she had an hour before Gathering. She dropped her backup Zippo into her pocket, slipped on her Hello Kitty slippers, and ankles aching, limped out the door and down a hallway leading to the Gathering of the Cyborgs.

The pews were vacant, and no votives flickered. The altar was bare, the brass lectern empty and dark. There was dust on the keys of the pipe organ. Lash used her Zippo to ignite a candle before bending down onto the kneeler, groaning from the pain as she descended. She'd barely settled in when a small, freckled redhead knelt next to her, bumping Lash's elbow.

"What, Bathory?" Lash said. Younger girls smelled of cactus lip gloss that made her want to puke.

"Problem," said the girl, breathing heavily.

"I don't play guessing games."

"Sorry," Bathory whispered, nodding toward the front of the room as if acknowledging her rudeness. "There's a girl bleeding in the armory. Bad."

"I told you little bitches to stay out of there," Lash hissed.

Meeting Lash's gaze, Bathory protested. "We don't know how she got hurt!"

Lash yanked off her slippers and sprinted barefoot out of the great hall, Bathory yelling for her to wait up. How in hell had the rug rats found a loaded weapon? Ammo was kept in a separate ammunition room. Had they broken into both?

In less than a minute, she was there. A group of girls huddled inside, where guns hung on the walls like artworks in a gallery. The kids surrounded a slightly older-looking student wearing a sports bra and cargo shorts. She dabbed her bloody thighs with what was likely her shirt.

"Got the thing for that," Lash snorted. She ripped open the armory's emergency kit.

"Some kind of invisible laser," the older girl said. Her name, Lash recalled, was Frida.

"I *hate* lasers," Bathory said, wrinkling her nose. She was winded from the run.

Lash tossed her a rare box of Tampax.

Frida tried to stand up. Then she fainted. The others caught her.

Bathory scratched her head. "Oh, right." She unwrapped a tampon. "For bleeding."

6

Lash screamed at the girls to get out of her armory. All together, they lifted bleeding Frida into the air, her eyelids fluttering a tad too dramatically. She looked like a rock star who'd intentionally fallen into a mosh pit.

They carried her away, Lash sneering at the girl's affected pose.

Bathory stayed behind, offering her best whipped-dog expression. "We weren't stealing," she insisted. She extended the Hello Kitty slippers.

Lash ignored them, staring angrily at the girl for a beat. "Tell me, Short-cake. How did you bypass the fingerprint recognition?"

"Gelatin."

"Go on."

Bathory sighed. "Took your print from a cafeteria glass, enhanced it with super-glue fumes. Then I snapped it with my camera, used Photoshop for contrast and—"

"You printed it on a transparency sheet."

Bathory angled her head in pleasant surprise. "Yes. Etched the transparency onto a printed circuit board—"

"And made a gelatin finger with the etching. Nice."

The younger girl smiled, raising her candied fingertip to wiggle it like a puppet. "I am *very* clever," she squeaked in a cartoon voice.

Lash commanded, "Get the forklift."

The girl wiped her mouth. "Yes, ma'am."

As Bathory went to retrieve the machine, Lash looked around the armory. Her eyes settled, in the nearest corner, on several stacked crates marked VAMPIR. It was an old NATO designation for the RPG-29, which the Russians had developed a year before the Soviet collapse. VAMPIR was a shoulder-launched tube that fired tank-busting warheads. Lash had boosted the crates from a casino mogul's fortress at the foot of Mount Charleston, far away from the Strip.

But not far enough. Indulging in survivalist fantasy had been fun until brutal reality swept in—bringing with it a cannibal mob like the one that feasted on the mogul and his family. While removing the munitions from his underground garage, emptied of its luxury vehicles, Lash and Dio had found skeletal fragments blackened from open-flame cooking over barrels. Some bones were small, including what was clearly the skull of a child. Lash had no chance to despair, as Richter's drones came out of nowhere.

He always seemed to know where and when to find Academy students. Pinned down behind travertine pillars along a barren pool, Lash and Dio almost abandoned the crates until Prof mapped Richter's line-of-sight signal with a clumsy weather-router. All it took then was a throwbot—a stealthy toss-and-terrorize—to isolate the downlink. Richter retreated.

Now, wiping dust from a crate with her hand, Lash thought about what she'd spent the last few years amassing. Her collection instilled her with confidence. Secretly, she kept the uncertain side of herself hidden from the others, projecting brashness and defiance to obscure her true feelings of hesitation, ambivalence. She knew that during her best moments, with the right team, she could use this arsenal to decimate bad guys. To slay the kid-eaters. To destroy all monsters. But during her worst moments, she knew that by continuously thrusting herself into harm's way, she wouldn't live to see her next birthday.

The sound of shifting gears entered the room. Lash indicated the crates and moved aside. Bathory, following the forklift on foot with a tablet in her hands, maneuvered the machine into place and raised the lift. Wood creaked, the weight of the RPGs shifting in their coffins.

Bathory reversed the machine out of the armory and brake-tapped. "Where am I going?"

"Loading dock," Lash said. "Dio and I are heading for the mines."

"The *gypsum* mines?"

Lash nodded. "We're working on something."

"Let me come."

She thought about this. "How old are you?"

"Thirteen. Well, next month. But I'm good at stuff. Like security hacks."

"I see that."

"Please," said Bathory, resting the tablet on top of her head, as if fending off rain.

"Move this trash can."

Bathory continued to remote the lift, walking behind it. Before turning off the armory lights, Lash saw a big rat sniffing around a mass spectrometer she'd forgotten to correctly store with the chemical-detection equipment. She quietly removed a bayonet from a carbine mounted on the wall. Gripping it by the blade, she drew her arm back and waited until the stirring creature showed its complete length.

She hurled the knife, impaling the rat through its back and onto the side of a crate. The rodent death-rattled, blood oozing from its wound.

"Heck was that?" said Bathory, peeking her head back into the armory.

"Dinner," Lash said.

7

After applying a blowtorch to the hairs, they waited for the rat to cool before cleaning it with steel wool in a plastic tub of water. After Bathory split it with a machete whack on a piece of aluminum siding for a cutting board, they salted the meat and took it back to Lash's room to fry thoroughly in a tin heated by grain alcohol and wood spirits—lazy Sterno. They garnished the meat with long-expired packages of airplane peanuts.

Good and greasy. Bathory's face glistened in the candlelight as she licked her fingers. Then she asked, "How did the rat survive?"

Lash shrugged. "Soap. Leather. They eat anything."

"I can't remember. Did burgers in America taste this good?"

"Better. When I was your age, no one ate rats. They were considered vermin. Like roaches."

"I *love* roaches. Fry them, dip them in sweet honey—yum!"

"Yeah, they're good. But french fries were a million times better. Fries and ketchup."

"Ketchup. The stuff in little red-and-white pouches?"

"Exactly. Vinegar, sugar, tomato paste."

Bathory scowled. At the Academy, vinegar was strictly a cleaning agent.

"If I find potatoes," added Lash, "I promise to cook you fries."

"Hold the ketchup," Bathory insisted. "I feel bad not sharing." She gnawed at strings of meat hanging from slender bone.

"We found and killed it. It's ours."

"I know. There's just nothing to eat anymore. Not even roaches. Only prickly pear."

"The military had plans, you know," said Lash, changing the subject. "To manipulate bugs by remote control. Called for implanting tiny neural electrodes into the backs of insects."

"Wow," Bathory said. "Food as surveillance bots. Crazy."

"Like I said. Roaches weren't food. But bugs were the first real cyborgs."

The younger girl made the sign of the cross at the cyborg mention or Lash's blasphemy or both. She placed the sucked-clean cartilage and joints into a chipped plastic bowl, wiped her hands on her shirt, stood up, and walked over to Lash's cheval.

"Mirror, mirror," Bathory said.

"Careful, Evil Queen." Finished, Lash scooped remnants into a bin for the incinerator. "It was my mother's."

Bathory ran her fingers along the decorated frame. "What was she like?"

"She was great," Lash said. "Hotel landscaper. Tended Bellagio's botanical gardens. Before it became a syrup distillery run by maniacs."

Bellagio was now controlled by the Harvesters. They'd expanded the hotel's old gardens to grow saguaro, a cactus fruit native to the Southwest. Saguaro had been brought to Las Vegas by the Tohono O'odham, desert Indians who abandoned their reservations when the government crumpled. A collective of psycho pagan sun-worshiping farmers, the Harvesters maintained neutrality and a truce with both the Academy and Richter, and they supplied the valley with saguaro fruit, juice, jam, and syrup. An eerie bunch, the Harvesters practiced human sacrifice and blood rituals to nurture the soil and enhance yields.

Lash knew this firsthand.

"Your mother," Bathory said. "She wasn't—"

"No. She died at UMC a few days before the Collapse. Cancer."

"I'm sorry."

"We leave tonight," Lash said. "Start packing."

Bathory's eyes opened wide in surprise. "Seriously?"

"Still have to convince Prof and Dio. But my own hacker should be onsite."

"I'm the best." Bathory approached Lash but didn't reach for her arm. "I'll check Koons's work."

"Don't check anything," Lash said. "Need you to watch for Richter."

"I can do that, too."

Lash gave her a mean stare. "Get ready. Prep satcom attacks and data-link jams."

Bathory raced off, leaving Lash to snuff the heat and wash dishes in a bucket of clean water. Shortcake was too young and untrained to fight Richter's forces, but the gelatin finger was impressive, inventive. It would've taken years for Koons to come up with that, if ever.

Koons was the last Academy student to vividly remember living with his parents in Las Vegas. He was eleven when the bombs fell and the world plunged into chaos. Sometimes Lash wished they could bond over their shared grief. But deep down, she knew this was impossible. Koons was obnoxious, a showoff and trash-talker. He enjoyed pleasing Prof at the expense of others' self-esteem. She and he had come to blows many times, Lash usually getting the advantage before another student intervened.

The last time, a week ago, she'd cut Koons's lip pretty good with her elbow. He glared at her with palpable hatred. She had to admit it thrilled her, to be bathed in such pure animosity. A buzz not unlike an Academy student's first sip of the Ritalin-spiked grape juice Prof gave out at Gathering to fool the kids into thinking a measure of cosmic transubstantiation had occurred. The amphetamine enhanced their alertness and cognition on critical missions. Prof didn't inform the kids of this, but Lash and Dio and probably Koons knew. They kept the secret for fear of losing special access to the stuff. Prof gave them their own scripts, which they renewed every thirty days with the Academy's robo-nurse. Lash had nicknamed the bot Dr. Feelgood.

She picked up her black Luxor hotel room phone and rang Dio in his lab. "How's the cannon?"

"A pain to move around."

"I want to bring Bathory."

"She isn't ready."

"Hear about the gelatin finger she made?"

Silence.

"Cakewalk for her."

More silence. Then Dio said, "Someday, you can tell me what a cakewalk involves."

"Richter will be there. We need an additional hacker."

"I'll let Prof know. But she's frickin' *twelve*, Lash. If she gets hurt—or worse—it's on you."

8

Koons would react badly to a second hacker, a freckle-speckled freshman at that. Too bad. Lash wasn't going to risk her life on a Koons-run mission. Richter assuming control of the excavator would be a disaster. Losing her weapons to him would be catastrophic. Bathory was one of Lash's hidden aces.

She knew Koons. No question he'd dragged a bolt-on robotics kit to the mine, making the excavator remotely operable. Koons would telecontrol line-of-sight from a Bobcat hundreds of yards away and install four tactical vignettes. The first, SHIELDS_UP, involved digging protective trenches. The second, GUNSLINGER, unleashed the devastating blade and Lash's RPGs. The third, WAGON_TRAIN, allowed for loading and unloading of drones and bots. The fourth, RESCUE_RECOVERY, provided for fetching bots—or dead Academy kids.

She'd have to fight Koons about installing a fifth: SELF_DESTRUCT. His ego would keep him from doing it. He strived for cyborg status, for ascension. To kill a machine as grandiose as an excavator would be like killing himself. What an idiot. She hoped Dio sided with her.

Another quirk of Koons troubled Lash. His insistence on voice commands. She hated it because of his nasal timbre. On top of that, anyone with a sneakbot could hear him coming for miles. Koons claimed more complex orders could be transmitted this way. Besides, he said, who heard anything with Lash's missiles exploding? She wouldn't disappoint on that front.

With her VAMPIRs dock-parked, she returned to her room to spin one of her dad's records, Black Sabbath's *Sabotage,* on her turntable. She grabbed a faded-blue Bishop Gorman High School duffel and packed an ultraviolet liter-bottle water filter, a vitamin D lamp, a tube of craft store-pinched titanium zinc for sunblock, and a Kevlar vest. And her favorite Italian shotgun, the Benelli M4 gas-operated 12-gauge semiauto that converted to pump action for door-breaching. For the Benelli, she'd fashioned her own ported sawtooth tool at the metallurgy, before Koons farted it up. She loved jamming the sawtooth, sharp enough to slice concrete, into a sealed door frame, then pulling hard and firing through the gap.

She also threw in a bag of coffee beans and a *mihmas,* a long-handled heavy iron pan for bean-roasting. She found her hand-woven Bedouin rug rolled up in the corner of her closet and tossed it in, too. A *Playgirl* magazine from the '80s with Mark Harmon on the cover for fire-starting. A bunch of classic-metal cassettes and her Walkman.

She removed her robe, donned a black Judas Priest shirt, camo cargos, and boots. She looked weary in the cheval's reflection, so she took a minute to kiss her eyelashes with some clumpy synthetic mascara a Fremont Street prostitute had handed her in exchange for accidentally snuffing her abusive pimp with a drone misfire. To keep from contracting pink eye and other diseases, Lash had sterilized the mascara with UV light.

She grabbed the duffel bag and a Metallica-stickered rifle case and headed to the dock to meet Dio and Bathory. They were waiting for her next to a trailer-based mobile-ops center attached to a beat-up, bullet-riddled, desert-camoed Ford F150. The VAMPIR crates were neatly stacked in the pickup bed.

"Oh yes." She pumped a fist.

Sitting on a folding chair, Dio put aside an old twentieth-century comic book, *Moon Knight,* about a silver-cloaked Egyptian ninja-vigilante. "Prof wants us at the mine tomorrow night at the latest. Koons claims he saw a drone and it wasn't ours."

"He heard a mosquito buzzing," Lash said. She opened the trailer door and placed her boot on the stepladder, keen to leave.

Ignoring them, Bathory clumsily hopped on a corrugated-cardboard pogo stick the younger kids were spitting out en masse on the school's recyclable-fed 3-D printer. The cardboard was stiffened with a blend of lake salt, manure, and saguaro wax, making it pinewood-tough.

"Still think it's a good idea?" asked Dio, indicating Bathory.

Bathory shrugged. "Does it even matter at this point?" This caused all three to fall silent.

"You heard Prof," Dio said. "Gathering first."

Lash groaned and said, "Damn that man's sleepy homilies."

9

Lash hated Prof's holo-sermons. They were steeped in a mélange of religious gibberish and an uninformed zeal for what the late scientist Hugo de Garis called "artilects," or artificial intellects. Prof believed the Cyborg-Christ would arrive when the Academy, or a group like it, constructed the ultimate autonomous drone. Prof didn't know de Garis from D'Angelo, but Lash had actually read *The Artilect War.* In it, the researcher posited a counterargument: Machines might assume control and erase humanity à la *The Terminator.* Lash felt this truth in her gut, but it was eat or be eaten and she intended to survive.

Lash, Dio, and Bathory rode an inclinator, the angled elevator unique to Luxor, down to join the throng of students, all wearing uniforms of black shirts and camo cargos and black boots, heading to the conference ballroom that had been repurposed for Gathering. Despite many of them having eaten, the scholar-runts were antsy with impending tedium. But they stayed composed under the cybernetic gaze of the Deacons. These machines—smaller and lighter-armed than warbots—prowled the old casino floor looking for anything that wasn't RFID-ed. They also enforced a no-talking-and-no-fooling-around policy in the main worship hall. Their cameras were part of God's Eye. Their 9 mm SIG Sauers, while never aimed at students, did succeed in intimidating the unruliest kids. Deacons were Prof's unspoken yet acknowledged instruments of corporal punishment. Lash didn't blame the headmaster for relying on them. Keeping students in line minus any adults on campus wouldn't be possible without bots. But what was good for discipline didn't suit Lash personally.

She walked by one of these clanking refuse bins now, staring it down while smacking her gum, an obvious violation. The bot didn't notice. Lash huffed, disappointed. Students gave her a wide berth. Dio and Bathory lagged behind, wary that she might go off and cause massive damage before being sedated by the Deacons and thrown into solitary.

It wasn't isolation per se that sparked fear in Lash. It was the agony of being alone without any books or music or any stimulation whatsoever. Left with her own memories, trapped with the ghosts of those she'd sent to hell, Lash suffered terribly.

The casino floor offered more than slot machines and table games. The Academy's survival program center installed a series of modular units, each overseeing a different need among Sin City's desperate souls. Getting access to services offered wasn't easy. Las Vegas residents who passed Prof's rigorous background and personality checks increased their odds of living more than a few years in the wasteland.

Lash had worked for a time in every program—for instance, the community learning center. It taught Academy rejects skills such as filtration, bucket-container gardening, and self-defense. The program was conducted off-campus and assisted by sunny old-world teens whose parents prohibited them from enrolling in the school yet wanted them to have something to do until the Second Coming.

Lash's favorite program was for seniors. Hardly anyone made it to age fifty today. Those who did could be drone-escorted to doctors and herbalists by Academy students. Lash enjoyed conversing with people her parents' and even grandparents' age and protecting them from predators. Old people were funny and cynical. They had a broader perspective on the End of

America. She admired their strength and tenacity and was envious of them. They'd taught her many skills. How to brew excellent coffee, for example. She'd resigned herself to not living long enough to join their ranks. She wondered about her own Gram, her father's mom. Hopefully, she'd made it to Guadalajara. A small percentage of elderly were said to have reached it before the Feds began carving up Las Vegas, killing tens of thousands.

Before Prof helped himself to the largest piece by taking control of the water supply.

Upon entering the Gathering, students brought the thumb, index, and middle fingers of their right hand to a point and made the sign of the cross. Lash skipped this and instead crossed her arms—partly in defiance, mainly because it was freezing and her headlights were high-beaming. Prof's earliest kids had converted this ballroom into a holy site, ripping out carpet and installing marble from a neighboring hotel's posh suites.

Kids dutifully filled aluminum-bleacher pews. Lash took a seat and watched the slideshow on two giant screens sandwiching the stage. It consisted of images that mixed the mechanical with the organic. Human organs and machine parts coalesced into bizarre, physically impossible forms. The pictures might've been an art historian's presentation on a history of surrealism, Dada, abstract expressionism. But Lash knew the drawings were Prof's, his concept sketches for students from a cyborgian near-future.

Eventually, the lights dimmed. Incense burned. Candles flickered on the altar. Electronic music burbled from massive black speakers mounted along the top of a concert stage assembled from scraps of a glam magician's former theater. Lash hated electronica. The completely synthetic sound tore at the thin fabric of tech-gouged minds like hers. Lash had thought long and hard about her and Dio's preference for heavy metal. Somehow the amplified clatter of vibrating steel strings provided relief in a violent cocoon of digital beeps, blips, dings, and buzzers. It also articulated the ongoing battle between good and evil. Light and dark. Beginnings and endings.

The techno burbled for several minutes before fading away as Prof, wearing his chrome-blue devotional vestment, ascended the pulpit, cue-ball head all spick and span. No one cheered or clapped or said anything. The utter silence was impressive, a testament to the respect—or the fear—the students had for their headmaster. The chaos and clamor that defined their drone ops in the substructures had evaporated. In this space, they were settled techno-angels of mercy. Pacified spawn of softly purring microchips.

Moments before he spoke, his giant image was suddenly projected before him, swallowing the pew-bound students. The hologram was a computer-generated 3-D environment that made Academy kids feel like they were engulfed by Prof, his words, his ideas regarding a religious Singularity. Haptic sensors allowed anyone to touch projections as if they were real, though Prof himself felt nothing when someone raised a hand to fondle his vestment. The hologram was stereo-immersive, too, his voice sounding divinely generated, as if speaking directly into one's brain.

"In the name of the Father and of the Son and of the Holy Spirit," Prof said. He was smiling his service smile, forced and fake. The wireless clip-on mic used reverb to make his voice sound immense, authoritative.

"Amen," the students murmured in unison, crossing themselves again.

From this point on, as always, the ritual became increasingly painful for Lash. A Rite of Blessing. Kyrie. Gloria. Opening prayer. Then the excruciating liturgical readings, whereby younger students onstage mechanically read aloud passages from the New Testament. The kids had no idea what they were reciting, any spiritual message lost amid stuttering mispronunciations.

Meanwhile, Lash's pulse accelerated. Perspiration dotted her upper lip. She drew ragged breaths. The room began spinning. She gripped the pew in front of her with both hands. She repeatedly bumped her forehead against whitened knuckles as if undergoing a mild seizure.

Seated beside Lash, Bathory whispered, "Lash."

It worked.

Lash opened her eyes and looked around. She saw other students glancing with worry at her before returning their attention to Prof. Bathory still looked concerned, however.

Dio had a theory about what Lash was enduring—a sporadic, subtler form of post-traumatic epilepsy. The result of a drone-induced head wound and injuries the Harvesters had inflicted upon Lash's body when they used it in a vile blood ritual that beggared description. Prof was aware Lash suffered during Gathering, yet believed her pain would be healed through perfect obedience to the cause.

Finally, the homily. But instead of delivering a sermon, Prof invited a student named Jamie onstage.

Lash opened her mouth, leveling a remorseless look at Dio. Rather than meet her gaze, he studied his scuffed Chuck Taylors resting helplessly on a kneeler. She knew he wasn't happy about this either. True, he believed in a lot of what Prof preached, but she knew he didn't appreciate the headmaster's hard-on for cyborgs any more than she did. Still, Dio offered no protest.

"As you know," Prof said, "Jamie here lost a limb during a successful yet arduous mission at Hoover Dam." He placed his hand on the pigtailed girl's shoulder, and she smiled. He was in campaign mode, fighting for the election of an idea—that students accept cyborg-tech implantation.

Prof continued. "Hacked through an insecure wireless connection, a sabotaging telepresence bot ripped Jamie's arm from her body and tossed it into the water. Poor Jamie here thought her Academy days were over. It was *not* the case. God provides."

"Hallelujah," said a student in the front row.

"When I heard what had happened," Prof said, "I immediately contacted my good friend Dr. Xin Fang, a surgeon with a specialty for this sort of case.

"Dr. Fang didn't want to attempt it remotely. He flew to Vegas to perform this procedure in the flesh, relying on the old facilities at University Medical Center. Show them, Jamie."

Still smiling, the girl raised her brain-controlled robotic arm, all shiny-silver, and performed fluid movements. Someone up front gasped in awe.

"It required a four-hour operation," Prof said. He gestured to another student, who threw him a sponge football. "Dr. Fang implanted two tiny grids of electrodes beneath her brain's surface, near the neurons that control hand and arm movement in the motor cortex."

Lash knew what Prof wasn't saying: The doctor removed parts of Jamie's brain.

Prof stepped away, until reaching a distance of about ten yards, and tossed Jamie the ball. She caught it one-handed with her cyborg arm. She passed it back, a tight spiral.

"It has taken Jamie three months to reach this point," said Prof, catching and cradling the ball like a coach. "Now she completes tasks with her new arm 91.6 percent of the time. She's back at her battle station, once more protecting Las Vegas."

Lash couldn't bear it anymore. Her temples throbbed. The space around her was starting to spin again. She stumbled out of her pew, stepping on the toes of classmates, and exited.

Once outside, her chest felt lighter, looser. She leaned against a pillar for a moment. She turned in the direction of the Gathering, expecting a Deacon to wheel at her with a demerit. Instead, Dio and Bathory approached, grim-faced yet ready to launch this mission.

"Sorry," Lash said to them.

"Don't be," Dio said.

"Well, the Deacons let us pass," Bathory noted. "Prof wants us to move, looks like."

"So let's move then," Lash said. "Before Richter turns us into cyborg fodder."

"Can it be that bad?" Bathory asked. "Jamie seems happy."

"That's because Dr. Fang performed a lobotomy."

"What? Wait, you really think—"

"Don't worry your pretty, unimplanted head about it, Bath."

Nothing more was said as they walked to the dock. What Lash didn't say—what Bathory and Dio didn't know—was that Fang had also put Lash's drone-split skull back together when she arrived at the Academy.

Lash suspected the surgeon had stuck something inside her head, a device. And that it was giving her seizures.

10

Driving a backfire-prone pickup with a poorly air-conditioned, satellite-festooned, drone-control station in tow from the Strip to the valley's north-ernmost edge was no easy feat. Add pothole-pocked roads, throat-slitting bandits, and Richter's Red Angel death-drones raking the skies like carrion-seeking vultures, and you had a probable fiasco. But on this journey, Lash and her team enjoyed elements in their favor. Steel-plated trailers and rec-reational vehicles—armed to the teeth with murderhole-nested AK-47s and UAV-crippling mortars—were all anyone dared maneuver through these treacherous streets. So the school's vehicular appearance was as common as radiation after the Collapse. Plus, if Richter happened to sniff Academy on them, their jammers would impede his ability to track and terminate them.

Dio pulled out of the Luxor parking garage and into a quarter-mile queue of post-apocalypse RVs waiting interminably for water from Mandalay Bay's trickling filtration pump. Guarded by Academy drones and warbots, the pump had once supplied swells for the hotel's wave-machine pool. Now it provided nomads with badly needed H_2O. A family traveling from, say,

Colorado to the Pacific Coast for food-bartering could stop here, hydrate, and fill their canteens before risking the long, dangerous drive down I-15.

Today, Lash saw the mustang that sometimes appeared at the fountain for a drink. Mustangs descended from the old domesticated Iberian horse, brought to North America centuries earlier by Spanish conquistadors through Mexico. Before the Collapse, the wild horses had free-roamed the state under government protection. In lawless Nevada, however, they were hunted to near extinction by hungry French-Canadian clowns, former Cirque du Soleil performers in Las Vegas. Horsemeat was a Parisian delicacy.

This mustang had a beautiful buckskin coat that glinted in the sunlight. Lash nicknamed him Sally and sometimes fed him carrots from Luxor's cafeteria and alfalfa hay, which nobody ever ate, from the student bucket-garden in the converted parking garage. Lash wished she could feed the horse now.

"Your boy's here," Dio said.

"I love him," Lash said. "So handsome."

Suddenly interested, Bathory put her face right up to the surveillance screens. Seeing no one worth mentioning, she said, "Heck are you talking about?"

"Horse." Dio sometimes teased Lash about capturing Sally and selling him to the clowns. But when he didn't, Lash knew he thought better of cracking the joke for Bathory now.

She didn't bother to cam-peek at the vehicles around her. She knew what these people looked like—ragged, starving, half-insane from a nomadic life on the edge of the abyss. Families were the hardest to stomach, especially children. She couldn't blame the RV crowd. Sometimes the best way to stay alive was to keep running. Many nonurban Nevadans had perished in Las Vegas, thinking the city might afford advantages. To tamp down desperation and violence, Prof maintained the fountain. Even knowing Richter's pilots occasionally drank from it, Prof looked the other way.

Although desert locked, Las Vegas wasn't much different from other major cities hit with bombs. The suburbs were rotting, cannibal-populated mazes of death where you took your chances upon entering. Safe harbors and small farming communities ringed the downtown core, where older and established vegetation thrived and what remained of the city's resources helped moderate the horror. What made Las Vegas unique was the vast skeleton of the Strip, mammoth hotel-casino husks standing like ancient

HAMMER OF THE DOGS

ruins in the sand, rendering the former tourist-teated boomtown older than it was. Las Vegas Boulevard, once a thrumming corridor of revelry, now stretched empty, a ghost-haunted cesarean-section scar running north to south, from one dead edge of the valley to the other.

Luxor housed the Academy. The Harvesters tended Bellagio's gardens. Other than these tenanted structures, only the hotel and condo towers of CityCenter showed signs of life, dim faces peering from windows during the day, lighted rooms glowing at night. All the while drones patrolled the sky around the complex, swooping down like aggressive seagulls to strafe or fire a rocket at a vehicle or individual drawing too close. Prof mentioned that, in recent weeks, Richter's Red Angels hovered like doom-delivering specters. This suggested he'd made a pact with the wealthy families sheltered at CityCenter.

Inside the trailer, Lash studied a map on a screen before speaking into her headset. "Clear."

In the front cabin, Dio punched the gas and turned the steering wheel hard. The RV's tires screeched dramatically—yet another parched, frantic family gambling to skip the epic wait and find quicker access to potable water.

Dio barreled behind Luxor and onto Frank Sinatra Drive, gunning it like everyone else, making good time up the road skirting the skeletal remains of the once-mighty Strip. New York-New York, Park MGM, Caesars Palace, the Mirage, and Resorts World, site of world-class traffic jams before the Collapse, now little more than a desert ghost town where drivers stopped for nothing, especially not the murderous crazies who suddenly stepped into the thoroughfare. Waving their arms in pretend distress was a ploy to trick newcomers into braking. Dio floored the accelerator. A group of them jumped out of the way, the fires of hatred and desperation blazing in their eyes.

Why didn't Prof drone-dice these scum? Was God's Eye cataracted? She mulled sending her own UAV but decided against it. Richter might be listening. The Academy didn't use cell phones for this reason. Phones were easily hacked, and no one hacked better than Richter.

Through the trailer's rear HD cam, Lash watched a roadway brigand. Having failed to halt Dio, the psycho mopped his sweaty, grinning, warped visage with a toddler's Dora the Explorer underwear. It was flecked with blood. Lash shivered. She gritted her teeth and considered asking Dio to

U-turn so she could rupture the man's forehead with her M4 and splatter his brains against the crumbling facade of Circus Circus.

Instead, she buried the impulse, kissed her crucifix, and said a prayer to Christopher, patron saint of travel. She said to Dio, "Never did get your learner's permit."

In his best Mexican bandit voice, he said. "We don't need no *steenkeen* learner's permit."

She laughed and said to Bathory, "Hope you brought food."

The girl nodded excitedly while tweaking her satcom jammer. Lash noticed an encryption-cracking algorithm percolating on her tablet screen. Little mama was getting busy.

"I love rat sushi," Lash added. "Pack any?"

"Desert truffles," Bathory said. She looked up to smile. "And scorpion jerky."

"Garlic or regular?" Lash returned the grin.

"Regular."

"Garlic's better for inflammation. Infection."

Dio struck a pothole. The trailer hauling Lash and Bathory reverberated with the aftershock.

"Sorry," Dio groaned in their headsets.

"Tell me that was a *human* speedbump," Lash joked.

"I'm disappointed in the people who gave me up."

Lash looked at the girl. Where did this come from all of a sudden? She considered a few responses, but then just played along. "Your parents? They gave you to the Academy. To Prof."

"But look at *your* parents. They didn't willingly hand you over to strangers."

"*Un*willingly then. So what?"

"They loved you. Would've kept you if they'd lived."

"You and I are here regardless."

Bathory dabbed her moist eyes with the sleeve of her shirt. She was clearly fighting off the temptation to blubber. "Weren't my parents responsible? For building this world?"

"No," said Lash, grinding her jaw. "Satan constructed *this* hell. With the help of fools."

Bathory looked at her dead-on now. "I was a baby," she said, hazel eyes piercing Lash's heart.

Uncomfortable with the intensity, Lash feigned interest in an HD cam.

Quiet for a time, Bathory said, "Anyhow, I know you'd never leave me."

Lash furrowed her brow. "How are you so sure?"

"I've earned your loyalty."

"Oh?"

"Yes. And when I help attack Richter with the excavator, we'll be best friends. Sisters!"

Lash laughed out loud. "Bathory, sisterhood is beside the point. This mission is about saving Las Vegas."

"*I* care," she muttered, returning her attention to the tablet, looking sheepish about her burst of enthusiasm.

Lash couldn't accept Bathory's love. Lash's friends never lived long. Lash wouldn't either. Better to keep her distance.

Bathory looked up again, forcing a smile. "I won't let you down."

"I know."

Suddenly the truck came to a halt. Anxiety seeped into the trailer.

"Dio," said Lash, peering at screens and observing empty streets. "What's up?"

"Hard to say," he said. "But *up* is why I stopped."

Lash nudged a joystick for the roof cam, pointing it at blue expanse. When an image came into focus, it took twenty seconds before she could process what she was seeing.

"Are those—"

"Blimps?" asked Bathory, over Lash's shoulder. "Really?"

"Inflatable airships," Lash said. "Frickin' zeppelins. How many?" She unsuccessfully tried to collect them into a single vid frame. She considered transmitting an encrypted photo to Prof.

"Looks like a dozen," Dio said. "No, fourteen."

"Let me guess," Lash said. "Heading north."

"Yep."

"Has to be Richter."

"Well, his drones *were* escorting the zeps, I noticed. Until a second ago."

"Then what?"

"Broke formation and retreated. A few ran out of fuel and crashed."

"Jammed?"

"Maybe. Or they got called away to deal with something else."

"Those blimps look strong enough, Dio. To transport an excavator."

"Probably. There are enough of them."

"Launching the Bride." She bent down to open a cabinet opposite the computers. She pulled out the rifle case with a Metallica sticker on it and leapt out of the trailer.

"Wait!" Dio called.

"What's the Bride?" Bathory wanted to know.

"Richter will have our location," Dio warned. "We're still twenty-five miles out!"

"Shouldn't have stopped," Lash said.

Dio lifted his foot off the brake, but it was too late. Lash had already assembled the old UAV her father had given her before he left her. The drone was different now in many ways. She'd cannibalized parts from the onboard computer of an old Northrop Grumman X-47B, once the pinnacle of drone design. The Bride was now a domestic-military hybrid boasting a parachute—she couldn't lose her cherished machine in a collision. Infracam. Autonomous navigation. Submachine gun. GPS-guided smartbombs. She adored smartbombs.

In other words, Lash's UAV was a havoc-wreaker.

But it was too heavy to hand-launch or bungee-shoot. So Lash kicked wide the slinger's tripod legs and cranked the drone into position.

"Dio?" Lash squinted at the slinger's real crosshairs before checking tablet coordinates.

"What?" His tone was flat.

"The name of the German blimp that caught fire and crashed."

"You mean on the famous album cover?" He was obviously brightening now. "*Led Zeppelin I?*"

"Yeah, was it Heineken?" She confirmed the multispectral real-time video mapping. She kissed her crucifix and said a prayer to Ignatius, patron saint of soldiers.

"Hindenburg!"

"Right. Fourteen of those flaming gasbags coming right up."

Bathory, outside now, watched Lash in action.

Lash glanced over at her and saw the wary admiration on Bathory's face, then catapulted the Bride heavenward.

11

Because of their multi-segmented bodies, the gray airships resembled the giant sandworms from the David Lynch film *Dune*. They hovered, according to Lash's high-res geo-corrected mosaic, somewhere above two thousand feet. This was her UAV's maximum altitude, but she wasn't worried. Smartbombs would reach them. The big, dumb, slow dirigibles could be deployed in an hour by popping them from standard crates. On the downside, they made for barn-size targets. Like shooting floating whales in nitroglycerin-lined barrels.

Lash was hot to exploit the downside.

The Bride minced the lead dirigible with a head-on shot that ruptured the engine's turbine blades. Fiery pieces ejected and landed on tent cities below, igniting conflagrations. With water too precious for nondrinking purposes and no fire departments, infernos raged. Soon, screams of people choking on smoke and burning alive began reaching Lash's ears.

But by then, a second and third round had been unleashed. One gashed a blimp's stabilizer, causing the hydrogen-stuffed behemoth to drift backward until it slammed into the spine of the Stratosphere Tower and exploded in an orange fireball, broken windows splintering in the blast zone. The third deflated the zeppelin like a toy. Surveillance drones projected images on Bathory's tablet of hydrogen gas poisoning people fleeing a bazaar, their twitching bodies squashed by cars and trampled by gas-masked shoppers.

Lash was wrecking an already-demolished city.

"Hadn't reckoned on the collateral damage," she admitted to Dio.

Overwhelmed and disgusted with themselves, they got out now to stand in front of the truck's headlights and survey the destruction. The sight of the Bride gutting three-hundred-foot-long UAVs was stirring, even if their sizzling carcasses inflicted severe damage and widespread suffering. Lash noticed that Dio was speechless, immobile, hypnotized. The sun began its descent as Las Vegas got its teeth bashed in.

The tableau mirrored the harrowing pain of her days after the Collapse. She cried, tears streaming. She'd unintentionally killed dozens, injured hundreds. Scared at what she'd unleashed, Lash touched the BASE option on her tablet to recall the Bride. She needed another way to harpoon the gray leviathans.

By that point, Bathory had snapped the encryptions like twigs. Back in the trailer, she pumped bogus weather-avoidance data through the control-station disrupter. Sure enough, alerted to a storm pushing in from the north, the blimps turned around and advanced toward the vivid landscape of what was once Red Rock National Conservation Area.

"Thank you," said Lash, meaning it.

Bathory had saved Las Vegas from Richter's excavator-transport scheme and the Bride's searing embrace. Clever girl. Lash considered giving Dio an I-told-you-she's-awesome look, but the moment wasn't right and anyway, he was on an encrypted call with Koons.

Dio hung up and said, "Koons is secure, but bots have him pinned. Richter delayed us."

"He wants to *kill* us," Bathory coldly stated. "For bringing down his blimps." She pointed at a Red Angel squadron slashing across a darkening sky, homing in on the Bride.

"They're back!" Dio yelled.

Lash tablet-tapped ATTACK. The Bride instantly pulped a Red Angel with a swift dogfight roll, followed by a point-blank smartbomb kill shot to another. Detonations curdling the atmosphere, a third Red Angel made it past the Bride, heading right for them.

Lash shoved Bathory into the trailer as Dio got the truck's engine to turn over and tire-marked the asphalt. A military-sourced projectile landed nearby, concussing the mobile ops center. The trailer echo-boomed. Lash's bones rattled; her organs shifted.

A nauseatingly familiar feeling.

"Hellfires!" she yelled into her headset. She recognized too well the impact of these missiles, her skull fractured by Hellfire shrapnel when she was twelve. A Predator had wiped out her Boulder City refugee camp to reinstate federal control over Hoover Dam. Later, official word on the strike was that domestic terrorists had infiltrated the camp. It was bunk, and everyone knew it. Lash didn't learn of the falsehood until much later, however. Her head wound had scrambled her lobes to such a degree that she stalked the talking ghost of her dead mother on foot, all the way to Bellagio—and right into the Harvester's uncanny fellowship.

"Bath, it's time to snap," Lash commanded.

But Bathory was already throwing out a fierce barrage of satcom-jamming and GPS-overriding pulse-waves. It saved them.

Jacked on adrenaline, Lash tablet-monitored the Bride, leaving it in autonomous mode. The drone was doing well. It cut down another Red Angel, then shadowed the Academy truck. The Bride would escort Lash and her team all the way to the mines. Dio had helped program her. He was the best.

Dio rocketed them down Charleston Boulevard, smashing through half-assed roadblocks that skin-cancered drifters had set up to slow down cars and beg for crumbs and water.

"Love your lead foot," she said to Dio from the trailer, her headset static-crackling.

Dio grunted affirmatively and punched the gas again. The RV clipped a shopping cart with a man who was, for whatever reason, dozing inside it. The trailer's rear-cam captured the guy flying from the cart, face bouncing off a light pole. He crumpled to the sidewalk. Lash closed her eyes and said a silent prayer for him. For the city she'd re-wounded.

Everyone was silent. Lash knew her team felt sorry for her and that they also, quite rightly, feared her even more now. They shunned her devastating wrath. She would've shunned it, too, in their shoes.

The sound of the RV was all they listened to for many minutes.

Finally, Bathory said, "Cracked and hacked." She meant the remaining Red Angels. She smirked mischievously and voice-commanded her tablet. "Greased Lightning."

Lash fretted. "What did you do?"

"Oh, nothing. Been working on synchronized UAV flying routines put to songs and I—"

"You hacked Richter's drones into performing a number from *Grease*."

"Yes!"

"The chicks'll cream," Lash recited. Her aunt had played the record for her many times. "Classic American musical."

Bathory cranked "Lightning" via her tablet speaker just as Lash projected Richter's dancing drones on the station monitors. They chortled, the redhead rocking in her chair.

"Lash, what were musicals like?"

"Fun. Well, except for *Phantom*."

"*The Phantom of the Opera*? No good, huh?"

"It was OK. The premise stunk."

"Which was?"

"A monster living underground."

So far, the mission hadn't gone well.

Lash thought about owning up to it after seeing the most disturbing evidence of the whole episode thus far. Studying the zeppelin damage close up via one of Bathory's surveillance drones, she observed a charred blimp-skin flake on the rubble-strewn road in the Academy truck's smog-trail with the letters USAF.

United States Air Force.

12

The highway leading to the mines was extensively damaged. The Feds had used it in vain attempts to exert control over the mineral extraction and reclamation plants. They badly misjudged the fury of two million people trapped in the valley with little water and no food other than skimpy FEMA emergency shipments that the desperate police, with advance knowledge of the drop zones, intercepted and used to enforce submission. Eventually, people gave up on the drops, learning to subsist on desert shrubs and rage. Or they died. Metro police, which had become increasingly militarized post-9/11, had tanks and drones to thwart Washington's advances. The battles were insane.

Lash deemed this the only good thing about her father dying early on. He was never forced to cut deals with drug cartels, only to end up killed by Uncle Sam-lobbed bunker busters a year later. With the cops defeated, the Fed's command chain roiled by assassinations in D.C., and the libertarian militia leaving to secure a mineral lode in California, the vacuum let Prof and Richter step in and carve up the valley. Neither warlord—Lash wasn't so naive as to deny Prof's true status—cared about road maintenance. Streets were for common citizens and thugs. Prof was clearly disinterested in what happened on byways, as long as general order was kept and people didn't tamper with water, power, and food. The elite conducted business remotely—in the air and over the desert.

It was a largely open secret that the cartels also supplied tech to the Academy. In exchange, Prof gave drug lords access to abandoned bases, black-ops centers, and the Test Site. The cartels—serving China, Canada, and Western Europe—dreamed of enriching uranium to irradiate the Ukrainian mob. The Test Site, for instance, stored waste that had never made it to a proposed dump at Yucca Mountain. An older student, now dead, had shared a particular nugget of information with Lash: every few years, for hardware, Prof graduated a student to work under drug lords and assassinate rival gangs.

But now the Academy had a plan to save Las Vegas. It involved hacking a colossal mine-saw to eradicate, once and for all, its rivals.

Bathory was sliding her tablet into its protective case when Dio hit another pothole. The computer slipped from her hands and struck the floor, the screen fubared in one corner.

The younger girl looked at Lash, grimacing with concern. "Sorry."

"Damn, Dio," Lash said.

"More than welcome to repave this road," he said.

"Sure. Then *you* can replace Bathory's tablet."

"What? C'mon, guys. Hold *onto* things, please!"

Lash asked Bathory, "Fixable?"

"It's a work-around." She opened the command menu, checking for touch-ability issues. Lash saw that the corner button, DEFEND, was problematic.

"Here," said Lash, offering her tablet.

Bathory shook her head. "Mine's customized."

"Suit yourself," Lash said. She put her gear away and glossed the screens.

"I—I have a question."

"Yes?"

"Richter's not jamming us back. Why?"

"He wants the excavator," Lash explained. "He's already at the mine."

"The blimps were a diversion?"

Lash didn't respond to the reminder that she'd taken on the military and blown whatever time advantage they might have had. But she still didn't want to burden Bathory with that information. Picking at a scab on her elbow where Koons's tooth had broken skin days prior, she lied. "Likely. The zeps were an effort to draw us out and reveal our location."

Dio hit another pothole, garbling Bathory's response. So she reached into her bag and took out a bag of dried meat. "Gives 'pet food' a whole new meaning," she said, handing over the largest slice.

Lash bit into the jerky, trying not to act starved.

"I hear you chewing," Dio intercommed. "Can I have some, please?"

"It's scorpion," warned Lash, her mouth full. "Doesn't meat gag you?"

"Bugs ain't meat," Dio insisted. "They're crunchy and protein-rich."

"Fine."

She looked at Bathory and put out her hand, on which the redhead placed another strip. Lash dug her other hand into a cabinet crawling with Korean-made grenadebots. Finding one with an onboard camera and magnetic claws, she placed the jerky in its pincers. She opened the blast-resistant sunroof to scoot the lobster-like bot across the trailer top.

Bathory laughed when Lash switched on the botcam. They watched the TNT-encrusted crustacean scuttle down the trailer's front end, across the hitch, over and around the VAMPIR crates, and through the truck's gun rack. Pothole impacts enhanced the humor of the bot's bumbling progress. Camera footage always seemed to add weight to people and, with his Kevlar on, Dio looked even more rotund. To Lash, anyway.

"Order up," she said.

Dio flinched when he saw the bot in the passenger seat. He exhaled loudly. "Not funny."

"Don't worry," she teased. "It's scorpion jerky, not a release pin."

He took the dried meat from the bot's pincers and stuffed it into his mouth.

"Good?" Bathory asked.

"I prefer the garlic," he said. "What about you, Lash?"

She was looking at something unrelated on the monitors. Behind them was a black Toyota 4Runner. It, too, towed a sat-dished trailer. Painted on the hood was Richter's insignia—a white jawless skull with an anarchy symbol on the brow. She spotted a mounted XM395 precision RPG. In seconds, it would be so close that jamming couldn't save them.

"Drive," said Lash, voice trembling.

"What do you think I'm doing?" Dio said. "Eating scorpion?"

"Go faster!"

13

Lash triggered the Bride's heatscope on the station keyboard, but Richter's infra-jamming technique was so gnarly that the virtual targeting froze up. Frustrated, she went handheld and toggled the joystick to wrench her drone out of spoof-default. It failed.

Above the Academy truck, the Bride circled slowly, unresponsive to any command. Richter's goons had toppled Lash's chessboard queen. Now they were coming for Lash's head.

Unaware of the approaching RPG, Bathory crowed, "Their drones are down. *So easy.*"

Lash glared at her with such contempt that the younger girl instinctively brought her knees up to her chest, as if about to endure a beating.

"Ladies," said Dio. His sudden acceleration suggested he'd seen the rocket. "Little help?"

"On it," Lash said.

With no options left, she grabbed the M4 and rifle-butted the unlatched sunroof wide open. Holding the shotgun vertically, she pushed it up and through, twisted, and used it to muscle-up, lifting herself over the improvised bar and on top of the trailer. Wind buffeting her, she crosshaired the 4Runner. It braked, backing down momentarily. Soon Richter's goons would zoom at her again when they saw she didn't have an RPG.

She planned on having one ready when they did.

But she needed another minute. She turned to snatch the grenadebot that had been retracing its path to the trailer sunroof. She accessed it via print scan, amped its magnetic and explosive levels, pulled the pin, and tossed it. Then she headed toward Dio.

The once-clownish bot instantly transformed into a grim decimator. Hurtling through the air, it spasmed its black pincers like a malevolent tarantula, landing on the 4Runner's windshield and slowly crystallizing the glass. Richter's men were prepared and shotgunned the spider through the windshield, which sent the bot spiraling forward. It detonated a millisecond later, ten yards in front of the truck. Shrapnel rained on them, slivering the headlights and causing the driver to graze the charred skeleton of a minivan and tailspin. He regained control but lost ground.

Lash had anticipated the sequence of events and gained the time she needed to clamber the length of the trailer, leaping onto the VAMPIR crates strapped to the flatbed. Her gun's sawtooth breaching tool butter-sliced the wood panels. She'd shoulder-strapped and armed the launch tubes months ago, so she took two and carefully stepped across the hitch. But then Dio called, "Hang on!" As he swerved to evade a sinkhole, she might've been thrown off the trailer had she not gripped its ladder.

The VAMPIRs were heavy and banged her vertebrae. She blocked out the pain and climbed on top in time to see the 4Runner coming within a hundred yards. GPS was useless and there was no time to aim properly, so she swung around the first tube, mounted it against her shoulder, and clicked off the safety.

"I am your hammer, God," she said, pulling the trigger.

The mortar missed, shrieking above the 4Runner. But the surprise of it, along with the rocket's profuse, vision-obscuring trail of ignition smoke and the impact of a pothole full of scrap metal, resulted in a blown front tire. Richter's men slowed to a useless creep as the tread unspooled completely to reveal a bare rim.

Lash climbed down through the sunroof. She pulled a stick of gum from her cargos and asked Bathory, "How's my baby?"

"I—I'm fine." She gazed at the VAMPIR leashed to Lash's back, her face changing from repulsion to attraction.

"I meant the Bride."

"Oh." Bathory checked the connection indicators. "She's back. Jammer's out of range."

"Great. Dio, how far?"

"Five miles."

The sun had disappeared. The Bride's night vision functioned beautifully. They could locate Koons lickety-split. But Richter-led ambushes enjoyed a higher success rate in the desert's total darkness. Dawn would be more advantageous for Lash's team.

"How's Koons?"

"All jammed up. But he has his crossbow."

Koons's crossbow was one of his better concepts. It shot an arrow that generated a short-range electromagnetic-pulse burst on impact. The burst fried microchips within a predetermined radius, turning a losing cyberwar or drone battle into a stalemate.

It wasn't in Lash's nature to appreciate a draw.

Lash had done Koons one better by taking his EMP idea, miniaturizing it, and sticking it onto a needle-drone, producing a flying hypodermic that injected poison milked from a blue-ringed octopus into a target. The squid had been pilfered from the seafood merchants of Shark Reef Aquarium. The venom caused instant paralysis, killing in seconds. Once the plunger depressed, a short-range EMP surge wiped out any droneware on the victim. Lash's stealthy syringe-UAV ensured that another mercenary couldn't pick up a fallen comrade's tablet and continue droning. She always got a little kick to think that her improvisation really needled Koons.

"Tell him not to use the crossbow. Cavalry arrives at sunrise."

"Pulling over now," Dio said.

Bathory applied ground-penetrating radar to the area. "Head due west. Caves, looks like."

Dio heeded her and stopped in front of a cluster of rock formations.

Lash was ambivalent about caves. They made escape impossible. But they also lowered heat signatures during the day and reduced the bite of the desert's cold wind after dark. All in all, it was a good night for a cave.

She and Bathory exited the trailer. The younger girl stretched, while Lash and Dio covered the truck and trailer with signal-masking tarp.

"Extra tarp, please," she said.

"Why?"

"Coffee."

"Not out here," Dio said.

"In the cave, of course. Hey, what's your problem? You love my brew."

"You need rest, Lash." He handed her a roll of material.

"When have you known me to sleep?"

"I'll be in the trailer," Dio said. "I get cranked just smelling your java."

After retrieving her duffel bag and gun, Lash stepped into the mouth of the cave. She clicked her Zippo and looked for tracks or any signs that an animal had used the shelter recently. There were none. Inside, it was critter-free—only sand, rocks, her own flickering, distortion-bending shadow. The cave was big enough not to have to worry about eating up all the oxygen with a fire and asphyxiating. She went outside and used her gum to tarp-cover the entrance, then sawtoothed an olive tree limb. Back inside, she used the old issue of *Playgirl* for kindling.

She roasted the beans in the *mihmas* like her Iranian neighbor Mr. Ali Hamad had taught her. At first, her mom had been suspicious about why an elderly taxi driver was teaching a teenage girl how to make coffee like a Bedouin tribesman. Lash knew the old man was tired of hearing her throw knives against the wooden fence between their houses and figured he should teach her a quieter, more useful skill, like making strong Arabic java.

She was grateful for his gift—as well as his protection in the days following the Collapse.

This most recent batch of Sumatra came from an Arizona family that had bartered with her after she replaced their car battery. The beans roasted well, and she ground them with a copper mortar and pestle. When the water was hot, she poured it over the coffee. It smelled so good she wanted to wake Dio now with a cup.

Sipping the steaming brew, she tried, and failed, to compartmentalize the mass injuries and deaths she'd inflicted on Las Vegas. Five years earlier, when a drone-launched Hellfire carnaged her life in the refugee camp in Boulder City, she'd considered drone pilots chickenshit thrill-killers who derived ghastly kicks from watching defenseless victims explode on camera. Gradually, after enrolling in the Academy, learning to remotely pilot missile-laden aircraft herself, and witnessing the killing of others by her own hand, she became not only inured to causing psychological and physical harm, but actually embraced the practice of digital aggression toward strangers.

Then again, maybe she embraced nothing. Compulsion was a better explanation. She knew little of the early twentieth-century Austrian psychoanalyst Sigmund Freud, but she'd stumbled onto his theory of the death drive in a musty old book, *Beyond the Pleasure Principle,* from her father's library. Searching for dirty-sex parts, she'd encountered an upsetting idea. Freud had observed how shell-shocked soldiers returning from World War I tended to repeat, reenact, and consistently dream of their traumatic experiences. It symbolized the desire to move from an organic to an inanimate state, from order to oblivion, from life to death. The death drive's fullest expression was in the collective instinct toward the destruction of the world.

Freud was onto something. What else were drones but the embodiment of man's ceaseless hunger for self-annihilation? Drones were especially pernicious, because they added a technological filter between the Cain-and-Abel ritual. Through a screen, everything was reduced to fantasy, a game. The cyber-eye of a vengeful machine wasn't the pilot's to pluck out.

A pilot was playing a role, doing his job. "The computer really did it!" was the compartment into which a remote killer routinely placed his or her guilt. Drone pilots never admitted it, but it was how they went to bed every night and slept the sleep of the just.

She was about to turn on the UV lamp for a D-vitamin charge when Bathory entered the cave wearing black Academy-issued pajamas and Lash's pink-and-white Hello Kitty slippers. They were dirty and scuffed now.

"Can I try your coffee, please?"

Lash forced a smile, poured the dregs, passed the girl the tin cup, and watched her squint.

"Ugh," said Bathory, handing it back. "Tastes like bitter earth."

"Keeps me awake."

"You don't sleep?"

"No."

"Too many nightmares?"

"Not enough dreams," Lash said.

14

They sat cross-legged in silence, listening to the wind and sweating from the oppressive heat in the cave. Somewhere outside a screech owl clapped its mandibles. A coyote yip-yapped in the distance, reminding Lash that she was hungry. A mouse twittered. Bathory said, "You're so close with your brother."

"Dio and I aren't related. People just assume that. We arrived at the Academy on the same evening. We bonded over that experience, I guess."

Bathory yawned. "What were your first days like?"

Lash didn't like rehashing the past, but strong coffee was coursing through her bloodstream and she didn't want to think about the zeppelins anymore.

"Frightening," she said. "Violent. Bloody. Back then, lots of students were dying. One or two every day. Richter was on a rampage. There was no time for training."

"Did you really kill your first merc at fourteen?"

"Yes, but I'd been flying since I was a toddler. Not kill-drones. My dad's line-of-sight, hand-launched, surveillance UAV. He was a cop. The idea is basically the same, whether you're plopped in a mission chair or tableting on the street. You put the wind—the air—to good use. Speed makes the air stronger. You want to avoid overcompensating."

"Wow," Bathory said. "You were a pilot before you learned to read."

"Fourteen?" Lash laughed. "I was reading comic books at age three. I'm an above-average pilot, but my strength is making weapons and mods, then using them to kill drones and bad guys."

"I don't know," Bathory said. "I'd hate to square off against the Bride with you piloting."

"Obviously, she's been updated for military engagement. Dio taught me everything I know about repair. He's my *real* teacher, not Prof."

"How does Dio know how to do everything?"

"Lowriders. His parents were members of Gesto Azteca, a classic-car chapter in Las Vegas. His family worked in body and auto shops along Industrial Road for decades. They spent all their time taking old Chevys down to the metal and building them back up. When he was eight, Dio was sandblasting Impala shells and using a grinder to level out welds."

Bathory looked interested, but also confused. "I *think* I get what you're saying."

"See, Dio was born into a world of iron and steel, not plastic. He's pretty mediocre at flying UAVs. But if you need a heavy tank for defense or require an assault bot, he's your dude. Prof's no idiot, so he made Dio his right-hand bot-boy."

Bathory's next question annoyed Lash. "Is Dio in love with you?"

Lash said nothing while trying to formulate an answer. Of course Dio loved her. *Duh.* And if she were any kind of comrade to him, she would return his affection. She would've already slept with him, given her tight body over to his chubby caresses, his cactus-yogurty fingers, and his little uncircumcised pecker hidden somewhere under the creases of his tummy. She knew it would please him. She knew if she asked him, he'd run away with her. After escaping the Academy, they could live together in a safe place like Guadalajara or—well, anywhere that wasn't Las Vegas.

But it wouldn't be fair to Dio. Lash wasn't cut out for marriage, children, or whatever conventional arrangements the old world enjoyed. At the same time, she recalled the many instances Dio had protected and comforted her for no reason other than that he adored her. Remembering his sacrifices over the years was painful, so she rejected the pain and focused on whatever their mission happened to be. There was another way she could make him happy—to utterly mince Richter into a merc-patty and cook him on a grill of vengeance.

Lash shrugged. "Dio's never said anything."

Bathory had already moved on to another subject. "Think any of the Academy boys my age are cute?"

"What?" Lash said. "Hell no. They're all worms. Get out. Go sleep in the trailer with Dio."

"Ugh," said Bathory, standing up to knock dust from her scrawny legs. "Smells like spoiled cactus juice in there."

"Too bad," said Lash, tablet-scanning a rendering of the excavator. "Goodnight, Bathory."

"Goodnight, Lash. No nightmares and more dreams."

"More dreams, Bath."

Lash had only opened the first schematic capture when the girl returned, hands pressed to her chest. Fright on her face gave her the aspect of an anime character. "What's wrong, Shortcake?"

"Something's out there."

Lash lunged for her shotgun, which made Bathory step forward and add, "It's *breathing*."

"Wounded merc." Lash, relieved it wasn't a kill-drone, bolt-loaded the Benelli with a solid slug. She'd barefoot-stalk whatever Bathory claimed was panting in the darkness. "Stay here," said Lash, twisting a suppressor onto the end of the barrel.

Crouched low, finger on the trigger, she ninja-pranced out of the cave. Above, the black sky was star-pricked. A slight breeze dried her cave sweat. She heard squeak-cries from a restless killdeer fifteen yards to her right. Otherwise, nothing. Dio's trailer was so silent and tarp-obscured, it took Lash a few seconds to locate it.

There was an intensity to nighttime engagement. She'd feared the dark until infra-vision taught her an important lesson, that no monsters roamed the desert—only lost souls, plus some mercs with a quarter of her instinct and skills. She reminded herself now that, if anything, *she* was the fiend dogging everyone's nerves.

Then she heard it. Snuffling. Digging. Clicking. Earlier, before the sun had completely set, Lash noticed a patch of prickly pears, from which the noises were currently emanating. She couldn't help it. She groaned in anticipation of fire-cooked meat.

The javelina grunted back at her, distressed and confused at having encountered a human.

The pig-like mammal scampered, kicking up dust, then froze in the beam of Lash's gun-mounted flashlight. The beast's staring eyes glowed green in the moment before Lash fired. The muzzle blast was audible, even with a silencer muffling the sonic signature. As long as no mercs were within a mile, Lash's strike team would be safe.

Perfect shot. The peccary squealed piercingly twice, in agony and terror. It trembled with a sudden convulsion, fell on its side, and lay still.

Dio rummaged inside the trailer. He swung open the side door, belly hanging over his boxer shorts, cradling a drone-dispatching tablet. "Tell me you're hunting."

"Javelina," Lash said. In recent years, with the ecosystem upended, the pigs had migrated to Nevada from Arizona. "I need a blade to clean it."

Dio yawned, dipping a hand into his boxers to scratch his balls. He went back inside and came out, grinning wickedly and holding up a big survival knife.

"Rambo-dacious," Lash approved.

An hour later, meat was roasting inside the cave. Coughing, Lash swatted grease-burning smoke in a vain effort to direct it outside. She used the knife to push fat-glistening chunks off the spit and onto enamel plates. Bathory devoured her share with gusto. Dio, an unrepentant cactus-yogurt addict, chose to sleep.

"There's an upshot," said Bathory through a mouthful of pig, "to being your friend."

"Highbrow conversation?" Lash laughed. She'd just finished relating to Bathory the absurd plot of her all-time favorite horror-comedy film, *Gremlins*.

"Great food."

15

Ritalin and coffee did the trick. Burping and farting and reading and sniffing her smoked-bacon fingers, she stayed awake, far away from sleep's black forest of nightmares and out of the thicket of seizures. She spent the rest of the night studying excavator blueprints and pinpointing areas of armament. Initially, she'd thought to fit RPGs along the boom arm. The idea became less appealing the longer she looked at the CAD drawings. There was a risk that a competing signal might lure away her rockets and slam them into the blade.

Damned if *she'd* be the one to cripple the excavator. Let that be Richter's challenge.

A subtle pink glow emanated from the horizon. She went to the trailer to stir snoring Dio and porcelain-doll Bathory in their sleeping bags. Then she cooked more coffee in the cave and brought them each a steaming cup. This time Bathory drank it without complaint.

"Tastes good now," Lash noted.

Bathory nodded, sipped, blinked.

They also tucked into more of the javelina meat, then Lash wrapped as much as she thought would survive till it could be refrigerated, whenever that might be.

Dio had somehow produced another shaving of yogurt-coated prickly pear. He gobbled it and wiped his hands on his DON'T DRONE ME, BRO shirt and belched. "Let's go save Koons."

"Make sure he knows we're here," said Lash, scanning the screens for trouble. The Bride's solar charge had wound down, so the drone was again bathing in sunlight. "I don't want him lobotomizing the Bride. EMP darts won't affect my shotgun in his face."

"He's well aware of the Bride," Dio said.

Bathory asked, "If everyone's jamming everyone else, how can we help?"

"Easy," Dio said with a crooked grin. "We drive the excavator out of there manually."

"Don't listen," Lash said to Bathory. "That monster hasn't moved in years. I'll check it out and see if it has enough fuel. The *right* fuel. That the treads function. When it's ready to roll, we insulate our bots and chips. Then Koons turns off the lights."

"With an electromagnetic pulse," Bathory confirmed.

"And then," Dio said. "*Texas Chainsaw Massacre* time."

Bathory tilted her head questioningly.

"Old horror flick," Lash explained. "Ready, Dio?"

"Yes."

They got in the truck and trailer and drove farther down Pabco Road. The terrain was Martian, lifeless and reddish-gray, until they saw in the distance Richter's jammed drones circling like cough-syruped buzzards. Bathory gasped when a UAV, drained of its charge, suddenly plunged to the ground. The Bride had already untethered from Lash's control, lapsing again into GPS-confused autopilot, thanks to Koons.

They also saw the excavator, looming like a tranquil glacier plunked into a desertscape. Its blade was magnificent, the morning rays giving the machine an unearthly aura.

"Might as well start jamming," Dio advised. "In case Koons's disrupter takes a dump."

Bathory added her own drone-paralyzing pulse to the deadlocked mix. She watched Lash slip into Kevlar before venturing a tentative, "Can I come?"

"Stay with Dio," said Lash, picking up the other VAMPIR and her M4.

"Fine."

She seemed to be pouting, her lower lip quivering. Or was it nerves? "Don't be scared," Lash said.

"That thing out there. Why did they build it?"

"To dig metals. Out of the land. Resources."

"Looks horrible. Like a nightmare."

"Yes."

"It's bigger than the Academy. Bigger than the hotels on the Strip."

"It's a piece of mining equipment. That's all."

"I'm not scared."

"Good."

"Does Koons know what he's doing?"

"Yes."

"Doesn't seem right. To hack something that size."

"We haven't hacked it yet. Might never."

"Promise me something."

"Yes."

"Destroy that thing. If we lose it to Richter, I mean."

"Why?"

"Because I don't want to have to think about it!" she exclaimed, sounding like the twelve-year-old girl she was. "That it might find us. At the Academy."

"Never. No chance. You have my word it won't."

"Promise?"

"I just did."

Bathory went up to Lash and hugged her. Being touched felt like a hot poker. When the girl's tears welled, Lash pushed her away. "Watch the skies."

"I will."

Lash stepped out of the trailer and trudged her way down a vast trench above a deeper pit in which sat the excavator. The first trench was a half-mile around in diameter and her boots sank into the soft calcite, pounded into fine powder long ago by mining companies. She could already feel grit getting into her shoes, weighing them down.

A crash-landed drone, one of Richter's, left pieces strewn about like a miniature plane wreck minus the passengers. She could identify the robotic architecture, every sensor and rotor, but couldn't recognize what it all amounted to.

On her hike, Lash had time to consider her craving for violence. But then the familiar ambivalence crept in. What if hacking military—or mining—tech was really the devil's work? What if Prof was wrong? That would make her no better than the pagan souls who sleepwalk toward oblivion.

The sun grew brighter, so she put on her sunglasses. She looked up at a firmament rife with lethargic, revolving drones.

A red dot from a sniper-scope fluttered across her face.

She instantly dropped to the ground. Dust in her mouth, she aimed the VAMPIR at a chain of craggy-debris mounds. There, someone was waving at her in friendly fashion, rifle in hand.

Koons.

She stood up, made her way to the piles of mining waste, and in a few minutes reached him.

"Took you long enough," he said, smiling, the cut on his lip still healing. Even sunburned, he exuded what had been called before the bombs a prepster vibe. Maybe he was Prof's puppy because, unlike Lash, he maintained an immaculate appearance. Koons was perpetually unruffled, hair combed, cheeks clean, despite being confined to an open-pit mine for days.

He offered his arm to pull her up the mound.

"One question," said Lash, before taking it.

"Yeah?"

"Will this work?"

"Like a charm."

She reached for his hand and ascended.

16

Koons was an Academy valedictorian, his grades higher than Lash's. When they built solarbots, Koons was peerless estimating angles and inputting operations data. His bots were flawlessly constructed and smoothly programmed. Lash's drones hiccupped, stalled, and tended to burst into flames. In the arena, however, her bots, despite their quirks and handicaps, routed anything Koons put forward. Her school rival had a sensible design genius, while she had a *realistic* killer instinct. He could build a wicked bot but couldn't handle it as lethally as she did.

The big reason Lash abhorred Koons? His interest in tech was competitive and passionless. Claiming good intentions, he really just wanted to outdo everyone, especially Lash, and make them look bad in Prof's eyes. Killing savage, valley-draining nonbelievers like Richter was a means to an end, not *the* end like it was for Lash.

They needed each other now, which is why Prof had smiled so strangely when giving her this mission. There was no way Lash could've hacked an excavator herself and no chance Koons could fight his way out of the mines while remotely steering an ogre-razor. If they were to achieve success, they needed to yin-yang their strengths together.

"Signs of Richter?" she asked, as Koons led her to his ops-center Bobcat. It was parked on the other side of the debris mound, tucked behind crates. A miner's four-wheel Hyster forklift, presumably hacked yet dead from jamming, baked in the sun ten yards away. The drone-disrupter box and EMP crossbow sat on a big, red flat-topped Igloo cooler. Towering in the sky and rooted in the adjacent and much deeper trench was the excavator. A boombox blasted AC/DC's "If You Want Blood," Bon Scott's pub-crawling, ladies-man screech not loud enough to drown out the buzz overhead. Koons loved hard rock and metal, too.

"No," he said. "His goons are all over this dusthole, though."

"Shoot any?"

"One. In the butt. He snagged a tripwire-flare near the excavator sometime after midnight."

"You have flares?"

"Designed them in chemistry," he bragged. "Your weakest subject."

"Sure, that's right. Dio tell you we encountered blimps?"

Koons shrugged. "Not convinced they were for the excavator. Or that they were Richter's."

"Whatever," said Lash, annoyed. "Let's start from the top. Gas."

"Heavy diesel. Enough to get home. But we'll have to synthesize something for the assault."

"Power."

"Look, can we skip this? It's operational, Lash."

She sighed. "Completely?"

"Can you just arm it? We need to move."

"Oh, I'll arm it. After you tell me the auto-destruct code."

"Lash."

"Koons."

"We're not destroying it," he said.

"You know the risk."

"What risk?" He checked his blond, feathered hair in the Bobcat's scratched-up blind-spot mirror. "It's all voice-command anyway. I'm the sole operator."

"You must have an Ebola-grade fever. No way you're firing my rockets."

Koons shot her his best don't-bust-my-balls look. "OK, tell you what. You and Dio install the tank-busters. I'll give you a destruct password and your own suitcase downlink. You can chuck grenades at will."

"Thank you so much, Koons," she said sarcastically. Of course, she had no intention of letting him operate the excavator either. She would break that news to him later.

"You'll thank me for something else. After we've taken control of the excavator and blasted our way out of here, I have a proposal."

"Is that so?"

Koons nodded. His humorless expression piqued her curiosity, but she was tired and wanted this mission finished. No more games. She indicated the forklift. "Manual?"

"Yes, but don't overload it. The fork sticks when you pile on more than a half-ton."

"OK."

She hopped into the Hyster and turned the ignition key. The puny eco-whine of an electric motor was an affront to her ears.

"Seriously?" she said, shaking her head at Koons. "You're a frickin' hippie."

"It's all I could find. Place was stripped. You know, maybe I should tell you—"

She accelerated before he could finish, just to piss him off. It would take an hour to get the RPGs into the trench. Time was critical. If Richter saw Prof's top students gathered in one location, he'd send more enforcers, large twenty-year-old males with mutilating inclinations. With the Bride and grenadebots jammed, Lash didn't look forward to hand-to-hand.

Spying an evened-out forklift groove with reduced incline, she happily went for it. "Here we go."

In minutes, she reached the truck. Visored, Dio was welding a gyro-mount to a launch tube. Under infra-kill tarp, Bathory was heating up more javelina over an electric stove.

"Save me some," Lash said.

"This one's a carnivore," said Dio, flipping up his welding mask.

Bathory smiled and sprinkled some kind of improvised seasoning on the meat.

"Smells good," Lash said. She patted Dio on the back. Together, they resealed the VAMPIRs, then dragged and heaved and stacked the crates onto the forklift. Lash was sweating now.

"Hate to say it," Dio said.

"Go on," Lash said. She grabbed her duffel bag and stuffed it under the lift's seat.

"Quiet."

"Before the storm."

"Maybe," Dio said. "Koons set any alarms?"

"Tripwires."

Dio nodded, then looked over at Bathory. "Seems to be working out."

"Don't ever doubt me."

He smiled, but then an overcast expression settled in. "Lash, I want you to know—"

"That I'm awesome?" she said, turning away. She frowned and shook her head. What was with these guys all of a sudden? Plenty of time after securing the excavator for sweet nothings from admirers and antagonists alike.

She got back in the forklift and drove into the trench. Going downhill, the electric engine didn't bother her so much. She laughed when she had to hit the brakes to keep from rolling forward and over. The bungee cords were tightly wrapped around the RPGs but were still elastic enough that she stopped several times to make sure she didn't damage anything.

Hunger scraped her stomach as she thought of Bathory savoring more pork. For a moment, Lash imagined the younger girl sucking the hot meat down to the bones and mangled bits of fire-roasted, sage-seasoned skin, but then tried to block out the gustatory fantasy.

When she arrived at the Bobcat, Koons had moved his boombox around the corner of the mound, out of sight. She heard him singing along to Cinderella's "Coming Home." His hair-metal power-ballad wail had improved, she'd give him that. Oddly, she sensed Koons was mocking the lyrics and the singer's strident falsetto.

"I'm back!" she called out, exiting the Hyster and popping some gum into her mouth. She left the M4 and VAMPIR strapped on her shoulder, along with her duffel bag. "With rockets."

Then a man in Kevlar and SWAT gear and wielding a Mossberg gun—and with a black motorized snakebot slithering around his neck and shoulders—stepped around the corner. The man whose voice she'd heard and not Koons's. A dark, lean enemy whose merciless visage was engraved in her imagination from years of watching Academy snuff feeds again and again. Scenes in which he brutally drone-splattered Prof's best and brightest. Images and sounds that proved him to be most despicable individual in bombed-out Las Vegas.

Lash had never seen Richter up close. She was frightened stock-still, a headlit deer.

She swallowed her gum.

Richter pointed his weapon at her and grinned.

The talking robo-pistol announced to its owner and Lash: *Pretty girl go bye-bye.*

17

Lash closed her eyes and waited for the bullet to rip her in half. It never came.

"Now, now," Richter gently scolded. "We can't have that."

Thinking he'd addressed her, she tried to look at him but was too petrified. Then she realized Richter was responding to what the weapon had uttered seconds earlier.

No bang-bang? the smartgun queried with its spooky lobotomized-android intonation.

"Moss, you don't shoot a rare and precious jewel like Lash. Not until she gives you reason."

It might've been a spine-chilling ventriloquist act. Except that the weapon's volume was so cranked, there could be no mistaking the chip-spawned speaker source.

Finally, she succeeded in looking at Richter. He was no longer aiming the gun at her. Even with her heart pounding out of her chest, she could see that he physically resembled a young *telenovela* star, with weapons and armor instead of a sports car and glamorous clothes.

It was difficult to return his hooded gaze, but she managed to say, "How do you know me?"

"The conversation with your classmate," said Richter, "helped immensely."

She looked past him, leaning forward to search for Koons. But all she saw was a smashed disrupter, which meant only Bathory was keeping Richter's drones at bay.

"Where's Koons?" she demanded through her terror.

"Is that his name? He's MIA. But speaking of names," Richter went on conversationally, "it wasn't the first time I'd heard the name Lash. You've made waves lately."

"Was that you stalking me in the Meadows?"

The snakebot, moving along Richter's frame, raised its vid-cam head, directing its full consideration on her, lens turning to focus. Richter was doubtlessly recording the encounter, to taunt the Academy with gruesome images of yet another student slaying.

"No," he admitted. "But my pilot brought the video of your escape to my attention. You're a scrappy, resourceful, young woman."

"Your favorite kind to shoot, right?"

Bang-bang! the mech-rifle blurted in agreement.

"Hush, Moss. Lash, you don't trouble me. I admire you."

She couldn't believe her ears, stunned speechless, though for only a moment. "What is it about me you think you admire?" If she was going to die on camera, she might as well go out sounding tough.

Richter smiled. "I have much to share with you. First, let's move the excavator."

"Can't. You killed the bot's only command source, which is the only way to override our jamming. Stalemate, I'm afraid."

Richter shook his head and, without smiling this time, leveled the smart-gun at her again.

"You mean this source?" The voice emanating from the weapon was now precisely Koons's.

Stunned again, Lash stood silent. What kind of nightmare was this? A sentient robo-pistol that was also an audio simulator? It pretzeled her brain to guess how he'd scored it. Or made it.

Richter was no longer looking at Lash. Something behind her was drawing his attention.

She turned to see that Dio had driven the truck to the lip of the crater. His face was visible through the windshield, and she could clearly see that what he was observing concerned him deeply. He slammed into reverse, tires slinging gravel into the hole, much of it landing on Lash and Richter.

Richter raised the weapon to point it at the truck. Lash's heart skipped a beat. Then another.

To her relief, the smartgun took out the ops center's disrupter dish on the trailer roof. The sound was like glass tinkling. The Academy's jamming waves were now smothered.

"Good job, Moss," said Richter, appreciatively.

"Wagon train," the weapon commanded, once more stealing her dead classmate's voice.

High in the air above them, the excavator wrenched itself to life, dragonlike, with a hefty exhalation of greasy smoke and a cosmic groan of metal scraping metal. Its blade began spinning. Treads started gnashing the desert. The ground beneath Lash's boots quaked.

The wind picked up, grew violent. Lash saw dust devils spinning wildly in the trench she and Richter occupied. It was as if a storm had joined the apocalyptic frenzy he'd unleashed.

How exactly, she had no earthly notion.

"Gunfighter." Koons's amplified ghost-cluck took on a mocking, menacing edge.

The excavator swerved its bladed boom arm across the pit, descended, and paused directly over Dio's puttering still-trying-to-escape truck. A guillotine poised to sever a housefly.

"No," she begged, remembering her promise to Bathory. "Please."

Just as suddenly, the boom raised, allowing Dio and Bathory to reach Pabco Road and flee.

A flying condorbot swooped in, landing on Lash's back. Metal talons ripped the M4, VAMPIR, and duffel bag from her shoulders, cutting her favorite shirt and abrading her flesh. She could already feel the wounds starting to ooze. The bird pushed off into flight mode and pounded its fiberglass wings, leaving Lash disarmed and helpless before Richter.

The Bobcat hummed next and began pushing the RPG-loaded forklift toward the excavator.

Shirt torn, skin cut, she gazed at Richter dead-on, waiting for his next move. It surprised her.

Richter let his gun arm drop and held out his other hand, expecting her to take it. "Ever ride a giant earth-moving machine straight into the heart of Las Vegas?"

"Why should I trust you?"

"Because I know things you don't. Things you have every right to learn. But I can't teach you if you fester in a school that is, in reality, a prison camp. With Prof as your warden."

"What should I learn?"

He stepped forward, still offering his hand, and said solemnly, "Where to find your father, for one."

She moaned wretchedly, clutching her chest as if she'd been spear-gouged, then fell to her knees. Tears erupted this time, and she couldn't quell them. Nausea plowed her guts with the force of a mallet. Inhuman wind knifed her eyes repeatedly with mine grit. At the same time, rage consumed her entirely, tearing down the fortress of her resolve. "I," she gasped, kneeling, arms swathed across her churning stomach, eyes of burning hate aimed at Richter. "Will. Kill. You."

"You can certainly try," he said. "Maybe you'll succeed. For now, though, we ride."

He holstered the smartgun and stooped to pick her up. As he carried her in his arms, she was paralyzed and wanted to die. Then she yearned to live. She hadn't slept in four days. Crippled from exhaustion, she felt herself slipping behind the wall of sleep. Or into a seizure.

The last thing she saw before closing her eyes and falling into a dream state was Richter. He snatched the crucifix from her neck and pocketed it.

Snakebot weaves across the limbs of a tree in a lush garden. Dio obeys a talking gun that Prof draws and reholsters and draws again at the front of a classroom of students. Richter sits alone on a blanket beside a stream reading a book of Greek myths. Bathory drifts in a canoe on Lake Mead, ripping pages from a Bible and carefully placing each onion-skin sheet on the water's surface.

Lash? Koons wants to say something to you now, Lash.

"Live or die."

Live. Or die.

Live.

And right before total and unmitigated slumber claimed her, she stood in the presence of her handsome father. He was dressed in his police uniform, ready to work another shift.

He brushed her hair softly with his calloused fingertips and kissed her cheek, his face soft and warm from having just shaved.

He told her not to be afraid.

"Live, *mija*," he said.

18

She woke in a beautiful arctic-white canopy bed. Sunlight streamed through bay windows, every glass pane clear and perfect. Vanilla-scented candles, carefully arranged on the tiled sink, shimmered like those home-furnishing catalogs her mother got in the mail and illuminated an antique wood-encased turntable. A record she recognized as Miles Davis's *Kind of Blue* was playing, every note a spiritual balm.

She pinched herself.

Her skin was clean and soap scented. Her hair, redolent of coconut cream, was damp from recent shampooing. She lifted a freshly laundered sheet to look at her toes. Dead and blistered skin no longer marred her feet. Someone had pampered her with care.

But she was irked. Her crucifix and Zippo were missing, her grubby battle clothes replaced with a soft cotton nightgown. Worried about Richter's sadism, she checked her crotch for tears, bruising. Nothing. Her back was bandaged where the condorbot's talons had scratched her. She took deep breaths and tried to relax. Panicking at this point wouldn't help. She should find her bearings before learning what Richter had meant when he told her he knew where her father was. If true, she would be reunited with the greatest man in her life and depart Las Vegas. Forever.

If false, Lash would fillet him in front of all his pilots.

The bigger question was why he hadn't killed her. Did he think her loyalty to the Academy was so weak that she would defect to the dark side after a nap and a bath? If he thought she was going to operate the excavator he'd stolen from her and Koons and use it to inflict evil, he was mistaken. Yes, she had big problems with Prof's cyborg prophecy, but at least he believed in a higher power. Everything Richter accepted as true was gore-streaked.

On the other hand, this was hardly a charnel house. Perhaps there was more to Richter than she'd been shown. Nothing would change the shocking carnage of those videos he'd shot. Killing Academy students on camera was bestial. Distributing the images was diabolical.

Then again, maybe it wasn't Richter sending them, but one of his deviant pilots. Or maybe, just maybe, it was Prof, shocking his own into loyalty, at which Richter already hinted.

She got out of bed and padded over to the majestic bookcase. The hardwood floor was warm and comfortable to walk on. The shelves were lined with classic novels—*Lord of the Flies, Ender's Game, The Time Machine*. She loved all these books, most of which her father had read aloud to her as a little girl. Some of the stories, like *Starship Troopers*, had terrified her. Others, like *Watership Down*, thrilled her endlessly. Part of her wanted to curl up in bed with these books now and read them straight through and waste the day.

After the bombs, though, no day in Las Vegas could be spent on anything less than survival.

A knock on the door. Lash quickly reshelved *Watership* and kept silent.

The door opened and in came a girl her own age. "Hello," the young woman said. "Lash?"

"Yes."

"Sleep well?"

"Very."

"Your bandage isn't too uncomfortable, I hope."

"Not at all. Um, my clothes—"

"Washed and folded. Top." She indicated the dresser.

Lash opened the drawer and took them out. Crisp to a fault.

"Did you iron these?"

"Yes," said the girl. "Well, *I* didn't. The staff."

"Staff."

"There's a dry-cleaning operation here."

"Where are we? Richter's mansion?"

"Gosh, no. My name is Helen." She approached with her fist kindly extended.

Lash bumped it and said, "I love your name. It's special."

"Oh? Why's that?"

"The city of ancient Troy housed a Princess Helen. In *The Iliad*?"

"That a videogame?"

"Book," Lash said. "Epic poem, actually."

"I'll seek it out."

"Whose are these?" Lash nodded at the shelves.

"Richter's. They were recovered from a library. They look great, don't they?"

"Richter has read all these?"

"I don't know. I assume so."

"How many hours did I sleep?"

"Try three days."

Lash couldn't believe it. Had she really been so fatigued? "You bathed me?"

Helen smiled with a tinge of impish humor. "I did. I'm afraid it was necessary. You weren't the freshest rose in our garden."

"I bet," said Lash, recalling the cave, javelina butchering, and filthy mine.

"Can I interest you in breakfast?"

Lash's stomach growled. Eating poisoned eggs crossed her paranoid mind. She let it go. Richter wouldn't kill her with an omelet.

"Get dressed," insisted Helen, "and I'll take you to the dining room. I'll wait in the hall."

"Thanks," Lash said. When the door closed, she removed the gown and stepped into her torn Judas Priest shirt and camo cargos and examined herself in the mirror. Her clothes looked and smelled a lot better. Her boots, polished and waxed, appeared nicer, too. She laced up, picked up a pearl-handled comb, brushed her hair in the mirror, then stepped into the hall.

Peering at the long row of doors down the corridor, she had a good idea where she was—in one of the many glass-encased CityCenter towers, time-share condos, or apartments that jutted from the Strip's core. They'd always been operational and heavily guarded, but until Prof mentioned it, she had no idea Richter was involved. He and his pilots were previously based in an industrial warehouse, an automated chicken-deboning facility that sat along the broken hobo-haunted rail lines no train dared travel. The chickens had long since been eaten, but Lash heard ghastly tales of disciplinary measures. In these accounts, Richter impaled disobedient pilots on hooks before activating a 3-D-vision system. A carving bot then executed leisurely planar cuts, slicing through ligaments and bone, leaving a mushy pile of human meat in a bucket. All details she'd heard from Prof.

CityCenter seemed to be a million miles away from such horror.

In the hall, Helen was picking up lint from the elegant carpet. Lash noticed that she was dressed impeccably, like a casino VIP host before the Collapse. She wore a black dress and low-cut jacket that projected confidence and allure.

Helen led Lash into an elevator and lit up the B button. Hard jazz—a Sonny Rollins number—burbled at a healthy but not distracting level. Helen smiled at Lash, giving her clothes the once-over twice.

"We, um, have a gift shop," Helen said. "If you're curious."

Lash glanced at her own laundered yet threadbare shirt. "To buy clothes, you mean?"

"Oh no. It's taken care of. Just pick out what you want."

They rode down to the bottom level. When the doors opened, delicious aromas from the dining room made Lash salivate.

"Smells like—is it sausage gravy?"

"Yes," Helen said. "Wonderful, isn't it?"

"Where does the sausage come from?"

Helen gave her a quizzical look. "Farms, of course."

"Farms," Lash repeated.

She was so hungry that she couldn't worry right then about where the pigs might be kept and how she would drone-hunt and barbecue them. She'd calculate that later.

"I ate already," Helen said. "May I sit with you?"

"Please," said Lash, food-shocked and famished.

She took a plastic tray, plate, and silverware, pushing them down a steam-table line. Soon her plate was piled with biscuits and gravy, fried eggs, and hash browns, food she never thought she'd taste again. Still, a stab of guilt tempered the indulgence, as she pictured skeletal Bathory eating roasted rat and fried scorpions and Dio subsisting on cactus yogurt. She couldn't help wondering if Bathory would even like this food, which she'd never experienced. Lash was also starting to feel a little queasy from how rich and filling it all was. She was weeping before she finished pouring an orange juice.

"You OK?" Helen asked gently.

"Yes. Just hungry. Tired. Can I ask you?"

"Yes."

"Are there sedatives?"

"Where?"

"In the food."

Confused, Helen shook her head.

Lash shoved a warm biscuit into her mouth. It melted.

"Coffee? It's good and strong."

"Maybe later," said Lash, fighting off the touch of nausea. "When's lunch, by the way?"

19

CityCenter, as Prof had always described it to Lash and her classmates, was where a handful of wealthy families resided. Armed guards, sonic-sensitive airborne minebots, and Hellfire-laden Reaper drones protected the towers. Very little came in, and nothing went out. The families were self-sufficient because of hydroponics, solar power, and a direct water line from Hoover Dam. Removed from the valley's desperate power plays, they didn't interact—or engage in combat—with the Academy. CityCenter was a symbol of aspiration, a bright and shining mansion on the figurative hill of an impoverished town. Over the years, Lash had occasionally gazed at the buttery window lights, wondering who lived in such a tantalizing cocoon of privilege and safety. She'd fantasized about the opulent decor, the different foods, the ability to bask in daylight.

Now, strolling its sunlit halls, she grasped that the place far and away exceeded her imagination.

"How do you feel?" She and Helen made their way to the exercise room.

"Better." Lash's discomfort from the food had dissipated. She wore a new shirt, a vintage sequined Celine Dion concert shirt circa 2010, that caused Helen to raise an eyebrow. As soon as she found a needle, thread, and sequins, Lash planned to stitch a shiny skull over the singer's face. A skull similar to Richter's emblem. Dio would appreciate it.

Maybe Richter, too.

"So," Lash said. "We get to see the boss now?"

"Not yet," Helen said. "Richter wants you to visit our new athletic facility before you meet."

"Why?"

Helen was moving briskly ahead of Lash. She turned to walk backward for a moment and shrugged. "He thinks you have a biased understanding of drones."

"That so? Oops, sorry. I'm dragging." She hastened, moving faster. "Normally, I can keep up better. I'm—well, dazed, honestly."

Helen slowed her pace. "There's no rush. Working in hospitality makes me move quickly."

"*That's* what you do? Industry's dead as a Kennedy, I thought."

Walking right beside Lash now, Helen said, unoffended, "Not anymore."

They reached a wide auto-sliding glass door. It opened, and they entered a lavish training space. A pleasing phalanx of machines and free weights occupied half the room. A mirrored wall tricked Lash for a second into thinking they were in a convention center.

But it was the track on the room's opposite end that startled her.

Four Eastern European men in gym clothes ran a rubberized oval, each pursued by a quadcopter. Lash held her breath, waiting for them to be shot to pieces or torched. She instinctively backed away toward the exit, never taking her eyes off the drones.

Observing Lash's reaction, Helen said, "Um, it's not what you think."

Looking more closely, she saw that the quads were foam-fendered and flying ahead of each runner, setting unique paces.

"Joggobots," Helen explained. "Pacesetting drones."

Lash's apprehension faded. "What? They're motivating?"

"They *can* be," Helen said. "Sometimes they function more like dogs, if you recall."

"I do." Lash thought of her family's Labrador, Nacho. He'd disappeared after the bombs fell. Probably run over by a car. Or killed and eaten.

Helen continued. "The bots have a setting that lets them react to a jogger like a companion."

"Bots as man's best friend," Lash scoffed. "Prof would love that."

"Do *you* like it?"

"I run with drones all day. *From* them, mainly."

"Come over here, Lash," Helen said. They walked to the weights area, where a muscular man reclined on a bench press. Sweaty and straining, he struggled to return the iron-laden bar back to its rest-holder. What looked like an attenuated warbot treaded up behind the lifter, spotting his press with slender hydraulic pincer-limbs. After the bar clanged into place, the man got up to yell triumphantly and flex in the mirror with absurd machismo.

"What a waste."

"How so?"

"People are dying." Lash suppressed her temper. "On the streets of Las Vegas, right in front of CityCenter. These bots should be assigned real work."

"What work is real?" Helen seemed interested, while indicating that Lash should follow her.

"Security," said Lash, heeding her. "Protection. So people have things like water."

"I understand." Helen, walking ahead of Lash, led her into the spa.

"Do you?"

Helen nodded, but Lash couldn't see her face. "I used to perform such work for Richter."

"How I see it?" Lash said. "He steals everything for himself."

They moved across the spa lobby. The warmth, steam, and candied scents restrained Lash's displeasure. She thought to ask Helen for time to sweat things out, then thought better of it.

"You believe Richter took all this from someone? From the people of Las Vegas?"

"Maybe." Lash tapped Helen's arm to get her to turn around. "Who are these men?"

Helen looked right at Lash, her expression aloof. "Guests. Wealthy *paying* guests."

"From where?"

"Everywhere *but* the US, which barely exists anymore."

"How can there be guests? The world economy was flushed."

"Is that what Prof says?"

Lash couldn't figure how to respond, so they stood silently, facing each other outside a room marked MASSAGE. All of a sudden, the Academy student detected a fellow assassin. "You're a Red Angel pilot."

"Retired," Helen said. "I teach now. Please." She made an *after-you* gesture with her arm.

Reminding herself that they'd have killed her sooner if they intended to do so, Lash closed her eyes and inhaled, taking in the spa's fragrances for a moment. Then she entered the massage room.

On adjacent tables lay a man and woman, facedown, naked save for white towels around their waists. Over each hummed a bot that, like the spotter, was non-weaponized.

"Massagebots?"

"We call them 'robossagers,'" Helen said. "Using sensors, they detect tension in the human body. They can pinpoint and focus on areas of stress."

They watched the bots use their mitts to apply pressure on the couple's backs, shoulders.

"What's on their hands?" Lash said. "Urethane?"

"Encased in silicone skin, yes."

"Still. Can't feel very organic." Lash was getting her nerd on. Koons, wherever he wound up, would be proud.

"Each hand is ninety-nine degrees and contains micro-airbags to modulate force. Feels human."

"Doubt it."

"Experience it yourself." Helen touched a tablet hanging on the wall.

"No thanks," said Lash, stepping back.

"Richter insists." Another robossager wheeled into the room, its humanoid hands odd, but nonthreatening.

"I'm *not* getting naked," said Lash, "so that a bot can touch me."

"Chill out, Lash. You can keep your clothes on."

"You don't get it. I build and arm bots. Fight alongside and *against* them. They can't cure me. They're not therapeutic. Besides, I'm wounded here."

Helen tsked and patted a table. "This isn't therapy. And you're scratched, not mauled."

Lash glowered at Helen. Still, her back muscles ached. Her whole body was sore, actually. Plus, she wasn't skittish.

So she stripped, wrapped a towel around her, and climbed on the table. She said to the robossager, "Bot, you'd better not touch my Band-Aids."

The bot's warm, oiled hands kneaded her lower back, careful not to disturb the bandages near her shoulders. Lash moaned loudly.

"Thank you," she sighed, without thinking.

20

Blissful from the massage, she re-dressed and met her host in the spa lobby, where Helen was chatting with another girl their age at the welcome desk. When Lash approached, she said to the girl, "Can you call them, please?"

"Where are we off to now?"

"One more stop before we see Richter."

Lash carped. "Seriously?"

"You didn't enjoy the massage?"

"I did. Immensely. But—Helen, what's going on, *mija*?"

"*Tu pelo*."

"My hair?"

"Come on," said Helen, giggling like a teenager now instead of hotel-toiling grown-up.

It stirred Lash. She hadn't heard that sound since the bombs. Today, the kids didn't laugh with any elation. They laughed with cynicism, sarcasm. Not even Bathory emitted such a joyful noise. Helen's giggle infected Lash, making her forget the bad things.

They ended up in a salon crowded with Eastern European women getting their dark roots blonded by bots. Scissors snipped. Clippers buzzed. Dryers blew. Women sat foil-haired, staring at tablets loaded with images of movie stars Lash couldn't identify. The ladies were Slavic-tongued, but the body language and emotional pitch were familiar. Lash thought of her mother. Despite her gnarly hotel landscaping job—manure, sod, chemicals—she loved to visit the Bellagio salon. Lash accompanied her, watched celeb-gossip shows on flatscreen TVs, and flipped through women's magazines while waiting for her mom to look wonderful. Which she did, every time. Then they headed home, baked a chicken, and waited for Lash's father to arrive. When he did, he said to his wife, without fail, "You're stunning." Then he put on a CD, played a song like "Prayer for Young Lovers," danced with his wife, and kissed her.

Sometimes late at night, Lash sang the lyrics to her mother's memory. A prayer. Requiem.

> Loveliest cowgirl,
> Wasn't it enough
> To drag my heart
> Through neon and dust?

Watching her parents kiss had never embarrassed Lash. She'd savored those exquisite scenes. The fealty of such moments. The security.

She felt secure enough now to sit in a chair as a salonbot wielded scissors above her head.

Helen handed her a reference tablet and said, "Choose it or lose it."

"Wow," said Lash, scrolling through images. "None of these are good."

"So what's cool?"

"Lana Del Rey circa 2012. *Born to Die* album."

"Weren't those extensions?" Helen retrieved the tablet, searching.

"Maybe. Ooh, Bettie Page!"

"Audrey Hepburn."

"Kim Gordon."

"Fantasia."

"Shakira."

"Lucy Liu."

"Sade."

"Salma Hayek."

"Hottest woman who ever lived?" Lash asked.

"Angelina Jolie?"

"No."

"Elizabeth Taylor."

"No."

"Who?"

"Carrie Fisher. *Star Wars*."

"Boys *love* that 'do, don't they?"

"Me, too."

"Here," said Helen, selecting the style.

The salonbot got to work, gliding Lash over the sink and reclining her to wet her long, dark hair. The scalp-rub and shampoo were delightful. That done, the bot returned Lash to her seat in front of an illuminated mirror and began trimming. By now, she was starting to become accustomed to taking pleasure from drone-dispensed excess, even being touched. It surprised her how quickly she stopped flinching—and wanting to deck the toucher.

Helen sat in the adjacent station's chair, casually observing. "I helped design these."

"These what?"

"Bots."

"How'd you think up the styling mechanism?"

"I didn't. It's based on Richter's imaging system."

Lash didn't say anything, so Helen continued.

"Funny story," she said, now scrutinizing her own locks in the mirror. "Stole the force-feedback algorithm from an old, automated poultry processor."

Lash remained silent.

"Back then, it was all about the meat-bone transition. So I enhanced the sensitivity to distinguish between hair and skin—"

The salonbot suddenly stopped cutting and wheel-reversed a few feet.

"Lash?" Helen shot up from her chair but didn't intervene. "Your face. What—"

Lash stood staring at her reflection, a single scissor-nick on her cheek. Red blood decanted from the tiny wound. She'd flinched when Helen mentioned the bird-carving tech.

Lash ripped the smock from her neck and spun around to confront the bot. She got down low as if ready to deliver a martial-arts strike.

"Stop," ordered Helen, taking a step forward.

Too late. Lash roundhoused the bot's urethane skull, severing it. The optical cable sizzled and sparked. Then the machine fell over, crashing mightily against a row of perm-cookers.

Customers, Czech women waiting for hair color to set in, momentarily looked up from their tablets. They evaluated Lash's bleeding face. Then they inspected the damaged bot. Seeing that justice was done, they shrugged and returned to their digi-gossip.

Lash was angry, ashamed, disgusted with herself for reacting so violently. Obviously, years of living on a knife edge would take more than a few days to recover from. If she even wanted to recover.

"It's OK," said Helen, her voice calm, neutral. "Let's get a bandage on that."

And they did. When they left the infirmary, they returned to the salon. Another bot finished Lash's Princess Leia cinnamon buns. Then they headed to the pool to finally meet Richter.

Helen said, "Sorry about the cut."

"My fault. Overreacted. Just a scratch."

"Walk it off, walk it off," Helen snorted.

They both broke into laughter. Lash found it easy to get along with Helen.

"The salon was too much," Helen insisted. "You've been through a lot."

"What do you know about me?" said Lash, prickly again.

"That you're an Academy student."

"What does that mean?"

"Luxor is a tough school."

"Life is tough everywhere. Not just at the Academy."

"Some places are easier."

"Which ones?"

"The school Richter started. Here at CityCenter."

"Since when?"

"This year."

"Oh? And what does he teach exactly? Thou shalt kill everyone?"

Helen stopped walking and studied Lash. "Richter isn't like you think."

"Maybe. But he disappeared a classmate and hijacked my excavator."

Helen's eyes narrowed. "What were *you* going to use it for?"

Lash said nothing. She stared back until she broke contact first. As soon as she did, Helen sighed and resumed walking.

Lash joined her and said, "So you're saying Richter's school is less rigorous."

"No, I meant easier on you personally," Helen said. "You'd be allowed to thrive here. No limits. No restrictions."

"I'll stick with the devil I know."

They entered the indoor pool area. The smell of chlorine was robust. Lash flashbacked to her water wings and childhood swim lessons with her father. The CityCenter pool was Olympic size. The sight of all that wasted drinkability rekindled her anger. Her drone-kicking session and awkward exchange with Helen had restored her doggedness.

Men in goggles and European bathing suits performed laps in the lanes. Outside the shallow end, in another section of the pool, a group of preadolescent kids stood along the edge, trying not to get wet. They wore uniforms, which made Lash assume they were students enrolled in Richter's pagan camp. She saw them leaning over and fiddling with some kind of underwater UAV demo. They were arguing over batteries.

"Lithium ion," griped one kid.

"Thought we had an adapter," bellyached another.

"These only go with—I don't even know," bleated a third.

Lash couldn't help herself. "Dudes, go with this bullet connector over here." She used her boot to lightly nudge a plastic toolbox full of battery mods.

The boys exchanged quiet, confused glances.

Then the first one said: "The polarity difference—"

"Just note it on the AR connector," she said. "Also put some more insulation covering on that or you'll end up with a shorted cell."

"Listen to the expert," said Richter, behind her. His voice was a stab of dread.

The boys stood straighter, tucking in their shirts.

Lash turned and saw that Richter wasn't wearing a snakebot or carrying his Koons-aping smartgun.

"Lash here is a great student," Richter told the boys. "And she'll make a superior teacher."

21

Richter's expression darkened as he noticed Lash's face. He approached, touched it. This time, she was astonished that she didn't recoil. Instead, she stood there, allowing his rough fingers to graze her bandaged cheek. She hated herself for somewhat enjoying it. She had to admit that he was attractive. She didn't know his age, figuring him to be older than Prof but younger than her dad; either way, in the redistributed demographics since the bombs fell, he was old. But he looked remarkably young. Unlike Prof, Richter had all his hair. Jet black and slicked back, it radiated . . . sensuality, though it disgusted her to admit it. A handsome killer. Yet he seemed concerned for her welfare. He acted like he cared. Maybe it was genuine. He hadn't shot her down like a dog in the desert, he intimated that Koons might still be alive, and he seemed to allow Dio and Bathory to escape. That meant something, right?

But what?

"Helen?" He was obviously perturbed.

The girl's nervousness was evident. She tugged her earlobe. "Salonbot malfunction."

"Did I request her hair to be styled?"

"No, sir."

"We were having fun," Lash intervened. "Besides, it's just a scratch."

Richter seemed satisfied with the explanation that the girls enjoyed each other's company. He said to the boys, snapping his fingers, "Back to class." They grabbed their ineffectual drone-sub and tools and hurried off.

"They seem pretty smart," Lash said. "Bit whiny, though. And weak on battery mods."

Richter smiled. "You can change that."

"Me?"

"Of course. As their instructor. I need a good one. The best."

"I'm not a teacher. I'm one of many Academy students. You continue to kill us."

"And here I thought your classmates were trying to kill *me*." He clasped his hands behind his back and turned away, then sauntered to the swim lanes.

Hotel guests stroked to and fro. The din of splashing echoed. "Including your boyfriend. Koons."

"Not my boyfriend. If he were, you'd be dead." She suppressed an urge to crush his larynx.

"Lash," Helen warned.

Richter raised his open palm at her, then said, "Prof is a good headmaster and a brilliant strategist. But let's be clear. His view of drones is daft. He believes, wrongly, that they offer a higher purpose."

"I don't agree with that," Lash said. "Make you happy?"

Richter's eyes were no longer wily, but mildly surprised, even pleased. "Yes."

"The Cyborg-Christ concept *is* nonsense," she added, wondering why she was divulging this. "But so is your nonbelief, I assure you."

"Well then," he said. "We have much to learn from each other."

"I'm not a missionary and don't wish to convert you. I need to know what *you* know."

"About your father."

Lash nodded.

"Helen, would you please excuse us?"

Before she did, she threw Lash a pleading glance.

When the girl left, Lash said, "Is he alive?"

Richter gazed up at skylights and said, "Yes. And I know where to find him." He cleared his throat, searching for language. "However."

Impatient, Lash said, "However *what?*" Then a lightbulb. "I see. I have to serve as a teacher in your school before I can see him. No deal, Richter."

He conveyed offense. "I don't cut deals. It's just that you might not be able to cope."

"With what?"

"Your father's mental integrity. It has deteriorated."

"Brain damage?"

"I'm not really sure."

"Take me to him."

"Absolutely. Only I can't right now."

"Give me a reason."

"Heard of the Penitents?"

Lash's heart lodged in her throat. Of course she'd heard of them.

The Penitents were a nomadic, leaderless herd of deplorable humanity.

They'd earned their name from inflicted agonies on one another for sport. They wandered the desert, living off sparse vegetation. When they weren't fighting or raping or killing or cannibalizing one another, they scavenged downed drone parts that they bartered for gas, paint, and cleansers to huff. Dangerous and unpredictable, they were beyond help. Many had tried, including Prof and the Academy.

An older student—now dead after a savage ambush by Richter—had even erected a camp for the Penitents. He'd affectionately named it the Penitentiary. It offered everything—latrines, running water, cooking pits. The camp was in an area no one contested. In less than a week, the Penitents stripped it of pipes, PVC tubes, urinal cakes, firewood, which they traded for kerosene. They used that to dampen rags, getting high until they staggered through the streets like zombies. There were communities, it was rumored, that shot Penitents on sight, in the head, because their behavior was so insurmountably depraved. Zombies.

For Lash, it had been sorrowful to watch a student's well-intentioned effort come to naught, rejected by the very creatures he sought to uplift. To hear that her father, a brave and morally upright man, had joined the Penitents sickened her. His psyche had to be in ribbons to be part of such a morbid, nihilistic crew.

"I don't care if he's among them," she said. "Doesn't scare me."

"I'm not trying to frighten you, Lash."

"If his mind has snapped, I'll do my best to mend it."

"And I'll help you."

"If I can't repair his soul, I'll—"

Richter waited. When she didn't continue, he said, "You'll do what?"

She looked down at her boots, which felt encased in lead. "I'll handle it."

"Come to that bridge first before you cross."

"Where are they?"

"Lash," he said. "The Penitents possess something that makes it hard to approach them."

"What's that?"

"Phantom Eye payload."

The Phantom Eye was a military UAV bomber armed with nuclear warheads.

Lash absorbed this. "Where are they keeping it?"

"Near Aliante," Richter said. It was an area bordering North Las Vegas.

"They carry the bomb around everywhere on a stretcher, detonation code at the ready. They coerce communities into handing over gasoline."

She shook her head, clarity the result. "Do you even know my father?"

"Met him briefly." He reached into his pocket, pulled out a shiny object, and handed it to Lash.

She couldn't believe it.

Her father's police badge.

22

The day before intercepting Lash at the mine, Richter and his mercs had lost an experimental drone because of an automated landing-system failure. The flight-termination parachute deployed in time, so they raced beyond what was once called the Centennial Hills neighborhood to recover the UAV.

When they arrived, the Penitents were waiting for them. They'd already severed the tensiles and clumsily folded the chute into a cardboard box. They were rock-clanging the drone's reinforced shell, trying to crack it open and rip out its tech-laden entrails.

Richter told Lash he didn't want to squander ammo on such a pointless bunch. But there was mission video on the UAV drive that he hoped no one would stumble upon, especially Prof. So he megaphoned the Penitents to immediately scatter or he'd use a laser-aimed PROPARMS 20 RCMK3 machine gun to whittle them down to bloody stumps.

That's when one of them waddled forward with a control display system rope-knotted to his waist and announced, "I have the code."

Richter asked, "To what?"

"The bomb." Behind him, the others hefted a metal object on a stretcher and moved forward.

Another Penitent approached. "I'm a police officer." He presented Richter with a badge.

Richter took it and saw it was Metro. "Am I under arrest?"

"Looking," the Penitent said hoarsely, "for my daughter."

"She might not be looking for you, though."

"Her name's Lash."

From the moniker, Richter pegged her for an Academy kid. "She happen to fly drones?"

"I taught her."

Richter was intrigued, but the stretcher was getting too close for comfort. He went to draw his smartgun at the bomb-bragger.

Moss, however, refused to leave his holster. *Sniff-sniffing live warhead,* said the gun, which housed a radiograph.

"Control system synched?" Richter asked.

Yep, yep, Moss confirmed. *Code inputted and awaiting command.*

Richter said he felt his chest ice up and backed away. He gave his pilots the drawdown signal, and they retreated.

Richter's drones conducted surveillance, tracking the Penitents as they dragged the nuke across the desert and into Aliante. The community's Geigers clacked faster the closer the radiation came. Security knew something hot was nearing and went to head it off.

"For fifty gallons of gas," negotiated the Penitents, "we don't trigger the bomb."

It was a lot of fuel, but the leadership of Aliante agreed to the terms. The leaders, it turned out, represented a solar-based farming commune with abundant backup systems. The atomic problem moved along.

That had been just hours before Richter took Lash to CityCenter. Now the Penitents were holed up inside the caves at the valley's edge, waiting for all that unleaded to be huffed or else evaporate. When it did, they would restart their grisly parade until someone without detection gear—or stupid or crazy or suicidal—made the error of attacking them.

As soon as his drones spotted them out in the open, Richter would work on neutralizing the nuclear threat. But he wanted to present Lash with a chance to save her father before that.

Now Lash and Richter were sitting at a table in the hotel's open-air coffee shop, water misters holding down the summer heat. He sipped an espresso. She guzzled something ice-blended and sweet. The sugar tasted real.

"Until then?" she said. "I can't sit on my hands."

"Don't. Meet my students. Talk with them."

"Your future drone pilots? I'm not interacting with my prospective murderers, Richter."

"No one wants to murder you."

"What about your condorbot?" Her shoulder wounds had mostly healed. "I'm going to trim that drone's talons."

"I promise my condorbot will never touch you again."

"And you're killing me with the Beatles soundtrack in here."

Richter smiled. "Not my cup either. But it worked for Steve Jobs. Anyhow, the kids need a positive musical ecosystem for now. When they get older, I'll hit 'em with Nirvana."

"Or a drone strike."

"Nonsense. We're rebuilding Las Vegas, Lash. Join us."

"You and I are at war."

"No, *Prof* is at war. In this place, we construct and operate hospitality bots."

"Is that why they don't display the same skull logo as your kill-drones?"

"The skulls are for show. Intimidation. They send a clear message. My men brandish the skulls to those who come between us and resources."

"*Those?* You mean Prof and me."

"Lash, Las Vegas is coming back. CityCenter occupancy is at 30 percent."

"Las Vegas is a wasteland. No one's coming here."

"Seen New York? California? You don't know what a wasteland is, *chica*."

"Resources are for the desperate. Not your wealthy guests from Poland."

"We make money. Lots of it."

"Worthless dollars, euros, rubles?"

"Sure. At some point in the future that we imagine here, they'll be worth something again. In the meantime? Silver, gold, platinum, palladium. Why do you think we coveted the excavator?"

"For you to buy weapons."

"To reinvest. Everything's already in place. The hotels and infrastructure. Do you know how many kids we've rescued from filth? They work here now."

"Took them away from their parents. Now they build a death army."

"C'mon, Lash. They build bots that draw guests. The kids get paid. Most of what they earn goes to their families. What does Prof give the parents from whom *he* takes children?"

She couldn't answer this, so she challenged him., "You're a hotel owner now? A job creator?"

He laughed. "Director of Entertainment and Security."

"And Hostile Acquisitions."

Richter sighed, showing what looked like some genuine exasperation. A shaft of sunlight through the roofless café drifted across his face, which prompted him to don shades. Then, apparently concluding it was socially awkward, he removed them to squint at Lash.

She considered how long it had been since she saw sunlight fall so easily, so naturally, on another person's face. On a face as handsome and beguiling as Richter's. She'd lived in a tomb for too long, under a thirty-story burial chamber. He was dragging her out of the cave of shadows and into the light of reality.

Somewhere, somehow, there had to be a catch.

"Why are you doing this, Richter? How did you land this gig exactly?"

Richter shrugged, sipped his coffee. "Priorities change. Think of this as my DIY approach to creating a future. My experiment with anarcho-libertarianism or whatever."

His subtly tremoring eyes gave him away. Lash knew he was lying but didn't press it.

"*Paleo*-libertarianism I get," she said. "At least they accept Christ."

"I really hope we're not talking religion and politics. I want you to teach these kids how to be productive and successful. You're the best candidate for the job. That so wrong?"

"Doesn't sound *right*."

"Let me show you. Please."

He stood and walked to a cascading waterfall, waiting for her to follow. Lash took out the badge and ran her thumb along the nickel plate and leather as if they were braille, reading the shield's curves, notches. Then she put it away, slurped her dregs, and got up.

The school was in the hotel's bowels, near the laundry. Unlike the sour-aired Academy, the halls here smelled of fresh detergent and thrummed with dazzling, chirpy order. Classrooms were vibrant. The youngest kids programmed pre-built bots to complete basic tasks, such as following a black line around a track or driving a certain distance and turning. From there, tasks escalated to become more intricate. Older students used color sensors to build bots that distinguished among and sorted different spectrum-hued objects, then advanced to conditional reasoning, repeatedly executing objectives via program loops.

The youngsters all smiled at Lash, mistaking her for someone's big sister. They invited her to sit with them and watch as they tested predictions and untangled glitches. The teachers were mostly older boys and girls, with a few bona fide instructors such as Helen, who was encouraging a group of hotshots to assemble their own rocket-enabled exoskeletons. The four other real teachers were male hacker-nerds, obviously National Security Agency subcontractors who'd found their way to Las Vegas because of the school or simply gotten stuck here.

The school didn't blast metal, opting for the smart, articulate sounds of jazz and classical and—the closest thing to rock—the Beatles and Bob Dylan. The uniforms weren't black. In their white Oxfords and khakis, the kids looked primed to tackle the problems of Las Vegas, pushing the city in a positive direction. They appeared well fed and content, like private-school students before the Collapse. They were obviously gifted, if a tad sheltered. They exuded the future, and the future looked bright. The picture Richter presented was seductive.

Lash felt like a wraith among angels.

Her heart softened further when she sat down with a group of whizzes to calculate missile-applied trigonometry. This is where she experienced what she never had before. She was checking a girl's math to determine the highest altitude of her rockets when the student—Duffy—busted out an old-school protractor.

"Where'd you find that?"

"My mother's," Duffy said.

"Nifty thing she packed you."

"She didn't pack me anything. She died when I was a baby. My father enrolled me here."

"Sorry to hear it. My mom's dead, too."

"They're in heaven together, I bet," Duffy said. Then she calculated her rocket's peak height.

Lash looked around, waiting for someone—Helen, Richter—to correct the girl's mention of an afterlife. It didn't happen. Then Duffy reached for Lash's hand, the very fist that had delivered myriad punches to the craniums of Academy students. She smiled and asked, "Be my study-buddy?"

"Sure," Lash agreed. She looked around and noticed Richter standing in the corner of the room, observing the exchange.

He smiled slyly.

23

Lash didn't think she would sleep, but her room was so comfortable and side one of the Dave Brubeck Quartet's *Time Out* was so soothing that she slid effortlessly behind the veil.

In the morning, after breakfasting with Helen on waffles—*fresh strawberry* waffles—Lash followed her new friend to CityCenter's school to teach her first class.

"Wait," Lash said. "I forgot to try the doughnuts."

"You can have them anytime," said Helen, laughing. "They're not seasonal, you know."

At the Academy, structure had been ironclad, the curriculum immutable. Students suffered boredom sitting in old wooden school desks to watch videos of Prof demonstrating drone-construction techniques and remote-kill methods. Experimenting or finding answers to tangential questions were actively discouraged. Peculiarly counterproductive, it seemed to Lash, because she, Dio, and Koons exhibited a tendency to trial-and-error everything. Their clever innovations had forced Prof to rely on them, albeit reluctantly. Clearly, he didn't want *all* his students thinking independently. Just his most advanced ones—and only for specific circumstances.

Richter's school was different. There were no desks or videos, no chairs, dry-erase boards, or projectors. Instead, a giant rectangular table filled the middle of every classroom. There were school supplies—paper, pencils, books—as well as devices such as tablet computers. Storage shelves in the walls housed an incredible assortment of Russian-made drone-tech parts. Fuel tanks. Gear lube. Flight cams. Servo cables.

"Why don't we assign you to Duffy's team?" Helen said. "She really likes you."

"I like her, too. And I guess I have a few tricks to show them."

Helen elbowed her friend. "No demolition derbies," she joked.

"That'll be their final exam," the drone-killer said.

"Your attention, please," announced Helen as she and Lash entered the classroom. The kids had been excitedly debating cell phone semiconduction, but quickly quieted down. "Let me introduce my friend Lash. Today, she'll be teaching a lesson on—what was it again, Lash?"

"How to build a Doughnut Monster."

The kids silently looked at one another.

Lash let it hang there, crossing her arms, waiting. There was no clock in the room, so she pantomimed glancing at her invisible wristwatch.

Finally, Duffy raised her hand. Lash nodded at her.

"What's a Doughnut Monster?"

"A dessert-snatching bot that we're going to scratch-build in the next hour and remote-stealth into the cafeteria," Lash answered. "Who's with me?"

All the students wrenched their arms high into the air, eager-eyed, smiling.

It took them only forty-five minutes to assemble the bot, including the doughnut-pinching pincer arm. Lash was impressed, especially since they didn't rely on a 3-D printer to punch out plastic parts. Obviously, serious resources and investment were happening here, which gave further credence to Richter's boast about resuscitating Las Vegas.

To Lash, anticipating a Bavarian crème she never thought she'd taste again, the world suddenly seemed to open with possibilities. The students were impressed by how easily their teacher maneuvered the bot with the limitations of a touchscreen tablet.

"Where'd you learn to *do* that?" one boy asked.

"My dad," she said, feeling guilty about having fun while he was trapped with the Penitents.

"He's dead?" asked a girl, suspecting yes for an answer.

"No," Lash said. "He's out there somewhere. In the desert."

"Do you know where?" Duffy asked.

"Yes," said Lash, cam-guiding the bot into the cafeteria and up to the desserts. The tablet showed rows of doughnuts, each on a ceramic plate. "When the time's right, I'll grab him."

She activated the pincer, which nabbed the nearest doughnut. But the grip wasn't solid. The circular piece of fried dough fell and rolled along the cafeteria floor.

"Bad omen," Lash said.

24

Lash rose from the canopy bed, spun Julie London's *Nice Girls Don't Stay for Breakfast* on the turntable, rinsed in a Kohler-fixtured shower, and put on her gift shop tourist attire.

She checked her look in the mirror. "Your heart's been gutshot," she quoted to her reflection. "And left to die."

She left her suite, scarfed fresh fruit, smoked fish, and toast with cream cheese, and drank black coffee in the cafeteria, then made her way up to Richter's command penthouse at the pinnacle of CityCenter's Vdara tower. It was where Richter and his men resided and spread terror across the valley with skull-emblazoned UAVs. She hoped they might update her on her cave-caged father.

With its dark and nasty vibe, the penthouse was a total contrast. There was no trace of CityCenter's shiny, happy, techno-utopian learning center. Here, Richter's mercs were battle-scarred, bloodthirsty, twenty-year-old thugs much older than Lash's students and Prof's Academy kids. These men had been gutter-spawned in the chaos-charred barrios of Las Vegas, Richter recruiting them at sixteen, their aggression and rage at peak levels. *In three years,* Prof often said, *Richter can turn an unfocused delinquent into a serial killer.* While not as gifted as Academy aces or even Lash's kids, mercs were fearsome and savage.

As soon as she entered the command center, the mercs made her skin crawl by ogling her with murderlust. Like she was a creature they might—if they whimmed it—bind, torture, eat, kill, and rape. In *that* order. They emanated famished brutality. Unfettered cruelty boiled in their blood. Blacklit posters of their heroes—Charles Manson, Adolph Hitler, Scarface, Hannibal Lecter, the Joker—adorned the walls. The room reeked of testicle musk and depravity.

They didn't intimidate her. She'd encountered their type. She showed them her own cobra-like gaze, letting them know she wasn't their prey. Rather, *she* would hurt *them,* or worse. With or without a drone, she would spill their blood to watch it pool, then bathe in it.

But then Richter entered the penthouse, glaring. They slunk back to their stations and resumed piloting the Red Angels that perimetered CityCenter. The mercs also neutralized stray federal supply trucks and goods-laden RVs, leaving them for Richter's scavengers in their black 4Runners to plunder. Sometimes they engaged in brief, vicious dogfights and deadly ground skirmishes with Academy drones and bots. She watched them spread misery for a few minutes, taking notes. Then she left to teach class.

The next morning, Richter's most lethal pilot, Vai, who physically resembled Dr. Moreau's vivisection experiment involving jackals and humans, greeted Lash with some snuff videos projected on the giant combat-theater screens. They comprised high-def footage of Vai's drone-recorded kills of Academy students, audio cranked to earsplitting decibels. The images and screams of Lash's dying classmates were meant to chase her away.

But Lash had tortured herself plenty with these inhuman sights and sounds on her own time. She was, in a sense, inured. All Vai and his men had done was broadcast her motive for revenge. They'd unknowingly played their own requiem. Lash stared down Vai with a Linda Blair-in-*The Exorcist* grin that made a few of the pilots' Adam's apples anxiously bob.

When they saw their boss coming, they shut off the Academy-kill loops and pretended to be busy droning again. She said nothing to Richter. She would deal with it her way.

"Your uglies ever train? They sit here staring at screens all day."

Richter laughed. "They conduct drills. Care to attend a session?"

Lash shrugged. "If I can join in, sure."

Intrigued, Richter said, "Yes." He bent forward, resting sinewy forearms along a railing, to study his mercs at work. Lash tried not to admire his stunning physique.

"What do *these* freaks have to do with your vision of a better tomorrow?"

"It remains a brutal planet out there. My mercs ensure it doesn't hamper our grander aims."

"What grand purpose does your school serve? Your shot at redemption? You're too young to sweat your legacy, Richter. Besides, your tombstone's written: Here Lies a Mass Murderer."

He smiled. "I was hoping for something more—*balanced*."

"Balanced. So at what point do you begin filling your dirty merc ranks with CityCenter's clean-cut students of sweetness and light?"

"Never," he said, standing up straight, suddenly very somber. He pierced her with his eyes, fervent with belief in an idea she couldn't yet wrap her mind around. "That won't happen."

"What will *definitely* happen," said Lash, "is that I'm going to tear your mercs a new one."

"You're really chomping at the bit, aren't you?"

"I bet your drills involve eating baked cactus chips while balancing tablets on their guts."

"Mercs have only one training exercise," Richter said. "Hunt and terminate."

"So who am I liquefying?"

Richter harrumphed. "My best pilot, Vai, would love a shot at you. Says he can tag you with a microdrone in sixty seconds. Maybe less."

"What a dreamer. Let me guess, Vai's the brain-damaged coyote? Mr. Toothpick-sucker?"

"That brain-damaged coyote you refer to holds the record for Academy student kills."

"I thought *you* held that record."

Richter smiled. "You suffer a lot of misconceptions. I'm far too busy to swat gnats."

"So am I. But I'll make an exception for Vai. He can chase me line-of-sight. In less than a minute, though, my hands will be choking the life from him."

"I'd like to see that," Richter said. He wasn't smiling. "I'd like to see that right now."

Moments later, Richter, a group of mercs, and Lash were inside Crystals, a quarter-mile stretch of what used to be a luxury mall that ran along the length of CityCenter. Once the architectural summit of high-end retail immersion in the US, where rich foreigners came to consume for the sake of gratuitous consumption, the facility had fallen into disrepair. Lash remembered strolling through here as a kid with her mother, awed by the extravagant waterfall shows and the dolled-up, high-heeled trophy wives and girlfriends, elegant in their Vuitton, Lepore, and Dolce & Gabbana. Shops gutted now, the space functioned as a beat-up combat-training environment. Drone fragments from previous exercises had been swept into corners. Standing on a crumbling second-floor terrace at the mall's south end with homicidal scum, Lash noticed bright-red paintball impacts on the walls.

"Your mercs drone-splatter each other with paint," Lash said to Richter. "Cute."

"Cute isn't an adjective usually applied to my men."

"So where's this Vai guy?"

"Wasting you will be short but sweet," said the merc, stepping up, toothpick in his mouth.

Lash moved toward him, not in his face, but close enough to strike. "You can try wasting me. But then I'll shatter you *and* your little toy."

Vai eye-razored her, baring his yellow bicuspids.

Amused by the standoff, Richter interjected. "Vai, you might recall we've seen vids of Lash coming out on top in desperate scenarios. You instigated one of them."

"So it was you," said Lash, not blinking or breaking eye contact with Vai. "In the Meadows."

"You got lucky," he replied, squinting.

"Let's test your theory, *princesa*," she said.

"Vai," said Richter, separating them to offer the merc a tablet. "Your microdrone is armed."

Lash saw it hovering to her right, the same wicked little bot that had nearly iced her during her search for flamethrower fuel, but in place of the sniper rifle, it now sported two double-barreled Goblin paintball guns. She made a mental note. The drone would be lighter, faster. Not necessarily to her disadvantage. Vai tended to overcorrect his turns.

"Lash," Richter said. "I'm curious to know if you can do this. You'll find a baseball bat and capture net on the first floor, second shop from the mall's opposite end, left-hand side."

"Not needed," she said.

"Head start's what you need," Vai cracked.

She feinted as if turning away, then hook-kicked the tablet from his hands. She heard the impact of the screen cracking. Vai would have to chase her now with a splintered device.

It went sliding down the corridor behind him. The crowd of mercs gathered to watch the contest gasped and laughed and hooted. As Vai spun to pursue the tablet, Lash booted his rear. He fell forward, knocking his chin hard against the floor. His fellow pilots winced and oohed. He roared in anger, shot up with an explosion of upper-body strength, and twisted into a martial arts stance. He was ready to brawl.

But Lash was already on the first floor, having banister-glided the stairs. Running, she kept to a path that threaded a row of palm tree installations, the green plastic fronds providing minimal cover. In seconds, she heard the drone's soft whir.

Vai stomp-clomped his boots on the floor above. She knew he couldn't see her, but his drone-cam would pick her up soon.

The drone clipped a frond, the noise tipping her off. Lash jumped into an open, ungated space as the Goblin fired a paintball. It fleck-bounced off the store entrance.

She ducked behind a clothing rack, scanning for something—maybe plastic hangers—to hurl at the drone. Then she heard Vai land hard against the floor outside the shop, no doubt having leapt from the escalator bank. He wasn't content to simply paint-splat her and win the game. He intended on landing a few fists as well.

Lash had other ideas.

The drone took a wide turn, so that Vai could cam-survey the entire room. Lash knew that he was taking his time to study the tablet's images through the fractured lines in the screen, so he'd eventually see the toes of her black Bedford lace-ups below the cobwebbed dresses hanging in a carousel-display rack.

When he did, he hissed, "Got you."

But then he muttered, "Damn . . ." and Lash knew he'd found her empty boots and used his surprise to turn the tables on him.

As the ceiling tiles above him crashed down, Vai sprung up to deliver a roundhouse kick. But a blow-dryer cord garroted his throat. Windpipe painfully compressed, he dropped the tablet to try to dig his fingers under the cord, desperate to allay the pressure. He choked, gagged, tongue jutting from his oxygen-depleted mouth. Saliva foamed his lips.

"How's it feel to be hunted?" she taunted, her hot lips moistening his ear.

Brought to his knees, blue-faced, Vai flail-punched behind him, but there was nothing. Finally, she let him figure out that she was strangling him from above, leveraging his shoulders with her bare feet while perched atop the ATM beside him.

"Die, Vai."

Obviously calling on a final reserve of strength, he heaved his body into the cash-dispensing machine, toppling it.

The cord came free. Vai gasped for air on all fours.

By now, the mercs had arrived, watching him with embarrassment. A girl had steamrolled the best among them. Some appeared sideswiped by Vai's quick defeat. Others looked away. A few rubbed their cheeks, barely stifling their snickers. One even gave a low whistle of astonishment.

Richter was satisfied, but not with Vai's performance.

The merc leader approached, placed his hand on Lash's shoulder. Instead of striking out at him, she welcomed his touch. It felt warm, medicinal. Black hair full of broken ceiling-tile fibers, still panting from exertion, she looked up and returned his admiration and, yes, his physical attraction. She clasped Vai's disabled drone under her arm.

"You were right. You didn't need the bat and net."

"Been doing this awhile," she huffed, still breathing hard. "I can kill any pilot. Destroy any bot."

Richter nodded. "I'm convinced of that now."

"And now you're going to accept my demands."

Richter withdrew contact but didn't seem surprised. He took a step back and listened.

"I want an update on my father and the Penitents every morning in the command center. No exceptions. Tell your Jeffrey Dahmer wannabes to stand down. Or I'll thrash them into bloody froth and show no mercy like I did here."

"Absolutely."

"And if my father isn't rescued very soon," she added, "bad things will happen. To everyone."

Richter clenched his jaw and raised his square chin, as if offering it for her to strike. She could see it in his eyes, how he looked at her differently now. Like she was his equal. Or even the object of his passion. "I understand."

"And I want a nondenominational meditation room installed on the same floor as the school," she said, smiling as she twisted the blade of compromise. She saw Richter as she saw herself. Obdurate. Unbending. "I need a place to collect my thoughts."

Richter nodded.

Still on the ground, Vai lay flat on his belly. The defeated merc coughed and moaned.

"Oh, and this?" she said, addressing the other pilots, holding Vai's drone above her head like a trophy. "Mine now."

25

As she'd expected, Lash claiming Vai's microdrone as a victory scalp intensified the enmity between her and the merc pilot. When she elevatored to the command center the next morning, she was well aware that trouble had been boiling in the kettle of Vai's mind. He didn't take losing well. And he wouldn't follow Richter's instructions to keep away from Lash.

She was walking down the carpeted pathway that led to the main tactical area when Vai came charging up the same ramp. He was challenging her to step aside and let him barrel past or confront him and risk getting steamrolled. A childish test of dominance.

So using her steel-toe-reinforced Bedfords, she went cold-faced and delivered a lightning-quick stab-kick to Vai's crotch. Because a ball-shot is never a surefire fight-ender, and because you never really know how well you've connected with an opponent's nutsack until he's on the ground crying, and because Vai's pain-stunned head was already down and in position for a finishing technique, Lash dropped her elbow against his ear, followed by a ruthless knee-strike that jetted blood from his nose.

Vai didn't get up.

As she stood over him, taking deep breaths to regain her equanimity, Richter came up behind her. He looked at Vai, flat on his back, immobile, moaning again as he'd done the first time Lash savaged him.

"Serves you right," he said, stamping the disobedient merc's head.

Testes-crushed, crimson-covered, Vai had to be bot-ferried to the infirmary. After that, his fellow wolves ceased shooting her lecherous looks.

The next morning, there were no incidents. She walked past Richter's chastened pilots and checked the screens to see if the petrol-sniffing Penitents had emerged yet. Thanks to infrascopes on Red Angels monitoring the area, she saw the feral gang's red-orange heat signatures clearly palpitating inside cavern-wombs like psychedelic fetuses.

One of those throbbing splotches was her father. Which, though? That spot there, mortally wounded by the others, signal fading to yellow, to green, then to nothing? Or was it this other static blob-blemish, inactive for hours and brain-dead after having huffed an oily hanky? Perhaps it was this ceaseless schizo-smudge over here, marching back and forth, jabbering about flesh-eating bugs and voices chattering and a bomb ticking on a stretcher.

Another patch of elevated temperatures registered near the caves. Lash assumed it was a hot spring. She'd hidden in one near Hoover Dam the night Uncle Sam's drones turned the refugee camp into a killing field and she'd escaped Boulder City. Listening to the machines hunt down and pick off the remaining survivors, she huddled in the warm, trickling pocket of quartz and limestone and waited. The water tasted salty, bitter, mineral-laced, but she drank it to keep from dehydrating. Cerebral fluid leaking from her cracked skull, she hallucinated, conversing—for what might have been hours or days—with her mother's ghost. Lash only exited the cave when the ghost led her out into the sunlight—and into the grim embrace of the Harvesters, the pagan-nature cult so mentally unhinged and reality-challenged, Lash doubted eviscerating them en masse would bring her any satisfaction.

But she would still execute them all given the chance.

She wanted to spearhead a raid, climb in, shoot through the Penitents, and rappel out with her father in her arms. But she didn't want to lose him to a psychotic freak's itchy tablet finger. To reach her dad only to watch him devoured by a cave-born nuke-blast would be worse than her own death. Richter was right on this point. It would be easier and more effective to sniper-shatter the control display system once the Penitents were in the open and vulnerable. Then, while drones encircled the warhead and kept the maniacs from setting it off manually, Lash would swoop in riding Richter's high-speed sandsurfer, an autonomous hoverbot for two, and pluck her father from the monster mass, bring him to CityCenter, and do her best to mend his broken mind. To restore his humanity. To show him that she loved him eternally.

And if it didn't work and his soul was kaput, she would do the necessary thing and kill him. *She* needed to do it. No one else. Better her than a stranger.

"Don't worry," assured Richter, seeing her irritation at having to wait yet another day. "Their gas will dry up. They'll come out, and we'll rescue your dad."

"Sometimes I think you just want the warhead."

"I want it *dismantled*," he said. "We're rebuilding Las Vegas. Loose nukes sink profits."

"Who's the *we* you keep mentioning?"

"My bosses. The Westphals. They own this hotel."

That sounded right. Prof always insisted a wealthy family was holed up at the top of Aria, the tallest tower at CityCenter.

"Can I meet them?"

Richter frowned. "Why?"

"I'd like to know who I'm working for."

The answer seemed to please him. "Certainly. The matriarch has suffered health problems of late, but she's recovering nicely. I'll let her know you're eager to make her acquaintance as soon as she's not, well, coughing herself into violent fits."

"Great."

He looked at her for a long moment. "Meanwhile, I want to show you something else."

She shrugged. "OK, I don't teach for another hour."

He led her to his Red Angel station. A pair of padded chairs and an array of video monitors beamed system-status updates and satellite-rendered maps of valley topography. Richter, taking a seat in the pilot's chair, gestured for Lash to sit in the adjacent seat, then keyboard-clacked a command.

"Who's your sensor operator these days?" she asked, getting comfortable.

"Only lazy pilots rely on sensors."

"Sure. And you have Red Angels in . . . what are we looking at?"

"That's a shantytown in Rio."

"Brazil?"

"We're *everywhere*," he said. "In every part of the world."

Lash felt gooseflesh on her arms.

The monitors seemed to confirm this. In the wake of the worldwide economic apocalypse, precarious dwellings of shantytowns and heaped-together encampments had completely taken over. Pushed against the main river port of the Amazon was now a city of millions. The streets and homes were made with scraps of wood, sheet metal, plastic, and cardboard. Looking at an infrared feed, Lash could make out figures moving through the cooking smoke.

Before the visuals grew too depressing, Richter toggled a switch. "It's not entirely hopeless out there. For example, the seaweed farmers in Bali."

She could make out farmers beyond the white-sand beaches by the tops of their conical sedge hats.

"And Versailles near Paris." Bathed in orange sunset, the ruins of the gardens, pools, and fountains of the chateau looked eerily Martian, trashed by unruly aliens. The boggy ground that workers had struggled to use as a foundation for King Louis XIV's palace was dried up. Lash hadn't seen anything so beautiful.

Richter switched again.

"Where is this?"

"Near the ancient city of Kaunos in Anatolia, Turkey," Richter told her.

"Underwater UAVs?" asked Lash, referring to dozens of dark blobs that trailed in the boat's wake.

"Loggerhead sea turtles."

He flipped another switch, accessing a view of a caravan of ten dromedaries trekking a dunescape, the sun stretching their shadows across the sand.

The massive dark-gray tale of a whale erupted from the ocean waters of what he identified as the Península Valdés in Argentina. The tip of the Karymskaya volcano farted ash into a Siberian sky. Squat red, green, and gray buildings huddled against endless ice around McMurdo Station in Antarctica.

"Got Guadalajara?"

Richter looked up the coordinates and tried to dial in the drone images, but all he got on the screen was static. "Not surprised. From Puerto Vallarta to the altiplano is completely controlled by the Chinese. They welcome anyone who can make it there, but they don't care for scrutiny. Never did."

Lash's yearning for Richter, her desire to be possessed by him, intensified on the spot. Maybe he'd visit her and her dad in Mexico.

"So there you have it," he said, smiling. "Anything else I can show you?"

"Nope. I remember how to find the school. On my way down there now."

"Wonderful. Oh, and Lash?"

"Yes."

"Eat something."

She ignored the inference that he was fattening her for slaughter. "Can't argue with food."

Lash scarfed a fruit smoothie, almond butter and jelly on cinnamon toast, and a Bavarian crème doughnut, drank freshly squeezed orange juice instead of black coffee, and exercised in the gym. She taught Richter's students drone design, repair, and piloting. She discovered that she fancied the new environment. Unlike the Academy's severe monastic character, Richter's school vibrated with upbeat, can-do spirit. Classmates fervently chatted among themselves. Electrical tools purred. Kids cheered as they watched each other triumph and fail during experiments.

Lash enjoyed running the desert bot-racing competition in the CityCenter convention hall on a course of simulated regolith. The first two groups did well enough for a while, until kicked-up sediment overwhelmed their systems. The third group, Duffy's, nailed it by gasket-sealing their bot's hardware inside the chassis, a dust-proof design NASA would've admired.

"Seals are key," Lash said to Duffy. They were waiting for the last bunch to run their bot. "Especially in the desert. That was smart of you."

"I thought of Harrison Schmitt when I was designing ours," Duffy said.

Lash rifled through her memory but came up short. "Who's that?"

"The Apollo 17 astronaut."

"Right." Lash snapped her fingers in recognition. "Lunar-dust-allergy guy."

Duffy snorted. "Made him itchy."

"Turned him into a moonwolf. Bet you didn't know that."

"Really?"

"Top-secret stuff. Back on Earth, whenever there was a full moon hanging in the sky, Schmitt transformed into a howling beast of hell. He chased chickens and ate women."

"What are you doing?" Duffy asked, seeing Lash scoop regolith in her palm.

"Nothing. Just studying this moon dust. Oops!" She blew powder at the twelve-year-old. Exactly Bathory's age. The two would make fast friends.

Duffy flinched and laughed. Then she gently howled, "*Ow-oooo*."

It was like this every day. The students displayed intelligence, creativity, and humor. Lash wondered if her newfound teaching role might work at the Academy.

Prof never presented learning as anything but a somber survival tool. In his view, schooling was the ultimate doom-bringing weapon in one's cyborg-striving arsenal. The effort was painful, risky. Woe to those acting to sabotage the illuminated path. A shining CyberCity on the Hill was coming soon, a municipality of man and machine.

Since arriving at CityCenter, Lash's eternal doubts about the Academy blossomed fully. There was a deeper recognition that the operation at Luxor was nothing but a death cult, obsessed with mortality and killing. Why should she, or anyone, double-down on an afterlife? She never really had, of course. But it was all she knew, having nothing to compare Prof's theology to.

Here, at Richter's school, a gilded, life-affirming community might actually succeed in the desert. She could see how these students would one day focus their energies on bettering things in *this* city. In *this* realm.

Another week passed. The students made huge strides under Lash's tutelage. Intrigued and challenged by her assignments, they loved having her as their instructor. Helen, who taught in the classrooms for half-days, noticed it. She praised Lash for her natural-born mentorship.

"You're so good," she said, sitting with Lash in the café one afternoon. A bot, what Richter's kids termed a robo-espresso, steamed milk with loud assurance. "Of course, they were brilliant when they got here. But now the students are honing their talents to a razor's edge. Expanding their skill sets. Soon they'll be able to do anything."

"Except they won't." Lash finished the last of her iced tea. What had felt awfully decadent before—sipping drinks in a coffee shop, for instance—now seemed normal. Which made her feel guilty again, wondering how hungry and desperate Dio and Bathory and the rest of the Academy worms might be at the moment. "They'll be stuck in this hotel-casino. Building better slot-machine bots and robo-dealers. Designing barber-droids. They could do more. *So* much more."

Helen put her hand on Lash's arm. Once again, Lash noticed that she no longer reacted badly to being touched. Back at the Academy, she'd have hauled off on anyone who kindly prodded her or drew too close.

"It's a way out," Helen said. "Grinding poverty grinds people. Into *graves*. The mystique of Las Vegas, the legends and images that the name evokes, remain intact. People are coming."

"Crazy to think so," Lash said. "All I want to do is escape from here." She tried to sound convincing, but knew she'd failed. Truth was, she'd never felt better. She'd gained weight. Her headaches had gone away, no longer requiring caffeine treatment. No seizures, either. She hadn't felt this healthy since before the bombs.

Helen ignored her comment, taking away her hand to sip coffee. "News on the Penitents?"

"Still spelunking," Lash said. "They'll be out of gas soon, so says Richter. I'm at his mercy."

"Richter will come through," Helen said. She glanced around the café before leaning in to share something of vital interest. "He needs you, Lash. More importantly, he admires you. He put his leadership on the line for you. The mercs don't trust him now. Dissension grows."

Lash looked right at Helen to make sure there was no confusion. "I don't care, Helen. All I want is my father back. When I reach that bridge, I'll figure out how to cross."

Helen nodded. "My folks are gone. Drone-smashed in front of me. I see things as you do."

"Oh," said Lash, dazed by Helen's admission. She wanted to ask but withheld. She couldn't share the story of the devastating loss of her own parents right now. Not yet. "I—"

"No worries," said Helen, as if she understood. "You know, I've been meaning to return something of yours." She reached into her jacket pocket and handed Lash her Zippo.

"Wow," said Lash, happy. Then she noticed that her black lighter now brandished Richter's haunting logo, a jawless white skull.

"I can get rid of it," insisted Helen, apologetically. "I thought it looked really cool."

Lash blankly examined the Zippo in her palm. She flicked the top, staring into yellow flame.

"Forget it," said Helen, leaning forward and reaching for the lighter. "Dumb. Let me—"

Lash closed the Zippo, hugged it to her chest. "Nope."

Helen looked relieved and leaned back in her chair.

"I should ask Richter to return my crucifix."

"Yes," Helen agreed.

"My shotgun, too. And the excavator!" she laughed, without humor. "He said he didn't intend to use it against the Academy. Can I trust him, Helen?"

"Yes. But like you said—"

"I'm at his mercy."

Helen smiled. "Is that such a bad thing?"

Lash didn't answer. She pocketed the lighter, raised her arm to apply pressure to the back of her neck. She could use another robossager session. She yawned, not covering her mouth. She hadn't yawned in a long time. Fear, Ritalin, and coffee had always jacked her up.

"Beat," she said. "Long day. Dinner later?"

"Sure. Rest, Lash."

"I will."

Lash went up to her suite and dumped the contents of her backpack on the desk, looking for her new Chapstick. Sold to guests of the hotel, it was petroleum-based. A miracle balm for Lash, who for years had rubbed sticky cactus goo on her lips in gloomy Luxor. Earlier, she'd spotted a pack of real chicle-based chewing gum. She would buy that next.

She noticed a picture Duffy had drawn for her today. A deft charcoal sketch of a slobbering werewolf, presumably the Apollo 17 astronaut, in what looked like an arena. The clawed and fanged wolfman squared off against a pugilist-bot as people roared their approval.

Lash used a CityCenter magnet to display the picture on the minibar.

She still found the atmosphere at CityCenter, along with Richter and the people with whom he surrounded himself, extraordinary. Everything was provided—food, clothing, bots. She had friends such as Helen now instead of irritating rivals like Koons. Despite the Vai conflict, her father being ensnared with the Penitents, and a nuclear threat hanging over the mission to rescue him, Lash had ironically found her place in the world. Before Richter had kidnapped her to his castle on the blackened Strip, she never would've considered teaching. All along, she'd believed she would die alone, a berserk martyr to the end. Now she saw another way.

Another life.

Maybe she could be a leader, an improved version of Richter. What had the biker-hoodlum Forge asked of her? To rule beside him as Queen of the Huns. Lash wondered if she could one day command her own tribe of Amazon drone-killers. She imagined standing before an assembly of women warriors like those in Greek mythology. Leading them into a righteous battle against the scum of Las Vegas. Committed to throwing spears accurately, Amazons were said to have burned off their right breasts. Lash's were scarred, so she had *that* going for her. Instead of javelins, her all-female army would hurl UAVs into the sky, keeping peace, preserving laws, and protecting the innocent.

There would be no secret kill lists or targeting of citizens like in pre-Collapse America, no computer algorithms to determine who lived and died. None of the inhuman policies that had slipped beyond the control of the Feds and their contractors and subcontractors. After she'd survived the drone-fired missiles that ripped apart the refugee camp, she promised herself something. Never again would she allow someone else—unknown military enforcer, shadow security agent, autistic Silicon Valleyboy—to dictate the terms of her world. Power is knowledge, and she knew *plenty* about killing people remotely, as well as face to face. She could construct deadly weapons with minimal materials. She could elude, outwit, and bring down any pilot intent on murdering her. She would share this dark wisdom with others until those running the planet ran it better. Ran it justly. Or ran away.

Or until they all perished in the crosshairs of her rage.

She'd initially thought her enemy was Richter. He turned out to be a complicated villain. He harbored cruelty in his heart, but his reasons weren't alien to Lash. Although he hadn't spoken of it, his trauma was familiar. She recognized his suppressed injuries in herself, and his view of drones might as well be her own.

There was a time when drones assured a dazzling tomorrow. Wars waged without American lives at risk. Repairs made to extreme structures too hostile for human intervention. Surveillance conducted to save the world from monsters that couldn't be perceived on the ground. Drones had promised to save African wildlife. Aid crop production. Deliver medicine and food. Monitor human rights abuses. Improve public safety. All of it lies, falsehoods cooked up by the industry's public relations to make Americans believe drones were innocuous.

In fact, drones were the final nail in the coffin that contained human dignity, the soul.

Lash had the wounds to prove it. Drones weren't responsible for all the damage on her body. But those she didn't pilot had consistently herded her into harm's way.

Drones and the ghosts of those she'd loved and lost.

26

She was walking the subterranean corridors when she spotted Richter. He was waiting outside her classroom, thumbs hooked on the belt loops of dark, tight jeans. A black, tailored-fit shirt. His eyes were exquisite, other-worldly, girlflesh-hungry. He was a vampire-rockabilly hunk ripped from the pages of one of those total-crap young adult novels published when Lash was a kid. Adults, including her Anglo aunts, had consumed these books voraciously, more so than the teenagers for whom they were intended. Lash never understood it.

But she would peruse such a book now if it featured a villain as splendidly feral as Richter.

Lash was disgusted with herself for two reasons. First, for having put on a hot-pink, tie-dye CityCenter shirt this morning. Second, for caring what she wore in Richter's presence.

There was definitely a carnal facet to his gaze now. She thought he might even kiss her. Her stomach fluttered at the prospect.

He let her approach and said, "Time to meet the queen bee."

"The Westphal matriarch?"

"She feels better this morning. She's ready for a guest."

"What about my class?"

"Helen's in there now."

"Let's go."

They headed to the employee elevator. Richter was obviously aware of Lash's anticipation and said, "Yes, I have an update."

"Tell me the Penitents are moving."

"Starting to. Perimeter-foraging for food, which is exhausted. As is the gas."

"So we get it done."

Richter pressed for the elevator. "The control display system can't be snipered in a cave. A little longer. Please, Lash."

There was a muted *ding*. She entered the elevator, did a quick 180, crossed her arms, and slammed her back against the wall, vibrating the compartment. "Donkey Kong," she said.

He hit the C button for the casino floor and rubbed the smile from his mouth. "Nobody wants it over more than me."

The light inside flickered for a second, as if a power drain were imminent. Richter briefly craned his neck to examine the elevator's ceiling bulbs. Then he continued.

"We're only starting to rebuild. Every day the nuke stays in the possession of unhinged rabble brings Las Vegas nearer to eternal ruin. Dims the whole continent's chances for recovery. Our city could be a major economic engine. Or we might end up sabotaging America's rise from the ashes."

"If you're considering sealing the Penitents inside the cave, put it out of your mind."

"No," Richter scoffed. "An atomic detonation would decimate Aliante. CityCenter requires their solar-tech support."

"How'd the Penitents *get* a nuke anyway? Haven't even heard about a Phantom Eye in years."

"Not *from* a Phantom Eye. *For.*"

"Huh?"

"The government got cut off from its California arsenal. Desperate to retain it, the Feds strapped the nukes to blimps for transport. But they were pursued and drone-diverted. *Squeezed*, essentially, into bringing it through Las Vegas."

"Squeezed by whom?"

The door opened, and they stepped onto the casino floor. Lash noticed a large and very loud group of men who looked and sounded Eastern European or Russian bellying up to the center bar. From the audio system pounded horrible electronica—a monstrous hybrid of house music and ethnic folk involving an eighteenth-century stringed instrument she'd seen tube vids of called a *balalaika*. The bot-tender didn't pour drinks into glasses, instead opening entire vodka bottles and placing them on the bar for the men to swig with overly masculine flair. Some of them danced—even together—dress shirts untucked, and sleeves rolled up. A fleshy woman in a sparkly dress stood barefoot atop a nearby table, gyrating for the enjoyment of several drunk guys trying not to fall off their stools. A serverbot prodded them kindly with a Stoli-loaded tray. Alcohol-numbed, they didn't react.

Except for one of them. Shirtless, he puked a chunky stream directly on the bot, causing it to short and freeze up. Lash made a mental note to teach her students how to sawdust-clean vomit-soaked robotics. The Collapse hadn't improved the behavior of tourists in Las Vegas.

"No one's sure," he said, walking beside her, ignoring the dismal scene of guests getting their CityCenter kicks. "We thought it was Prof. But our spybots tell us he thinks *we're* responsible. Another theory is that the Chinese are working with a third outfit. Unlikely, though. Only two groups in this region have real firepower. The Academy and us."

"Back up," Lash said. "You have audiodrones inside Luxor?"

"C'mon," Richter sneered. "It's an anthill in there. Minus the organization. You can't frequency-tag a swarming multitude like that."

"OK," she said. "Someone funneled government blimps our way. Who brought 'em down?"

"Don't know. Prof was jamming our Red Angels when one of the zeps crashed. Which is why we had no idea the Penitents had stumbled onto an apocalypse device. Blind luck we discovered it."

He led her to the main guest elevator. Inside, he tapped the top-floor button. "We need to recover the nuke. And rescue your father."

"Only one zep creamed? Sure about that?" She immediately regretted saying it. Her voice had quavered slightly. Her armpits felt damp. She prayed her face wasn't reddening from mortification, from the effort of concealing her shame. That she'd unintentionally birthed a problem for everyone. For Richter. Prof. Her father. Herself.

Richter stared at her now. "Far as we know. Why, did you see them?"

She shook her head, frowning at her fingernails in an effort to exude disinterest in her own words. "No blimps. Just a 4Runner. Your men aren't the greatest drivers."

Richter harrumphed. "Manned vehicles, sure. Crow all you want, but on the whole, no other drone pilots on earth can beat my guys. Not even Prof's gifted guppies."

"Can your mercs fend off the Feds? The government will want its bomb."

The door opened. They padded down a carpeted hallway, crystal-teardrop chandeliers and spotless mirrors framed with decorative wood molding.

She let Richter walk well ahead, since she had no idea which suite was the Westphal grande dame's. Probably all of them.

"They don't deserve to have it back," said Richter, conviction edging into his voice.

Lash found his timbre familiar and troubling. It was something she would say.

They reached the end of the hallway. An iron entry door was engraved with the numbers 7301. Richter rang the bell. As they waited, he told Lash, sounding apologetic, "Not that I can influence you, but Westphal doesn't appreciate dark humor or attitude."

"I'm housebroken."

Richter chuckled.

A bot in French maid attire opened the doors and moved aside, allowing them entry. The preposterous sight brought to mind a comic book her father had read to her.

They went in.

27

She identified the odor immediately, even though it had been years since she and her father pressure-washed pigeon droppings from the roof of her grandmother's house in the neighboring city of Henderson. The smell inside 7301 was viscerally familiar and stronger than that long-ago afternoon spent spraying water and filling gaps between the orange Spanish tiles.

The room was pink, a concentrated rubicund that rivaled the intensity of Lash's neon tourist shirt. The vivid color wasn't bulb-powered. It was achieved instead by the sheer quantity of unusually tall and bulky flamingos inside the Westphal suite. Some posed on single, bony legs. Others ambulated about or out of Lash's path, with all the dramatic high-stepping of a karaoke drag-diva, before briefly dithering their useless wings.

Lash stopped counting birds, there were so many.

The carpetless floor was concrete-smooth. She easily avoided the grayish poop piles. But something touched her leg, and Richter had to grab her arm. She'd almost sunk a boot into a burbling puddle of blue-green algae.

"Flamingo food," he said, scrunching his nose in revulsion.

"Is that how their feathers get so pink?" said Lash, dazzled. "It's like we've been swallowed by a radioactive desert sunset."

"Pigment. Same dye they feed commercial salmon. There's other gross stuff in there."

She thought she saw something move in the algae, then hurried to keep up with Richter.

The coral-rose sea parted, fussy flamingos squawk-quacking. Irona the Mechanical Maid led them into the living chambers. Pink balloons sporting the CityCenter logo floated around the room, tops glide-scraping along a vaulted ceiling. The inflatables were weird, as if a children's birthday party were scheduled to occur here.

Westphal was reclining in a dainty and ultra-feminine Victorian luxury sofa that looked handmade in Europe. The velvety tassels, candy-shaped pillow cushions, and brass-swan side arm with an elongated neck coalesced into a vision of regal leisure. Above her, hanging from the soaring rafters, was a six-foot-long, gilt-caked chandelier. Behind her, through giant windows, was the blue-morning firmament of Las Vegas.

She faced her guests, pretending to partake of tobacco via a flapper-era cigarette holder. Lash could tell the woman wasn't inhaling smoke. She wore a long, sinuous, lace-edged dress that screamed Mucha. The scene was a death-kissed, art nouveau-inspired nightmare, fouling up the forced optimism Lash had summoned before the door opened.

"Good morning, Richter," wrinkled Westphal said. Her elderly appearance was like an unwrapped female mummy that had raided Daisy Buchanan's wardrobe. She wasn't getting up. "You must be Lash. I have heard so many astounding things about you. Welcome."

Lash toyed with the idea of kneeling sarcastically before the rasping Queen of Dead Vegas. "Thank you. Glad to be here. The drone students of CityCenter are remarkable."

"A considerable compliment," said Westphal, "coming from the Academy's preeminent graduate. As much bloodshed as Richter endures from, and in turn inflicts upon, Prof's disciples, you must realize the man standing next to you deeply respects the warrior spirit Luxor shapes in every child."

Richter coughed into his fist.

Westphal took the hint. "Of course, we look forward to both sides laying down arms and working together, hand in hand, to save Las Vegas. I believe it was Thomas Jefferson who said, 'Those who hammer their guns into plows will plow for those who do not.'"

"It's a tall order." Lash cut to the chase. "Prof insists resources should be shared, equally distributed. To funnel them into a single complex for the purposes of jump-starting a broken industry violates his moral code. Won't matter how many kids you rescue from dire circumstances or how much their drone service uplifts their families."

"We understand," Westphal said. "It shouldn't surprise you, then, that we hope you'll report to Prof, at some point in the near future, what you've seen and experienced here. Let him know we're not the monsters we're whispered to be. That we have love for our fellow man and that our means, while harsh in the short term, will soon justify communal ends."

A flamingo snort-shrieked. Lash thought the sudden noise punctuated, even punctured, the husk-lady's bloated comments.

"There are moments I'm convinced of what you say," Lash said. "No doubt Richter's kids possess the talent and selfless outlook necessary to rebuild a better town. But Sin City 2.0 isn't what we require. This place *earned* its nickname. Your guests, Russian speculators and carpetbaggers made wealthy from America's undoing, aren't worthy of such hospitality. And this bizarrely opulent suite incites nausea."

Westphal cackled. "I was warned you wield a sharp, unforgiving tongue. I feel its barbs now. But let me ask a question, Lash. What do you think of my gorgeous pets?"

"I think they'll taste excellent once they've been throat-slit, bled, plucked, gutted, seasoned, rotisseried over a fire, and browned to a mouthwatering crust."

The desiccated hag cackled again. Several birds not comprehending Lash's preparation instructions for roast flamingo joined Mrs. Westphal in conjuring a frightful din.

"It's not easy growing old," she said, mirth conceding to melancholy. "Though my late husband would have disagreed—right up until his dying breath."

Lash got the distinct impression that she murdered him.

"The silly trappings of one's heyday are difficult to surrender. Such is the case here. What you see is a woman of advanced age with tastes and habits of a bygone era. I look outrageous in your eyes. I realize that. But please know this. I have no intention of dividing the precious few remaining local resources so that we can allocate microscopic portions of water, food, and medicine. For more supplies to be shipped in or to materialize, we must use resources shrewdly. With the aim of enhancing the future, not triaging the past."

"Do what you feel you must," said Lash, playing her only card. "Just know that if I'm reunited with my father, who's currently caught up with the Penitents, I'll travel to hell and back to see that your goal of having a fully trained drone-ops force is reached."

"Thank you, Lash," Westphal said. "I'm sure I speak for Richter when I say we're doing everything we can to ensure your father is recovered from the Aliante caves."

With that, the bejeweled crone nodded at Richter. He broke his motionless poise and turned toward Lash, signaling that the meeting had satisfactorily concluded.

"Goodbye," said Lash to Madam Methuselah.

"Till next time," she said, waving the cigarette holder like a tiny parade flag.

Lash and Richter walked back, minus the maid, through the chattering mass of crimson-peach plumage and out into the hallway once again. Safe, for now, from the mad empress on an aviary throne, believing Vegas could be revived by coddling Russkies.

This time Lash was familiar with the music playing from the in-house speakers, a strangely appealing classical synth version of the Iron Maiden ballad "Wasted Years." One of her and Dio's favorite bands. The song made her miss her brother-in-arms. At the same time, if he got in the way of her reaching her father, she would kill Dio. She hummed along now, pleased with her tough performance and the compromise she'd made to be with her father.

Her sole regret was her pink shirt. It had made her look like another flamingo in there.

"Might've gone better if you hadn't threatened to barbecue her birds," Richter said.

"Hey, at least she laughed."

"She only laughs when she's PO-ed."

"Are *you* angry, Mr. Richter?" It came out flirtier than she wanted.

"No."

"You seemed anxious back there."

"I don't like those overgrown squawkers."

"They're ridiculous."

"Lash, they're *carnivorous*. Those birds eat human flesh. That pool of gross algae you nearly stepped in? A hand was sticking out of it. Westphal had them genetically modified in Russia, specially trained to kill people and bring down drones. The Russians are comped at the hotel."

"You're kidding." But then she remembered the beaks of those birds and something brushing her leg. She shuddered, then stifled her fear with the confidence that she could handle a flock of dumb, overgrown pigeons.

Richter shook his head, obviously disgusted by Westphal's aviary. "Man-eating fowl," he muttered, slowing his pace in the hallway back to the elevator. They were walking side by side now.

"I'm a man-eater, too." Lash was trying to lighten the mood, smiling at him in a way she didn't know she was capable of.

He didn't return the favor. Not exactly, anyway. Instead, he looked at her with ravenous intent and said, "I don't want anything to happen to you, Lash. Ever."

"Too late," she said. "Something's happening now."

They got into the elevator. On their way down to the casino floor, he suddenly and savagely pulled her to his tautly muscled frame, his face right up against hers. His expression was desire-racked, yet alien. Inscrutable. She longed to punch him, caress him.

He raised his hand. She brought up her arm to block him or throw a nose-bloodying jab. But it was obvious he intended no harm. He sought to batter something other than her body.

"*Tiene cuidado,*" she cooed, grinding her hips against his sturdy legs. "I bite."

"I see those sharp girl-teeth of yours," he seethed. "Already feel them on my heart."

She had no idea what that meant. She kissed him anyway. He tasted of ozone and citrus with a hint of kerosene. The most amazing flavor her mouth had ever encountered. His reciprocation was long, lingering, toe-curling. He was, apparently, savoring her as much as she was him.

She stopped him to ask, "Cameras? The mercs will make fun."

"I'll trash the files." He resumed his seductive tactics.

"I want you," she told him.

"Have me." His soft, wet lips brushed her ear, turning her insides to jelly.

"To give me back my crucifix."

He withdrew, breathing hard, and handed it over.

The elevator door opened. She exited, glancing back to say, in her sauciest voice, "Counting on you, Richter. Don't let me down."

"Expect to hear from me." He smiled, rebuttoning as the doors began to close. "Very soon."

En route to the employee elevator that sank into the hotel's descending colon, she noticed the Russians still at it. Drinking. Dancing. Debauching. The disco thickened into increasingly dismal, downbeat, throbbing sludge. Grotesque music and clinking glasses and heaving guests filled the air. An ongoing inundation of sonic misery. And all, as Richter said, on the house.

She ducked into a restroom to check her face and hair. None the worse. Once again, she had her crucifix. She'd missed its impression on her skin, its minuscule weight and comforting symbolism. Ovaries on fire, panties soaked, she considered masturbating in the stall. But Richter's drones might be listening for the sound of her orgasm.

She exited the restroom and took the elevator up to the school.

It wasn't until she stepped into the classroom to show the kids how to best password-hack an old FAA-regulated system that it suddenly dawned on her. She was surprised at how something that wasn't there could nonetheless chill her spine.

The casino floor lacked a casino. It didn't offer a single table game. No blackjack, baccarat, or craps. No Texas Hold 'em. No keno lounge or sports book. Not even one single slot machine to be seen.

28

Another day of teaching passed quickly. After Lash wrapped up a lesson on suppressing collision-avoidance systems, Helen popped into the classroom and made an offer no one in post-apocalyptic Las Vegas could've refused. "Wanna pet my dog? I need yarn for a sweater I'm knitting."

"No idea how those activities are related," Lash said. "But OK."

She accompanied Helen to her quarters in a Sky Villa in Aria tower. Night fell in the dead west. The suite's panoramic windows looked out over the darkened Strip. Thousands of barrel fires flickered tragically, like futile votives lit to honor a vanished god in a demolished church. It was a breathtaking sight. Outside, a drone puttered by, yards from the glass. Lash pressed her face against it, dark enough so she could see her reflection, a smeared specter hovering in a black doom-mirror. The villa behind her was lavish, white, mahogany-furnished with a living room, powder room, and a spa-like bathroom sanctuary. Lash longed to draw a hot bath. She wanted to impose.

Helen had a turntable like the one in Lash's suite. When they entered, the tonearm automatically lifted, swiveled, and dropped its stylus on a punk record Lash imagined Richter cherished. The Clash's *Combat Rock*.

She wondered if Richter had seduced Helen in this suite. If Helen had let him ravish her. Pangs of jealousy throbbed in Lash's guts.

Helen indeed owned a mongrel—smelly, long-haired, thick-coated. The friendly mutt had made itself comfortable on a mound of throw pillows. When the girls came closer, the animal panted and wiggled its tail without getting up. Gray-snouted, milky-eyed, the dog was advanced in age, maybe fifteen years old.

Lash thought of Argos, a puppy when Odysseus had sailed for Troy. The faithful hound waited twenty years for his master's return. When Odysseus showed up, he was dressed like a hobo to deceive his wife's suitors. Although covered in fleas and dung, Argos recognized him. The ancient pooch had enough strength to drop its ears and wag its tail before expiring from joy. It brought a tear to Odysseus's eye, touching the heart of a slaughterer of thousands.

The simple beauty of that relationship was something Lash feared she'd never know.

Helen grabbed a comb from under a pillow the dog was lying on and began brushing. The comb-teeth pulled hair from the animal. Helen gathered it, collecting it into a fluff wad.

"Passes the time," Helen said. "Calms me on nights when Richter and his pilots are busy securing resources for CityCenter."

"Therapeutic," agreed Lash, clenching her jaw, indignant at Helen's suggestion that she was Richter's girl. And that thieving Richter *secured* anything. "I imagine, anyway."

"Care to brush him?"

Lash nodded. She sat down on the dog's other side, taking the comb Helen handed her.

"What's his name?"

"Cerberus."

Lash comically scanned the room. "I *knew* this was a portal to hell."

"I don't get the reference," Helen said.

"Cerberus? The multiheaded watchdog at the gates of Hades?"

"Oh. Well, Richter named him."

Lash bit her lip to keep from asking the real question and began gently brushing Cerberus. "Richter gave you a puppy for your birthday?"

Helen laughed. She crossed her legs to perform what a yoganaut would call lotus position, closed her eyes, and said, "I rescued Cerberus from a slaughterhouse. Guy was selling dog fur, breeding puppies for his junkyard chopping block. He flayed them alive, leaving them to die slowly, skinless, before selling the meat. The cries were nightmarish."

Lash nodded. With civilization's veneer stripped away, man's cruelty to animals escalated.

Helen grabbed a fur wad, pulled the hairs along a straight line, twisted the end of the doggie-down between her thumb and finger to make a pointed end, and attached it to a drop-spindle. The spindle was a desk lamp with the post in the middle and an alligator clip pushed into the post. She twisted the first length of fur until she had a long enough piece of hair for the spindle to work, then wrapped the twisted fiber around the post several times, leaving a few inches hanging from the tip. Turning it clockwise, she inch-wormed the hair around and around. Slowly but surely, Helen was making dog yarn.

"Pretty cool," Lash said. "Going to be a funky sweater, though."

"I wash the finished yarn in warm soap and water."

"Sewing. Stitching. I was *way* too butch to learn all that stuff." She was reminded of her friend Dio. He was a lowrider lad, but also highly skilled at domestic crafting.

"You're so beautiful."

Lash felt her face blush. She looked down at the carpet, picked up a snip of stray fluff, and gave it to Helen. "As a little girl, I was drawn to boys. They were, I don't know, *action*-oriented. I wanted to be like them. Go on adventures like Tom Sawyer."

"Sawyer," Helen repeated. "He's the blond shorty in One Direction?"

Lash let loose a giggle that turned into a tiny pig-snort. Both girls were laughing now.

After they stopped, Lash waited a moment before saying, "C'mon, Helen, we're the same age. You didn't read books in school?"

"Never attended school," said Helen, picking up her knitting needles. "My parents were libertarians. I was educated at home. Only book I recall reading was *The Fountainhead*."

Lash had heard of it. "What was it like," she wanted to know, having a cop for a father, "growing up in a libertarian family?"

Helen puffed her cheeks, mulling the question. "When I was younger, things were ideal. My family was content, my father always working. Then so much changed so quickly. The economy crashed as the culture turned sinister, violent, and perverse. Celebrities were worshiped. We felt under siege by technology."

"Smartglasses telling you details about total strangers based on visual cues," Lash chimed in. "Cloud computing storing your most personal data and selling it to everyone, then claiming it was a hack."

"Yeah, and law-enforcement and homeowners-association drones spying on your car and house," Helen added. "Police emailing you tickets for violations in places you didn't remember even driving through. Levying fines for infractions no one could actually see on the ground."

Lash nodded.

"Sure, you were there, too," Helen said. "So you know. My parents were proud of being independent and entrepreneurial, so their options started running out. They were driven deeper and deeper underground."

"Were your parents Oath Keepers?"

The Oath Keepers were a libertarian militia of veterans and police officers from around the Southwest. They'd served as the valley's only line of defense, putting up a fight after the Feds slaughtered Metro and came for Hoover Dam's energy and water. They threw everything they had at taking control of a mine brimming with rare-earth minerals needed to make and fix drones, trying to blunt the Feds' technological edge. The government finally vaporized the Oath Keepers in a nuke strike at Mountain Pass, California, sixty miles southwest of Las Vegas. In the process, however, they also destroyed the mine. Which explained why they were resorting to blimps.

"No, my folks weren't Oath Keepers," Helen said. "But what happened at Mountain Pass tore out the last stitch of my father's sanity. He refused to accept rations the Academy had begun to dole out, believing the Chinese were poisoning us. My mom and dad were caught stealing banana-yucca fruit from federal land in Moapa Valley and were drone-murdered there."

"You saw them die."

Helen nodded, dropping her needles. "The drone spared me, for some reason. A man in a pickup found me weeping on the highway, covered in blood. He took me as far as Pahrump, dumping me on a brothel madam.

She took me in, but not out of any compassion. I was popular among her clients, Fed soldiers."

"I'm so sorry, Helen."

Helen shrugged, knitting again. "I'm over it. Richter saved me from that hell when he liberated the Nye County brothels, taking the youngest girls with him. That's how I got here."

"Richter did that?" Lash was stunned by Helen's tale.

"Yes. He's not the monster people think he is. He has empathy and genuinely wants to save Las Vegas. Sure, he's brutal, but he has to be. Others, like Prof, stand in his way, forcing him to make difficult choices."

"Like founding a drone-pilot school?"

"Yes, but that was always his dream," Helen said. "To create a learning environment free of institutional psychosis. Actually, Richter's concessions lie in his alliance with Westphal and the Russians. That's where he's in trouble."

Outrage stirred in Lash's chest. "But they're the source of his power."

"Power is secondary," Helen insisted. "His primary motivation is reprisal for having lost his girlfriend to a drone strike. He plans to stick it to the Feds by cutting them off from the dam forever. By building a self-sufficient city in these ruins. By teaching a generation of kids how to protect themselves and their children from the government."

Lash's mother used to tell her that power stemmed from making good things in the world. From creating beauty, rather than military might—what Helen maintained Richter was after. New Eden. If so, he was planting a garden with bad seeds.

"Richter had a girlfriend? I can't imagine any woman warming to him."

Helen looked at Lash like she was nuts.

"Kidding!" Lash yelped. "OK, I admit he has the tortured, romantic aura of Heathcliff."

"The cartoon cat?" said Helen, perplexed.

Lash facepalmed herself. "Sister, after you teach me to knit a dog-hair sweater, I'm paying you back with a summer reading list. You can start with the bookshelf in my room."

Helen laughed. "Deal."

They made more yarn. After a while, Helen announced she was hungry and ordered french fries through room service. A bot tapped on the door fifteen minutes later with a piping-hot platter. The fries were fresh from the grease and stung her fingertips. She blew on a spud sliver before popping it into her mouth. It was a real potato cooked in real beef tallow, better than the acrylamide-coated product McDonald's served before the bombs fell.

Lash suddenly remembered the pledge she'd made to Bathory. Another broken promise among many. She began to cry as she chewed.

Mistaking her friend's sorrow for gratitude, Helen said, "They're awesome, right?"

Lash nodded, swallowing. She tasted the salt from her own tears in her mouthful of starch.

A phone beside the stereo suddenly rang.

"It's the front desk," said Helen, standing up to get it. "Guest complaint, I bet. Excuse me."

She took the phone with her into the master bedroom, leaving Lash alone with cooling fries and snoring Cerberus and the guilt from having abandoned Bathory to Ritalin-fueled bot building.

Lash wiped her hands on her cargo shorts and went back to the windows. This time she opened the sliding-glass door and stepped outside. There was no wind and very little smoke in the air, despite the barrel fires. Perfect drone-flying conditions. She worried for a moment that Vai might be on duty and try to drone-strike her on Helen's balcony. But the Red Angels were in sentry mode, looking for hostiles coming from outside rather than within.

They'd missed something very small. An insect-size drone.

The Academy had trained Lash's ears to detect the Fed's nano air vehicles. Impossible to arm, flybots were nonlethal. She didn't bother to evade the one approaching her now. Normally, she would've hand-swatted the servomotored wings into polyester crumbs. But she was curious to know if the government was monitoring CityCenter.

Lash extended her palm, hoping the microdrone would plop down. It did.

She peered into its miniature structure. A two-winged job comprising a hollow carbon-fiber frame, lithium battery, and familiar Chinese wireless receiver. It was an Academy drone, likely piloted by a stealth-shrouded smartphone somewhere down below.

The flybot offered something else. A single headphone bud she could only assume was from Prof.

She glanced back and saw that Helen was still in the bedroom. Coast clear, Lash carefully inserted the bud—and the entire bug—into her ear.

"What's up, Prof?"

"Lash," said her headmaster, voice static-crackling. "Thank the Cyborg-Christ you're safe."

"At the moment. That'll change if they catch me chatting."

"I won't endanger you. Just confirming you're not dead." Pause. "And that you haven't joined Richter."

She waited for him to say more. When he didn't, she asked, "Who told you I'd joined Richter?"

"We have audiodrones inside CityCenter. It's difficult to sift what we're hearing, to determine what's true and what's not."

"Not that it matters to you," she said. "But I have, in fact, formed a temporary alliance with Richter. And let me stress the temporary part. He found my dad, and we're rescuing him very soon. Then I'm leaving Vegas."

There was a hissing noise, electrical interference. But Prof seemed to have heard her.

She added, "I'm sorry. But I don't belong at the Academy anymore. I belong with my father."

"I understand, Lash. All I ask is that you're careful with Richter. He's a deceiver. A liar. He'll say anything to turn you into one of his savage merc pilots. You'd be quite the coup."

Tears welled in her eyes again. She raised her hand to rip the drone from her ear. She stopped herself and asked, "Dio recover the Bride?"

"Yes. It's safe and waiting for you here."

"Is Bathory OK?"

"I can't see the evidence as you can." Prof ignored her question. "If there's a chance—the slightest—that your father's alive and Richter knows his location, you have no choice. You have my blessing. You have the Academy's prayers."

She didn't want his blessing or prayers but needed something else from him. "Give Dio a message for me?"

"Of course."

She sniffled. "Tell him I'm sorry. That he should forgive me. For bringing down the blimps."

Prof chuckled. "Blimps? I'm sure Dio forgives you, Lash. Richter is another matter."

"They weren't Richter's." She'd said too much. Her effort to warn Dio was clumsy, inept.

"Lash, the signal's hazy. I think you said—"

She removed the drone from her head and hurled it to the floor. It buzzed, struggling to launch itself into the air, but its wings were crippled. She smashed it with her boot and kicked its debris bits under the rail and off the balcony.

"Everything good?" said Helen, sliding open the glass door to step outside and join her friend.

Lash turned around and smiled. She coolly accepted the tumbler of caramel-colored soda on ice that Helen was extending. "Absolutely. Resolve the complaint?"

Helen sighed. "Yes. The expectations of a small percentage of our guests are unrealistic. They don't seem to take into account the fact that this hotel sits in a ruined valley."

"Who knew caviar was so hard to come by in a post-apocalyptic desert?" Lash snarked. She sipped her drink. It was cane-sugared Coca-Cola, imported from Mexico in glass bottles.

"Yes. As is potato-based vodka. Most everything we serve is synthetic. It does the trick, but some customers are sticklers for soda and liquor."

"This MexiCoke sure isn't ersatz. It's the real deal."

Helen nodded. "Coke and french fries are genuine. A heavenly combination." Helen raised her tumbler in a toast. "To the finer things. Can I get an amen?"

"Amen."

They clinked their carbonated beverages and giggled. Red Angels glided past them, oblivious to their little celebration.

"Where's all the gambling? The casino floor lacks a casino. No slots or anything."

Helen looked out at the barrel fires and crunched her ice cubes. "Thieves scavenged CityCenter's machines and tables in the immediate aftermath of the bombs. We're working on getting gambling online again. We hope by year's end."

Lash, not satisfied, said, "No bets of any kind?"

"Sports wagering," Helen said. "You know, on fights. Mixed martial arts. Stuff like that."

"Can't believe people still find televised bloodsport compelling enough to watch—what with uglier, more intense spectacles all around us, right? I'm glad Richter has the kids learning physical combat, though. Duffy's tough, I imagine."

Helen was about to say something else, but an explosion on the Strip below cut her off.

They leaned over the balcony rail to take a look. Lash could make out Red Angels Hellfire-shredding a camp people had assembled near CityCenter's refuse bins. Desperate souls seeking food scraps were being served up shrapnel instead.

"Damn it, Helen," said Lash, fists clenched, teeth gritted. A headache began building as she witnessed the drones going wild.

"I know," Helen said, angry. "It's terrible."

"Those people don't pose any threat to CityCenter. Richter should know better."

"Not his policy," Helen said. "Westphal's."

"Why?"

"She's paranoid. Thinks the Feds have plants everywhere. Even among the destitute."

"Well, sure, it's likely. Doesn't mean they can reach us."

"Westphal is nuts, Lash. She believes Prof infested CityCenter with nano drones. It's why she engineered her flamingo army. They eat bugs. Westphal claims her birds protect her from eavesdropping bots. *Crazy* stuff. Richter needs to figure out what to do with her—before she decides to do something with him."

Lash was silent. Flamingos were a good idea after all. She finished her Coke, then chewed the ice.

Helen said, "The worst part is—ugh, I shouldn't even tell you."

"Go on."

"The inedible scraps those wretches are dying for? Hotel leftovers are shipped to pig farms in Mesquite. Las Vegans are starved and strafed by drones, so our guests can eat bacon."

"You're kidding." Lash felt a seizure coming on. She took a deep breath.

Helen shook her head. "Like I told you, Lash. Richter cut a deal."

"Why doesn't he kill Westphal?"

Helen smiled and winked at Lash. Then downed the rest of her own Coke.

Lash smiled, too, pleased with the revelation that Richter had a plan. Her temples continued throbbing, though.

"She's not that easy to kill, number one. And two, she's sick. Richter believes she'll either expire or self-destruct from her hunger for power."

Together they watched the survivors tend to their wounded and burn their dead. It was a grim process. The horrid smell of charred flesh reached them in their glittering tower.

"Can't watch this," Lash said. "Then again, I've watched it all my life."

"Same here," Helen said.

Impotent and upset, they went back inside and closed the door. There was nothing Helen and Lash could do for the time being. Except add the sight of even more senseless carnage to their grievances. And memories.

They got under the covers together in Helen's king bed, listened to the second side of *Combat Rock,* ate cold fries, and watched a muted VHS cartoon from the '80s called *Thundarr the Barbarian.* It was dubbed in Portuguese and lacked English subtitles, but they followed the plot well enough. Lash's head soon felt better.

After Helen fell asleep, Lash studied her friend's features in the flickering TV light.

"Richter is mine," she said.

29

The next morning, she exercised, ate, and showered. Instead of immediately heading for the command center in Vdara, she took a moment to bask in the meditation chapel she'd ordered Richter to install for her. He'd converted a suite and done a good job, adding exposed overhead beams, wooden floors with carpeted floor runners, pews with cushioned kneelers. Large clear-glass windows behind the altar offered unobstructed views of the mountains on the valley's western edge. It was much brighter here than in the dimly lit Gathering of the Cyborgs buried deep in Luxor's lower colon. Of course, there was no cross on display here. But it was a start and a big concession on secular-humanist Richter's part, a nod toward the spiritual that Lash had pushed him to make. She took pleasure in bending him, if only slightly. She knew she couldn't get him to bow completely.

Lash wasn't surprised when he showed up. Bit creepy that he always knew where she was. Probably the audiodrones kept him apprised of her where-abouts. Or the RFID locator in her crucifix. Anyhow, he wanted to see her satisfied in the flesh and she wouldn't deny him. She smiled, showing him her *girl-teeth,* whatever that meant. She was no girl. He looked striking in his Amebix shirt and dark jeans. His hair was rockabilly-slicked to perfection.

"It's beautiful here," she said. She almost said thank you but nipped it.

Richter smiled bashfully. "You deserve nothing less. I hear only raves about you as an instructor. As a friend to Helen."

She didn't want to talk about Helen. "Hurt to carve out a pious spot in your secular hotel?"

He shrugged. "I learned to meditate in high school. Still rely on it for dealing with tension. It's a good idea to have this here, Lash. For you, the students, and me."

"What's stressful," insisted Lash, "is seeing a defenseless gleaner camp drone-strafed."

He nodded sorrowfully, looking right at her. "I'm sorry about last night. Westphal's policy and one I loathe."

"Get her to change it."

Richter sighed. "I choose my battles. Right now, my focus is on growing CityCenter's resources and keeping Las Vegas safe from atomic detonations."

"So you can take on the Feds and use their own nuke against them."

He shook his head. "Unlike you, I'm not on a suicide mission. And I don't relish murder."

"All killing isn't murder," Lash said.

Now he frowned, then handed her the bag he'd brought. "I'm sure you're sick of the jazz records in your suite. Here's your Walkman and cassettes."

Having her metal soundtrack returned thrilled her. "Listen to any of it?"

He nodded. "I didn't realize how *punk* much of it sounds. Metal always seemed overblown and cheesy. But it's ideal drone-fighting music. I see why you like it. *Screaming for Vengeance* is a great album."

"Oh yes." Pleased with his evaluation, Lash removed a few tapes—Iron Maiden's *Powerslave*. Metallica's *Master of Puppets*. Slayer's *South of Heaven*. "Heard these?"

"I'll listen to them," he said. "On a condition."

"I'm not heavy petting with you. In *here,* anyway."

30

Hungry and running low on inhalants, the Penitents were agitated. Or so Richter claimed. How he knew this, Lash couldn't tell. Their heat signals registered the same. If anything, the Penitents were moving less, dragging their feet ponderously, falling asleep or just still.

Richter insisted that it was now, finally, time.

"Going to need a few things," she told him.

Richter smiled. "You'll get your gun back when we reach the caves."

She shrugged. "Iron pan. Welding torch. Coffee."

"You want us awake for this mission? Fine."

The two of them piled into an armor-plated 4Runner as dawn first appeared. They dashed to the valley's northern edge, spewing a dust cloud behind them. The plan was to downlink a line-of-sight attack with combat-drone support. Richter would peer through a sniper-scope to answer an age-old question: to shoot a nuclear football cradled by a zombie or not to shoot?

She felt confident Richter would pull the trigger. If not, she'd gladly handle it.

They stopped two miles from the caves and got out. The landscape was monotonous. To their right, low hills and scrubland. To their left, low hills and scrubland. They walked along an old cow path that meandered around creosote, then trod-crunched over a small rise into a dip of more scrub until they could discern a scabrous assemblage of caves a mile away. She made coffee with a hotel chef's skillet and a Meco Midget. The beans, ground Peaberry Kona, were packaged pre-Collapse. Didn't taste bad at all. Scalded her stomach and cleared her head.

"Good stuff," agreed Richter, downing it quickly. "Our café is hiring, you know."

"Hah."

Then he reached into his backpack and pulled out binoculars, head-phones, and a mission-ops tablet. They lay flat on their stomachs to gaze at where they hoped to rescue Lash's dad and neutralize The Bomb That Would Permanently End Las Vegas.

"Tell me when you see it," Richter said.

The snakebot cyber-writhed around his neck. His holstered smartgun was still and silent, waiting patiently to be drawn. His condorbot glided overhead. Lash was fascinated by these devices, a little unsettled, but not frightened. She wanted badly to thrash the condorbot for having hurt her.

She squinted into the distance.

A solar panel was winking in the sunlight about two hundred yards from the caves. She raised the binoculars Richter had given her. Next to the panel was something Prof once showed her how to make, an anemometer or wind-speed sensor. The sensor wasn't in place to benefit them, however. It was there to provide the Red Angels with navigational intel.

Lash also noticed a camo-sponged microphone on a tripod next to what looked like a brown tackle box on steroids. Richter had installed a sound database amid a heavy blanket of desert silence. A visually subtle yet powerful eavesdropping setup that even an über-snoop like J. Edgar Hoover would've admired, after changing his lingerie.

"Sweet mic," Lash said.

"It captures ground-based sounds from miles away," Richter said. "Penetrates the deepest, densest caves. Catches noise generated from orbit."

"You mean we get to hear the impending alien invasion?"

"Especially useful for IDing military UAVs by sound. I know *you* can, Lash."

"I'm better at distinguishing drone-missile blasts. Serving as a human target for the Feds in a refugee camp ingrained that skill in me."

"You were at Boulder City? Sorry to hear it. That was a tragedy."

"Can't the Penitents find this?" she said, changing the subject. "They love stealing tech."

"Everything's encased in steel conduits and sealed inside a bulletproof trunk. There's also a sound-pressure meter."

"What's it do?"

"Triggers a phosphorus bomb." Richter blew into the lenses of his binocs, clearing dust.

"That might dissuade the crazies."

"Crystal-clear acoustics, too. Red Angels won't be here for a few. Care to listen?"

"I only wear headphones for Judas Priest. But for you, I'll make an exception."

Smiling, he offered his wireless chrome aviators. The thick ear pads were comfortable, immersive, plunging her into a rich soundscape. When she and Richter arrived at this area, Lash was struck by its remoteness, its otherworldly silence. After donning the Fostex TH-900 cans, she realized how congested and raucous the terrain really was.

The sustained and theatrical breath of the breeze was like a continuous spectral exhalation. Against it, she heard a baby bird cry out for its mother. It caused Lash's eyes to pool. The cry was followed by a mystery sound—a high, warbled yelp that could've been anything. Crow. Coyote. Bobcat. Normally, the commotion of creatures roused her hunger, inspiring her to hunt. Not this time. This time she was hearing the music. The world hadn't ended.

She detected other animals—crickets, rodents. The land was alive with fauna. Underground, a hot spring burbled as it had for centuries. She considered the prospect that the planet would survive, though people might not. Earth's dust would cover civilizations for millennia to come. The desert, like a giant Etch A Sketch, would erase all traces of humanity.

Who cared about the future, though? Here was the patter of two hearts, hers and Richter's. They beat dumbly in a dry yet teeming Eden. That's all that mattered.

Outside, she'd always cherished silence. Whatever had obscured stillness was to be avoided, destroyed, or eaten. She'd long wanted to inhabit absolute quiet. She didn't until now comprehend that there was no such thing as true peace. Maybe in heaven. Or in Richter's faithless void. He didn't accept Christ yet was attuned to cosmic mysteries.

"Let's push deeper," he said, adjusting levels on a small mixing-board app on the tablet.

She heard the Penitents, their noises a chasm of agony. Mumbling incoherently. Shuffling without direction. Coughing constantly. She heard the shaking of a nearly dry gas can, followed by a sharp inhalation. Another. Then a dissatisfied and pained growl, the plastic container thrown, smacking against a rock wall. Prolonged addict-howls. Gruff junkie moans. Long, unkempt fingernails raking against flaking skin. Scratching of the doomed.

Richter was right. The Penitents were irritated. They exuded despair, impatience. Lash sensed that, very soon, they would leave the cave for more gas.

Then she heard it. Her father's singing voice. He was still alive, thank God.

> *Loveliest cowgirl,*
> *Wasn't it enough*
> *To drag my heart*
> *Through neon and dust?*

His favorite song. He'd often played it for Lash and her mom upon arriving home.

Tears came pouring. She tried not to blubber. Her father sang weakly, defeatedly, throat ravaged by dust, soul fractured by grief. Still, it was more than enough to give Lash hope. As soon as the Red Angels arrived, Richter would sniper the nuke controls as she Hellfire-hammered the lunatics into seared bits. Then she would be with her father and care for him until he was as strong as he'd been before the Collapse. Stronger. She needed to be careful not to set off the bomb, though. She trusted Richter to neutralize that threat.

She would be thorough, destroying anyone threatening her reunion. Kill them all, Richter had suggested. God would cull the blessed from the damned. With the exception of her father, the Penitents were destined for Italian poet Dante's seventh circle, middle ring, reserved for the violently insane. Chased and mauled by ferocious dogs for all eternity.

A fitting punishment. Maybe it would be hers, too.

"Thanks," she said, wiping her face. She didn't care if Richter saw her cry. She was grateful. She'd smidgened Helen's mascara on her eyes. Lash hoped it wasn't running.

Richter nodded at her reaction. He understood her sadness, she thought. He had, at some point, maybe not that long ago, experienced a similar epiphany.

After she returned the cans, he binoculared the caves and said, "Technology doesn't have to bludgeon or buzz. Sometimes it can reveal the beauty of what we take for granted."

She held up his statement to the light and perceived a flaw. "You used a similar arrangement to eavesdrop on Koons and me. It's how you intercepted the excavator."

Richter shrugged. "Stalking Academy kids isn't why I learned to do this."

"Tell me. We have a minute."

"The summer the bombs fell, I was finishing an internship for a college credit at a desert-tortoise conservation center in the Mojave Valley."

"What did you do?"

He blew out a long, mournful breath. "I'd been assigned to a scientist with the National Park Service. Once a month, I carried a tote bag of computer components for her. She was studying the impact of synthetic noise on biodiversity. We'd drive to different soundscape stations, switch out data cards, and calibrate the mics."

Sensing that the scientist might be the girlfriend Helen had mentioned, Lash wondered what else they did at the soundscape stations. "Were you out there when the bombs fell?"

He dropped the binocs and turned to stare at her. He propped himself on an elbow, swatted dust from his jeans, and looked back in the direction from which they'd traversed. The snakebot fell still, responding to Richter's mood, immobilized by his anguished memories.

"Helen says you got your Zippo back," he said finally. "Can I borrow it?"

Lash pulled it from her pocket and handed it over.

He took out an ultra-rare pack of Marlboros and removed a cigarette.

"Stop," said Lash, snatching back her lighter. "I use that to kill drones. Don't waste fuel."

He groaned and slipped the cigarette back into the pack. "You don't want to hear my story."

"Tell me," she said. "Please, Richter."

She gave him back her Zippo, so he could light up.

31

Sagebrush seasoned the air the day nineteen-year-old Richter, in a canary-yellow Sonic Youth *Goo* shirt and jeans, watched the world end.

The valley was hot, quiet save for cattle chewing cheatgrass. He and a gorgeous, recently divorced scientist—Priscilla Paglen—had just refreshed a sound station. They were climbing back into their SUV when an aircraft appeared above the mountains.

As it approached, they saw it wasn't a jet, but a drone.

"It's circling over something," Richter said.

"What?"

"Don't know."

"Let's go see," Paglen insisted.

They jostled down a dirt road in the SUV, kicking up a cloud. The unmanned aircraft's pilot, wherever he was, apparently noticed them. The drone turned around and headed back to the mountains.

"Saw us?" Paglen hunched over the wheel for a windshield-view of the retreating drone.

"Watch out!"

She braked, hard, stopping the truck. "What?"

"There." He pointed at a canister half-buried in the sand next to a patch of cheatgrass fifty feet ahead.

"Stay here." Paglen got out and approached the thing.

The buzz of a distant propeller attracted his attention. It was the whirring thrum of the same Predator from before, making a beeline for the scientist.

He saw Paglen raise her hands in a gesture of surrender; slowly backing away, she took a white bandana out of a front pocket and began waving it like a flag, the international symbol of please-don't-shoot.

Richter, meanwhile, had already broken into a sprint, bolting away from the truck.

It saved him.

When he heard a hissing sound, he instinctively hit the ground. Or he tried to. When the missile slammed behind him with apocalyptic ferocity, the impact threw his body forward a great distance, knocking him unconscious.

Discomfort prodded him awake. His ears were ringing. His body was starting to burn on the inside. He pulled up his shirt to examine blood oozing from a quarter-size wound. He tried to focus on the rocket-scorched truck—burnt, bent, twisted, and left to smolder. Somewhere in the debris was what was left of his scientist lover. He made a promise to himself that, if he survived, he'd gain mastery of remote slaying to never again be on the receiving end of a drone strike.

Hearing another engine in the distance, Richter turned to see a dust cloud billowing where the road met the highway.

Someone was coming.

Body aching, he scrambled into a dense cluster of Joshua trees and craggy sandstone and got low.

A black Ford pickup chewed up the distance, rushing past the husk of the SUV and pulling up directly in front of the device. Three men in white radiation suits, black gas masks, and heavy boots emerged. They scanned the area briefly with a radiograph and approached the bomb. They didn't seem to care about the blown-up car. Instead, they rolled the bomb, barrel-like, to the rear of the F250 and heaved it onto the bed. Richter spotted crucifixes hanging from the necks of these radiation-suited figures as they climbed into the cab.

The truck turned and headed for the highway, back to Las Vegas.

Richter limped toward the dirt road that led to the two-lane blacktop to the highway. He moved from Joshua tree cluster to Joshua tree cluster, desperate for shade. It was hotter than hell. He'd lose a quart of water every hour from perspiration. He had two hours to find a drink.

"I won't die here," he rasped, barely able to coax the sounds out of his seared throat. His cracked lips began bleeding. His tongue felt like a tumor.

He moved on. He had no idea how long it took or how he did it, but he reached the highway. An old Mexican guy in a beat-up minivan slowed to take a long look at Richter as he passed, then stopped.

The man took one look at Richter and reached behind him to grab a small plastic bottle. Richter downed the warm water in one desperate guzzle, choking and spewing the last few ounces onto the dashboard.

They'd driven miles in silence, past Mesquite and Valley of Fire, toward the setting sun, when the man finally spoke up. "*Qué pasó?*"

"*Un robot.*" Richter made a flying-aircraft gesture. "Drone."

The driver's eyes got big for a moment. He gripped the steering wheel tighter, whistled sharply, and said, "*Mis amigos* run from drones. When they come across the border from Mexico."

"Your friends ever been hit by drone *missiles?*"

"*Ahora, no. En la futura? Sí, es posible.*"

"There's a proverb that goes like this," Richter said. "Create a world where anything can happen, and anything will happen."

"*No sé.* Do you change the world? Or does the world change you?"

"If I don't die in your minivan, señor, I'll find the answer."

"Ay!" the man exclaimed suddenly, face glowing from the brightness before them. "Fireworks. *Qué magníficos!*"

Perplexed, Richter gazed at the illuminated valley and tried to recall the date.

It wasn't a holiday.

32

"Before driving into the city to try to rescue his family, the Good Samaritan dropped me off at a giant rave being held at the Speedway," Richter said to Lash. "Tons of medical personnel were working the event, treating dehydration, ODs, and rapes. So the place ended up being a hospital. I was triaged in and mending before the first wave of bomb victims arrived."

"After that, you enlisted in the US DroneCorps program," said Lash, comprehending what Richter had gone through to become who he was. Lovely monster. Damaged innocent.

"Conscripted," he clarified. "The government was desperate to take control. They enacted martial law, forcing everyone between the ages of sixteen and twenty-four into service at Creech. At fourteen, you were too young, which is why you were banished to a Boulder City death pit."

Boulder. The word alone made her wince. Richter was right about it being a one-way trip to the cemetery. But it had been a luxury spa compared to what the Harvesters put her through.

Richter noted her expression and changed the subject. "The government tore the lid off Pandora's box by going completely apeshit with UAVs after 9/11 and went into overdrive after the Collapse. Didn't take long for guys like Prof and me to make connections with financiers in Russia, China, Africa. A month after my first drone op, I went AWOL. I took the gnarliest pilots with me—creeps like Vai—and went full-on merc. I never looked back."

"What about your parents?"

He closed his eyes and shrugged. "Missing. Dead, most likely. I mean, of course, I *hope* they're alive somewhere in Las Vegas. I would do anything to spend one more minute with them. And my twin brother and younger sister."

She thought he might tell her something else, but he didn't. So she said, "Why are you here?"

"To fix what others never should have broken. To rebuild the world."

"Why didn't you and Prof team up?"

Richter laughed at the suggestion. "Problem with you Academy folk is that you're always waiting, forever praying, for an even worse tomorrow—so you can leave the rest of us behind to suffer further punishment. Prof believes he's Mother Teresa of the Las Vegas Strip—protecting the poor, nourishing the hungry, clothing the naked. He prefers treating symptoms, rather than the disease itself. Why he does it, I have no idea. He must be motivated by some tremendous guilt. You know, half the thugs you Academy kids waste time saving would just as soon cut your throats as accept your handouts. Only cretins and psychos stick around here. With CityCenter back online, I can change that."

"OK, you're not Mother Teresa," Lash said. "Who are you then, Jim Jones?"

"I'm Richter, and I plan to build this city on rock 'n' roll."

"By stealing everyone's resources for Westphal?"

"By restoring the town's economic engine. Join or get out of the way."

Lash shook her head and smiled. "Let me verify something. After being skull-humped by a drone, you imagine you saw members of a weird cult that destroyed Las Vegas."

"I imagined nothing," he said, pretending not to be offended. "A nuke went off. Paglen and I apparently got caught up in something we couldn't decipher. Wrong place, wrong time. Maybe the military, trying to neutralize the cult's bomb, made an error, thought *we* were the bad guys, and sent a UAV after us. The real mass murderers, whatever kind of cult they might've belonged to, went on to trigger the bomb."

"Well, you *are* a bad guy, Richter." It came out all wrong. Or maybe it came out perfectly, because she very much wanted to kiss him now.

He was about to say something, then considered her expression and stopped.

She didn't have to tell him the snakebot irked her. He pulled it from his neck and tossed it into a clump of cholla. Since he and Lash were down low on their bellies, he elbow-crawled closer, brushed her hair with his fingertips, closed his eyes, and kissed her lips.

First gently. The second time was much harder.

Lash reciprocated, pushing her tongue into his mouth, delighting in his taste, his hot breath reminiscent of black coffee and molten steel.

Between Richter's gift of letting her hear her father sing and his account of how he was nearly blendered by a drone before Las Vegas died, her heart had taken a beating.

KO-ed, she emitted the tiniest moan.

When they disengaged to come up for air, he said, "I saw what you did to Vai. He's afraid to look at you now."

"Turn you on?" she said, rubbing her nose against Richter's stubbled coyote jaw, from which she wanted to hang like a scrap of meat. "Watching me smash other boys?"

"A powerful woman does it for me, yes." He placed his rough hand inside her Celine Dion sweatshirt. "A woman with beautiful scars."

He cupped her breast and pinched her nipple. First gently.

"Richter," she said. "The ground is moving beneath me."

"Cheesy," he said, teeth against her neck, ready to vampire-kiss it. "I'll let it slide."

"No, I mean it! The ground's moving!"

It was true. The earth shook beneath them.

Richter grabbed his binocs but saw nothing in front of the caves. He thrust the mission-ops tablet into her hands and stood to don his headphones. He listened.

"Not an earthquake," he said, confused.

Heart skipping every other beat, Lash knew what it was. Last summer, she'd hacked something spectacular from an abandoned intake project at the bottom of Lake Mead. Prof hadn't used it against Richter, because you could feel it coming for miles. And there'd been no practical application for it. Until now.

"You're hearing blades," she said, standing up, too. "A machine grinding through rock."

He looked at her and Lash could tell he was surprised and irritated that she'd pinpointed the sound before he did, and without the benefit of fancy microphones. "How did you—?"

"It's the Driller," she went on, head spinning, stomach turning. She could sense a seizure looming, trying to insinuate itself into her neurons. Goose flesh erupted all over her skin. She felt a numbness, accompanied by the sensation of standing on the edge of a steep precipice. The impending plummet symbolized a violation of her flawed yet critical bond with the Academy. A severing of kinship's tether. A breach.

"A fifty-foot-tall reservoir-boring beast," she continued. "The rotating cutter head has forty-eight ridged disks, each weighing three hundred pounds. Slow but effective. It's close, Richter."

"Lash," he said, stern voice dropping an interval. "Will you please tell me what in the hell an underground tunnel digger is doing here? And who's operating it? Oh. Don't tell me."

She said it anyway, the seizure building more strongly in her brain, murder in her heart. "Prof."

Shadows fell over them. In the sky, Richter's kill-drones had arrived, thrumming with the excitement of a slaughter-focused mission. They wouldn't get the chance. Incapable of tunneling, Red Angels were completely ineffective below the earth's surface.

Her command tablet asked with a pop-up if she wished to connect to a program module called RED_ANGEL_DEATH_SONG. She tapped CANCEL and looked right at Richter.

He seemed startled by the wild-eyed, battle-starved creature he suddenly saw standing before him. His mouth moved without sound as he struggled to find the words.

She said them for him. "No choice but to kill Prof now. He can't have my father. Or the nuke."

Eyes narrowed, mouth agape in uncertainty, headphones collaring his neck, Richter still said nothing and had yet to move.

Another beat. Then, "You'll find your gun in the truck."

She went running down the slope. Through the open window of Richter's 4Runner, she grabbed her Benelli M4 and ammo belt from the backseat. It felt great to hold the shotgun again, even if the anxiety of what she was about to do clawed at her guts.

She raced back up the incline where the villain she loved waited for her. Waited to join her in an attack against a Prof-piloted Godzilla-awl currently digging a subterranean path to steal a city-erasing bomb.

Winded, she reached the hilltop. He grabbed her arm, hard. For a moment, she thought he'd second-guessed himself and wanted her gun back now. Then he pushed her away. He poured the weird light of his pain-haunted eyes into hers and said, "This is a trap. You tipped off Prof. I heard you speaking to his flybot. I trusted you, Lash."

She threw a punch. He lunged forward in an effort to smother it. Her fist was already on its way, so he covered his head and moved inside the strike. The forceful blow glanced off his shielding arm. He grabbed her throat, wrenching her face toward his.

She kissed him deeply, sensually. He loosened his grip to return her kiss.

She could do nothing about it. Nor he. Either she'd trounced his godless nihilism, or he'd conquered her violent-martyr soul. Or love had defeated them both, trampling their pride, their physical and psychological scars, under its equalizing chariot wheels.

In any case, she broke off the kiss to say what needed to be said. "It's true that I stupidly said too much to Prof when he contacted me. But I haven't sided with the Academy since the mines, and you know it. In a few minutes, Prof will have my father and the nuke. I suggest we stop him."

"Oh yeah? How?"

"Annihilate him."

Mouth open, Richter threw the Fostex cans to the ground and clutched his chest, looking anguished. But the fire returned to his eyes, and he snatched his still-tendriling snakebot from off the cactus and unholstered Moss. "Prof was your headmaster," he said, summoning an aura of fierce, conscientious leadership. "I respect that, even if you don't. We'll bargain if there's a chance. If Prof doesn't goad the Penitents into blowing us all up."

I smell warhead, Moss confirmed, voice in androgynous-droid default setting.

"Prof is forcing their hand," Lash said.

"Prof never gives anyone a chance," Richter said. "I suspect he's somehow figured out how to neutralize the nuke. I'll tell you this, Lash. If the Academy thinks they're leaving here with a fission-powered device, they're wrong."

Staring back at him, she gritted her teeth. "Let's show them *how* wrong they are."

33

Richter summoned his sandsurfer, stepped aboard, and extended an arm. "Come on."

"I don't ride bitch." Her rule. Dio aside, she didn't trust anyone's piloting.

"Lash," he insisted, realizing she wasn't joking.

Her love for him allowed her to relent.

She took his hand. He hauled her onto the hoverbot. She wrapped her arms around his chest, pressing her body tightly against his, her cheek up against his muscular back. Whenever they made physical contact, it felt like the cruelest, loveliest destiny. Love was changing her for the better, mending her.

They launched, riding an invisible wave of air that carried them off the ground.

The sandsurfer coasted to a stop. Weapons drawn, they scurried toward the wide mouth of the largest cavern. A rocky shelf extended above the opening, filling it with shadow. Given the reverberations, Lash had expected the psycho-horde to come running out. They didn't. Even from this distance, the odor emanating from the cave was sickening—fecal matter, body odor, fuel. The Penitents were unrepentantly foul, relieving themselves in the cave instead of digging a hole in the surrounding area. Animals knew better.

"Abandon all hope," said Lash, citing an epic poem from the Middle Ages. Ready to journey into vile darkness, she turned on the halogen flash wire-hangered to the barrel of her M4.

Richter said, "I'll be your poet of violence."

"No infra-goggles?"

"Didn't plan for underground warfare. We'll do it old-school. And Moss here is quick."

"Better be." She'd wanted to ask Richter about his gun but didn't want to appear impressed. Moss heard everything. Why give a personality-augmented pistol the pleasure?

She kissed her crucifix and said a prayer to Benedict of Nursia, patron saint of speleologists. Although her heart drummed partridge-like within her, she advanced without hesitation, immediately gagging in revulsion. The growing stench made her wish she'd brought a gas mask. Her gunlight flooded the cavern's interior. It was devoid of occupants. A dry, overturned, red-plastic gas can and a few rags were scattered on the ground. Fat green flies encompassed a shit pile. She led the way, Richter behind her, his smart-gun projecting its own long-throw LED. With it, she got a better view of the deepening, expanding recess. The reek of diesel fumes competed with the malevolent whiff of Penitents. The low-end rumbling intensified.

"Driller's here," Lash said.

A growling sound ahead, coming from the pitch.

Richter stooped, gently nudging her to the side. Pulling the snakebot by its tail and from off his neck, he set it on the ground.

The mechanical serpent shot-slithered forward at an incredible rate of speed, its head springing up cobra-like to explode in an incandescent penumbra. Shielding his eyes with a scabbed arm, a naked Penitent swung at the bot with a strip of spiny shrub, howling as he missed.

It wasn't Lash's father.

Richter didn't miss. Moss devastated, as if from the inside, the space above the maniac's wild eyes. The Penitent collapsed backward, twitching as his blood soaked the sand. Judging by the damage, Lash believed Moss was firing 5.66 mm Le Mas frangible rounds. They penetrated steel, but not human flesh. Instead, the bullet exploded inside the target's body, ravaging tissue in all directions, creating untreatable wounds. She'd heard of frangibles, but never found a stash to try. Now she knew: the results were frightening.

Shoot 'em in the head, quipped the smartgun dumbly.

"Richter," Lash snarled. "God help you and your girly-voiced pop toy if my dad's hit."

"Don't worry," he said, trying to ease her fears. "Moss, you're upsetting my friend."

Ahead of them, the snakebot crawled, whirred, and lit up another Penitent, this one female, her breasts stretched and ravaged by the elements and the sexual depravities of other lunatics. She hissed like a Perseus-cornered Gorgon. Moss was busy annihilating her from the inside out, a mercy killing. Lash heard a noise between the gun's bullet-bursts.

An unfamiliar cough-groan sounded from above, where another Penitent had been waiting on a ledge. He jumped down. Lash instinctively trigger-pulled, gunlight flashing for a millisecond on the wild-haired, lesion-covered, rotten-toothed schizoid falling at her. Not her dad. The semiauto kicked in, six Remington game loads ripping the lunatic's face and crashing him into the wall. The body crumpled, a heap of buckshot-shredded skin and bones and blood.

A hot mist of gore rained down on her. She bent over to puke a thin stream of black coffee.

First rodeo, Moss said to Lash, circuits chuckling. It crossed her mind that Richter's gun was jealous of her. It seemed to enjoy stoking a competition and antagonizing her.

"Hush," Richter said.

She laughed at this bizarre triangle. She made a note to "accidentally" and irreparably break Moss before she, Richter, and her father relocated to Puerto Vallarta or vicinity. She wiped bile from her mouth with the inside of her wrist and reloaded the Benelli with slugs from her ammo belt. She took a moment to squat down and stymie the urge to vomit again. She'd been through revolting ordeals, but this was beyond horrific. Trip into the Inferno, indeed.

"All right," Richter said. "I'll lead."

He did so, pushing onward. Lash steeled herself and sprung up to follow.

The roar of the Driller stopped. They heard the crack and echo of small-arms gunfire.

"Move!" said Richter, breaking into a run.

Lash couldn't tell if he was commanding his bots to enter the cave or simply yelling at her to get into motion. She sprinted behind him until the passage narrowed. She had to stoop and scuttle sideways, left hand above her head to avoid colliding with the serrated cave roof.

The space expanded again into a sloping, boulder-strewn chamber. The snakebot projected a broad, prevailing light. Everything inside was inert. Surrounded by dirt and rocks, the Driller's diamond-studded boring tool had erupted through the floor. The machine was damaged, inoperable. Slabs of metal dangled, and wiring was exposed. Smoke lingered.

Lash and Richter flinched when sparks ignited.

A broken machine was predictable, given that Koons and Lash had been Prof's best hackers. Whomever the Academy assigned to steer this contraption must've collided with every limestone deposit from Luxor to here. Even so, it got the job done.

Richter remained frozen, listening intently, trying to determine if Prof was hiding somewhere, a lethal ghost haunting the machine.

"Auto-destruct sequence?" Lash asked Moss.

Nope, said the smartgun.

A few Penitents lay motionless in the dust. After checking the corpses for booby traps—a shameful tactic Prof sometimes adopted when dealing with Richter—she flipped over each body searching for her dad's face and praying she wouldn't see it. She breathed a sigh of relief when she didn't. But anxiety seeped in again.

"The nuke?" she said to Richter.

She saw the answer when he tore away the cracked control pad that had been strapped to a now-lifeless Penitent. Disgusted, Richter threw it to the ground.

The stretchered bomb was gone.

She examined the corpse to find more galling evidence. Her needlebot—the one she'd made using octopus venom and a micro-EMP blaster—was sticking like a pin in the cushion of the dead Penitent's throat. No wonder the crazies hadn't triggered the nuke the moment they felt the tremors. The Academy had deployed her beta drone, and it worked perfectly. It pained her to know that her alma mater had stolen her father from her by tele-operating a bot of her own design and driving an underground super-drill of her own discovery.

Lash noticed something else lying in the sand and nudged it with her boot.

A half-eaten slice of yogurt-covered prickly pear.

Richter leapt on top of the Driller's bit-maw. He peered down the length of it and into the burrow-pit the machine had tunneled on its trajectory under and up into the cave.

Me go, master, Moss said. The smartgun leapt from Richter's hand, parts shifting to form a grotesque wasp-like body. Tiny twin copter blades popped out, whirring to life. Shining an LED again, Moss descended into the hole. Lash walked all around the cave, looking for any sign of her father. For a cranny where he might be hiding. For a clue he might've left her. She realized it was pointless. He might as well never have been here.

She wanted to jump into the cavity, too, and track Prof back to his Egyptian tomb-hotel. But without compression suits, which Prof and his students had to have worn to maneuver the machine underground, she and Richter couldn't dare jump into such a deep shaft. The pressure would crush eardrums and lungs, causing severe injury or death.

A minute passed before Moss levitated back up into the chamber to confirm it.

"Damn," Richter said. He paced in a complete circle, running his hand through his slicked hair and mussing it in exasperation. "We're too late." He rubbed his eyes with one hand and raised the other like a falconer waiting for his hawk to return to the glove.

As Moss was flittering back to Richter, an Academy warbot quietly unpacked itself like a foldout stepladder to emerge from the dim nook of the Driller's operator booth.

Before she knew what she was doing, she charged Richter, hoping to knock him to the ground. He was about to be shot by a warbot she'd personally armed at the Academy.

She didn't reach him in time.

34

The lighting was eerie, shadow-plagued, as the snakebot inched its way up and across an outcropping of stone fragments for a better vantage from which to illuminate the enemy.

The warbot's M249 light machine gun chattered. She saw Richter backpedaling, but not fast enough. Hit in the neck, he groaned in pain before rolling into a prone firing position. He squashed the wound with one hand, trying to staunch blood loss. In the other, Moss blasted away.

The smartgun's bullets easily penetrated the bot's armor yet failed to hit anything vital.

In trying to save Richter, Lash nearly threw herself into the crossfire. She tucked and somersault-tumbled between him and the armored mech, smacking her cranium with her own shoulder-strapped gun so hard she saw stars and almost fell on her face.

Moss's deafening rounds knocked the bot backward, pushing it into a defensive posture from which it couldn't return fire. Meanwhile, Lash adopted a rice-paddy squat, feet flat on the ground, bending forward, making sure her elbows and knees didn't join. Bone-to-meat was the only way to level a firearm. And she knew a warbot's vulnerability better than anyone.

She targeted the shielded sensor and expended all six cartridges, shattering the opticals.

Realizing his bot was blind, the Academy pilot—maybe it was Dio—went to Gatling mode, indiscriminately swiveling the M249 back and forth, hoping to chance-shoot someone.

Suddenly a VAMPIR-launched TBG-29V thermobaric antipersonnel round boomed, rending the bot into countless metal fragments.

A few crashed down on Lash's half-deafened head.

Hands still covering her ears and lying on her gut, Lash squint-opened an eye. She saw Vai smirk with pleasure from dismembering a deadly unmanned ground vehicle.

"Nice shot," she said to the merc whose nuts she'd bruised. "With *my* frickin' RPG."

Vai gave her a blank gaze and reloaded the tube.

"Help."

Richter's jugular was intact; blood wasn't spurting. His vocal cords weren't damaged; he was speaking. She used her gunlight to confirm his spine wasn't hit. The wound was a graze, having ripped tendons and meat. Painful, but not life-threatening.

Moss, however, lay in pieces on the ground. The warbot had gotten in a lucky shot. More likely, the smartgun had sacrificed itself to protect its master.

Reassured, Lash stood over Richter and removed her Celine Dion sweatshirt, then her bra. Crucifix between her bare breasts, one hand wielding the halogen flash, she pulled Richter off his elbows and upright and used the shirt to apply direct pressure and absorb the blood, tightening the improvised bandage with her bra. She popped a piece of old cactus gum, got it sticky, and adhered the sleeves around his neck, bandage-like.

Lash noticed that Vai was enjoying her topless ministrations.

"You're a piece of work," she told him.

Arriving in the nick of time—in the moment before she would've given in to temptation and gun butt-bashed Vai's face—was the sandsurfer.

"Don't just stand there," she said.

Vai grunted and helped her lay Richter on his back atop the hoverbot. Lash used the thin bungee straps underneath the board to secure him snugly, as if to an ambulance gurney, then pressed the GPS-autopilot function. Into the command console, she said, "CityCenter."

As the sandsurfer mapped an exit route, Richter said, "Look, I know I can't stop you."

"You're right," she said. "You can't."

"I need you to wait for me to heal. Before you go after your father."

"I'll bring back your nuke."

He grimaced in pain. "Something I should tell you."

"Say it."

"Not here." He darted his eyes in Vai's direction to let her know why.

"Fine," she said, playing along. Then she lied. "I'll wait."

"Meet me in the infirmary."

"OK, the infirmary." To the hoverbot: "Go."

It went, taking Richter. Slowly at first, through the narrow passage and then, she imagined, across the desert and back into the luxury hotel where the bot-conductor could resume dreaming of a restored Las Vegas.

That left Lash, her naked torso covered in Richter's blood, alone with Vai. Resting the RPG on his shoulder, he stared at her chest, wearing his stupid, evil smirk.

"We started a conversation," she said. "We should finish it."

In the radiant cast of the snakebot, which remained perched atop some boulders as if eager to observe what happened next, Vai stopped grinning.

He now projected a look of furious contempt, of utter hatred. He was ready to fight. To kill.

She tossed her Benelli into the dust and adopted a combat stance. She'd assumed Vai would throw aside the VAMPIR and get into position, giving him too much credit. Instead, he pulled the RPG over his shoulder and aimed it point-blank at Lash.

Her stomach dropped. She cursed herself, then yelled, "Coward!"

He launched the rocket. The grenade, which didn't arm or come alive until it reached five meters, bounced off Lash's instinctively raised forearms. The rocket kept moving and detonated into the side of the cavern. The boom was teeth-rattling and triggered a cave-in.

The autonomous snakebot, in an act of self-preservation, went slither-dashing for the outlet, taking the chamber's only light source with it. A falling rock pinned it. Its light began to die.

Vai's eyes bulged. He looked around in panic, obviously trying to recall the way out of the cave.

Dust stirred by toppling debris filled the air. Darkness congealed around them. But she saw the gunlight still glowing in the sand where she'd hurled her Benelli.

She dove for it, turned over into a kneeling position, aimed, and spotlit her target.

The first round splintered the top of Vai's head, giving him a blood Mohawk. His shocked and agony-contorted expression was priceless. His face became a red mask.

The second round hit him solidly in the right upper pectoral, spinning him around in a ghoulish pirouette. He gasped, lungs filling with gore.

He collapsed to his hands and knees, reared back animal-like, scream-gurgling in anguish.

Lash opted to save ammo. She was walking up to him to boot-bash his skull to pieces when a large stalactite fell, smashing Vai into the ground with a sickening crunch.

"Vai died," she said aloud, savoring the statement as the thrill-killing, high-flying freak perished in the fading light of an imploding underground grotto. *Oh, the irony.*

Then another clump of stone came down, badly abrading and dislocating her shoulder. Her gunlight was shattered.

She found herself alone in a dark and sealed cave. Trapped beside a giant underground drill she'd discovered years ago, now too damaged to drive out of here.

Then she blacked out.

35

When she regained consciousness, with her good arm, Lash fumbled around in wet-grit pitch for her Benelli and located its barrel. She couldn't unwedge it from under a heavy rock. The cave-in had stopped, but there was a sound of rushing water. Hot water. The chamber was filling with geothermally cooked water from the hot spring.

If a lack of oxygen didn't snuff her, drowning surely would.

She blocked out her throbbing limb. Gathering her composure, she slowed her breathing. She flicked her Zippo and began grinding into the darkness. If she could keep her mind under control, she might make it. She shut the lighter and searched for a pinpoint. All she could discern was a barely perceptible strip of color. She had no choice but to seek it out.

Ankle deep now, the water flow was constant. She figured she had, at best, ten minutes until the cave filled. Maybe the water pressure would force rocks loose, allowing her to escape. Maybe she wasn't consigned to death just yet.

After a few false leads, she ran into a narrowing of the cave. Whatever light was softly palpitating in the distance lay beyond. She would have to squeeze through to reach it.

She would need to be birthed from this boiling womb.

A snapping sound. The rushing of water became suddenly biblical, a full-on flood. Time was running out. She had to exit the cave or grow gills.

She pushed her already-battered body farther into the gummy crack. Silt and sand scraped her bare nipples, stomach, and back. Water ran over her thighs.

The realization that water was driving her into the cavern's recesses jolted her. It was as if a strobe went off inches from her face, triggering her body to perform stupid actions. She started breathing hard, jamming her way forward with irresponsible, uncoordinated urgency. Panic would kill her before the water did.

After a few fear-spasms, her sanity returned. She considered her situation. She was lodged inside a prehistoric coffin. The water pouring against her was too strong to fight. A rock cluster inside the passage blocked her path forward. She felt a seizure coming on.

She intentionally went catatonic. Clasped in heated sediment, held firmly by the boulders around her, she closed her eyes and concentrated on visualizing a way out.

She clenched her jaw and kissed her crucifix. She said another prayer to the cave saint. She wrenched herself through a slightly larger length of passage and closer to the light. It was a thin shaft, the opening a few feet higher. The ray projected from a stone cropping that faced the direction in which Lash was moving.

Now sharp rocks and razored minerals chafed her flesh. Despite a powerful limestone aroma, she smelled her own blood, its metallic pinch and iron tang. It was mixing with Richter's now. A bizarre thought entered her mind. This might end up being the only instance in which the two of them shared bodily fluids.

Torrential, the waist-high water burned. She wondered if the temperature was third-degreeing her. It was similar to a flash flood, which Lash had survived years ago. The difference here was that she was in a scalding cave.

She reached another obstacle of rocky debris in the enlarged passage. Through the water engulfing her, she gave the cluster as hard a kick as she could.

It crumbled. She inhaled dust, coughing. She plunged forward and pivoted inside a deeper, more daggered recess to get a better look at the opening. It was small, no bigger than an apple. She had no idea what, if anything, was on the other side. Even if she could make the opening bigger, she had no leverage with which to raise herself.

She used her fist as a battering ram, expecting to strike rock. Instead, it was soft, soil-like. Breathing hard when she initially pushed, she choked on dirt clods falling into her mouth.

Water reached her neck.

Standing on her booted toes, she was about to pull more sand and pebbles onto her head when she sensed a vibration. Then she heard metal clanging against rocks and a roaring diesel engine. Suddenly, an avalanche of debris landed on her, muddying the water, turning it into quicksand that sloshed her hair and slushed into her ears and eyes.

She clawed at the edges of the recess, fingernails breaking off.

Out of nowhere, a hand grabbed her. Then another. Someone was pulling her out of the muck and into the daylight.

Lash set foot on something like solid ground. She staggered forward as sludge-mire oozed from the hole in the side of a sandstone formation. She kept walking, grimy-eyed.

Helen said, "Good morning, lobster."

"Hot spring," Lash explained. "Toasty in there."

Wiping her hands on her shirt, Helen fetched a tablet stuffed in her cargos. The backhoe near the volcanoing spring reverse-beeped, backing away from the encroaching gunk-wave.

"Your blouse? And bra?"

"Bandage—for Richter's neck wound."

Helen, taking that in, was silent, then said, "Your arm?"

"Dislocated."

They were both warriors. Nothing more needed to be said between them.

Resting her arm for a second, Lash bent her elbow at a ninety-degree angle. Helen helped rotate the arm and shoulder inward, toward Lash's chest, to make an L shape. Slowly but steadily, Helen rotated the arm and shoulder outward while keeping the upper arm stationary. She held on to Lash's wrist with her other arm and pushed slowly.

Lash screamed as Helen coaxed the shoulder back into the shoulder joint.

"How-*OW*," Lash gasped from the pain, yet also the relief, "did you find me?"

"Crucifix," Helen said.

"You knew it was frequency-tagged?"

Helen laughed. "Richter's been using it to track you and record your conversations."

Lash removed the crucifix and placed it on a slab on the ground. She grabbed another rock and shattered the cross she'd kissed a thousand times for help escaping dire situations.

"Richter could destroy the Academy," she said to Helen, "by mimicking the frequency."

"Richter has bigger problems." After parking the backhoe one hundred yards away, Helen restuffed the tablet down her shorts. She walked toward the machine, indicating Lash should follow.

"Like?"

"Now that he's injured, Westphal will find another merc to get the job done."

"Forgive me," said Lash, "but I can't recall the job."

"Appropriating resources for CityCenter."

"So what's the problem? Let someone else do it."

"You don't understand," said Helen, stopping in front of the backhoe. She rested her boot on the rubber-coated step-up. "Westphal has Richter's brother and sister."

Lash groaned with displeasure. Her blackheart Romeo was more deeply compromised than she even knew. She would forgive him, though. She had no choice. She was a girl in love.

"Educate me, Helen."

"Deal went like this. The sooner Richter took control of the valley and its resources—water, farms, mines—the sooner Richter's family would be returned to him. He's out of commission now, so the agreement is off. What Westphal plans to do with his folks—with Richter—is unclear. Richter's siblings are plant scientists, making them valuable. Westphal wants her own crops, instead of relying on the Harvesters and the Aliante operation. She wants absolute rule."

"Nasty old hag," Lash said. "Why didn't you guys tell me this?"

Helen silently looked down at the desert scrub. "Richter kept telling us he had a plan to get Westphal out of the way." She inhaled, then exhaled, slowly. "You see, Westphal's husband, Henry, was the principal in McCurdy-Bongo, the venture-capital firm that MGM sold CityCenter to before the Collapse. Henry and Richter shared a similar vision for the revival of Vegas, but when he died—"

"How?"

"Sepsis. After being bitten by a flamingo."

Lash grimaced.

"Henry was barely buried when Mrs. Westphal started living out her totalitarian fantasies. She'd obviously been dreaming about it for a long time. She's very good at it. She and the Russians."

Helen appraised Lash, topless, bloodied, and muddied. She grabbed a shirt from the driver's cabin and tossed it at her muck-encrusted friend. "He loves you, you know."

"I love him, too," said Lash, pulling the clean shirt over her filthy, scraped-up torso. She saw unrequited, jealous hurt in Helen's eyes and stopped talking.

Then she said, "Wait, *you're* in love with me, too?"

"*Coño, hija,*" said Helen, laughing as she wiped away tears. "You're such an idiot sometimes. Get in."

"Only if I'm hitching a ride to Luxor."

"CityCenter first."

"No. Prof has my dad."

"Help me kill Westphal. We'll grab the excavator. You need it to fight Prof. Only I can give you the command platform."

Lash said nothing. She wondered where Helen got the commands. Koons?

"Get in, Lash. Last chance. Otherwise, I'm leaving you."

She got in, doing her best to hide her giddiness.

36

"Another thing," said Helen, driving the NorthStar Trencherman back to CityCenter. "With Richter immobilized and vulnerable, he can no longer protect your students."

"My students can handle themselves," said Lash, unhappy to be riding bitch. The engine under the plastic seat they were sharing vibrated her butt uncomfortably. Crater-size potholes plaguing North Martin L. King Boulevard didn't help. "I trained them."

"You didn't teach them just to build and fight drones, Lash."

"I didn't?"

"You unknowingly prepared the best for the Magnus bouts."

"What the hell are the Magnus bouts?"

"Reason there's no gambling in CityCenter is because Westphal found a better way to rake in money," Helen said. "Human-versus-robot combat competitions."

Bot against man, or in this case children. Young flesh opposing deadly metal machines. Such bloodsport was illegal everywhere in the world. But in a ruined Las Vegas, it was anything goes, as long as it fills the house's coffers. Not so different, in the end, from pre-ruined Las Vegas.

"The wagers are staggering, in size *and* number,"

"You're saying—"

"Our students are ring fodder."

"Now I have an entirely different reason to feed Westphal to her own flamingos."

"Have to get through Richter's pilots first."

"That won't be hard."

Helen stiffened, brought the backhoe to a stop, and shut off the engine. She wanted to very clearly hear Lash's reply to her next question. "You killed Vai?"

"Yes."

"Good," Helen said. She was quiet for a time, before adding, "He hurt me. I was happy for a moment to hear you say he's dead. Now I'm unhappy for not killing him myself."

"Oh, Helen."

"I wanted to be strong."

Lash said nothing. Waiting for her friend to start the Trencherman again, she wondered if Richter knew, but knew better than to ask. Helen's shoulders began to shake as she sobbed quietly, so Lash wrapped her arms around the other girl and held her close and said the only thing she could say.

Helen blew her nose into the sleeve of her shirt and rested her forehead on the steering wheel. She might've mumbled a prayer. Or a curse.

Lash rested her cheek between Helen's shoulder blades, inhaling her sweet rage and sour grief. She felt a deep surge of pity. Or was it sympathy? Lash realized that pleasure and pain were two sides of the same coin. On the one hand, since she'd met Helen, her heart had fully awakened and opened to others. On the other, to feel powerful emotions and not be able to muffle them was excruciating.

She was happy to know such exquisite agony again.

She buried her face in Helen's thick mass of shampoo-clean hair and murmured.

"Tickles!" said Helen, laughing and crying. "What did you say?"

"Coffee," Lash said. "I need caffeine before placing Westphal's head on a chopping block."

"You got it."

"Sorry about Richter," Lash said. "Had no idea."

"Don't apologize. You got lucky, babe."

"If I'd known—"

"Stop. Please."

A troubling question popped into Lash's head. "Did you save me because we're friends? Or because you want to make Richter happy?"

"Because we're friends." Then Helen shrugged. "OK, both. Does it matter?"

"Not really. Thank you."

"Don't thank me. You have a lot of bastards to slaughter now."

"My kill list," Lash confirmed, "is epic."

Helen cranked the backhoe's engine and pushed on. The sun was beautiful and warm, the desert sky vast and blue. Clinging to Helen, Lash believed they were never going to die. Despite a shrapnel- and rock-bashed body and sore muscles, she'd never felt more alive, more dangerous. She searched the air for drones and for the first time in months, years, didn't see any. Being pulled from a boiling chasm had an effect. She felt reborn. Resurrected.

The Trencherman tortoise-crawled through the empty tracts of North Las Vegas at 30 mph before sputtering out of gas on the northern edge of downtown Las Vegas. They'd have to travel the rest of the way on foot. But not without a drone escort.

Helen grabbed her tablet. Within minutes, a dozen Red Angel drones were circling above like buzzards, Hellfire-armed.

"Can't Richter's pilots hack these drones?"

"My own fleet," Helen explained. "The mercs would have to crack serious encryption."

"Yeah, but it's the same network."

Helen shook her head. "Got my own servers."

"Where are the Magnus bouts staged?"

"In Aria. The old Cirque du Soleil theater. The season's first competition is tonight."

"Will Westphal be there?"

"Presiding over the event with her birds," said Helen, pausing to squat and scoop up some crickets, which she placed in her mouth to chew like popcorn. "She doubles as a ring-card girl. Which earns her some boos. A few dudes end up puking in their beers."

"Gross."

Helen stopped chewing to look at Lash quizzically, a cricket leg hanging from her lips.

"I meant Westphal." Lash realized she was hungry. She grabbed an insect from Helen's palm and scarfed it. "But I can't kill her if I don't know where she's holding Richter's brother and sister."

Helen drilled Lash with a don't-let-up-now look. "I'll find Richter's family. Go in tonight, kill Westphal, and rescue Duffy."

"Duffy?"

"It's her debut. She fights under the name Moonwolf."

Lash thought of the drawing Duffy had done for her. A coded distress signal she'd failed to decipher or even identify. Magnetized to her room's minibar.

"Let me borrow your Red Angels."

"No chance. Everything outside the ring is jammed to prevent cheat-hacks."

Lash sighed. "Fine. I'll need some things."

"Like what?"

"Depends. Got access to an armory?"

"Of course. What do you need?"

"Antipersonnel bomb. Phosphorus. Combat knife. Hydrogen tank. Industrial floor dryer. A bunch of those pink CityCenter promotional balloons. Oh, and a rifle."

"How will you get Westphal to step on a mine? Lash, remember that Duffy will be in the ring. And the ring will be surrounded by mercs and drunk tourists."

"No one has to move. The balloon's coming to them. Been thinking about the zeppelins I blew up a few weeks ago."

"That was you!" said Helen, impressed.

Lash nodded. "Shooting them down reminded me of Japanese fire balloons. *Fu-Go.*"

"What on earth are you planning?"

37

It took all afternoon and a gallon of coffee. Lash had a pink hydrogen-pumped CityCenter balloon with a phosphorus-encased bomb hanging from it prepped for takeoff on the nosebleed level of the old theater. Kevlar-jacketed, she tethered the mini-dirigible to a rail in a darkened handicap-accessible area with the seats stripped. She improvised a ballast shot bag using a backpack and ball bearings. The industrial fan was plugged in, go-light glowing green.

The plan was to push the inflatable over the crowd. Lash would pop the balloon with a Polish bolt-action Bor rifle borrowed from Helen. The antipersonnel mine would fall into the recessed seating area, detonating shrapnel and sending fire everywhere except on the elevated stage where Duffy would be fighting. Lash intended to snipe Westphal, then lead Duffy down a corridor where a hacked salonbot was programmed with instructions.

From there, they would head to the docks where Helen waited in the excavator, her Red Angel squadron above. Lash shared this strategy with her friend except for one part.

Lash had it in mind to rescue Richter, too.

A non-security camera designed to capture the Magnus action whirred nearby. Lash was situated well behind it and saw that its base rotated ninety degrees. It made her nervous, so she chewed cactus gum and stuffed it into the swivel-mount to make sure it wouldn't move too far. She checked her boot to make sure the Kershaw military knife was in place. She couldn't wait to use it. It required close-quarter combat, and she liked to get her hands dirty.

Her hunch was right. An abundance of CityCenter-branded products multiplied throughout the theater and coagulated into a pink mass—banners, balloons, bots, even birds. Westphal's flamingos preened, squawked, and were generally annoying. They strutted through the aisles and posed like vapid supermodels in need of food and attention. Unsettling.

The birds and the Russians didn't faze one another. The men—and they were *all* men—began piling in an hour before the first bout, carousing, buffooning, singing songs, and, naturally, drinking vodka. To Lash's revulsion, she saw a sheets-to-the-wind tourist cuddling with a feathered companion from Westphal's bizarre aviary. To Lash's further dismay, the bird reciprocated.

When the theater was half full, music began blasting—terrible, distorted Eurobeat that stabbed and twisted the pleasure centers in Lash's brain. Footage from previous combat competitions looped on four *kaiju*-size monitors hanging above the ring. Alcohol-vending bots marched up and down the aisles, wading into the folding chairs ringside, pushing plastic cups of booze into the mitts of revelers, letting them run their credit cards through blinking swipe grids on their chests.

The music became less grating as more and more bodies absorbed the echoes bouncing off the stands. The crowd's energy was surging in anticipation of a popular yet forbidden ritual. Lash saw spectators were hungry for blood, eager to witness flesh destroyed by metal and vice versa.

The theater seated twenty-five hundred, but standing-room tickets had been sold and the place was packed. For the first time, Lash noticed a robo-whore circulating. Similar to a robossager, it boasted silicone facsimiles of women's body parts—mouth, breasts, vagina, anus—with the genitalia purposefully moved to different places on the bot, for the sake of sexually deranged variety. One chest-sprouted an erect penis and balls, ersatz veins throbbing. The men, some stone-cold sober, were smitten, fondling the bot openly, pressing their tongues against fleshy boobs installed in the bot's rear end, fingerbanging a snatch-face until the bot coquettishly pushed away and moved on to the next lecher for a card swipe.

It was all in preparation for an even stranger, more terrible ritual of violence. Lash thought back to Prof's boring homilies, the patience-fraying liturgical readings by her classmates. They'd been quaint, not even in the same league as the bestiality she currently observed. Yet Gathering at the Academy had injured her more.

Without fanfare, pugilist-bots climbed into the ring and began fighting. One on one. Two on one. Four against four. Smashing and sawing each other into bits and broken chips. There were no rules, no emcee. Westphal hadn't shown up yet. Instead, a housekeeping hoverbot armed with a dustpan and broom simply hovered to the edge of the canvas, scooping and vacuuming mechanical entrails to deposit them into a dumpster in the corner of the theater.

Finally, the lights dimmed. A spotlight landed on the ring. A ghetto-blaster-faced, spider-limbed bot climbed through the ropes and into the center, then stood up straight to comically brush himself off and reached up for a wireless microphone that was flying toward him.

"Ladies and gentlemen," he announced, a synthetic voice laced with static and digital effects, with an emphasis on "Ladies" as if it knew none were present. "The final bout of the evening. A ten-rounder pitting the Chopper against Moonwolf!"

Amid applause, the emcee-bot's image was projected on the giant screens, occasionally interspersed with a straight betting line: Chopper –3, Moonwolf +3. The point spread made no sense to Lash. She looked at the numbers again.

Those weren't points, but limb losses. Mortal wounds.

"In this corner, from Foxxconn factory in China's Jiangxi province, I give you—the Chopper!"

The spotlight transitioned to a hooded figure. The crowd booed. Someone sailed a paper airplane into the ring. The bot bent stiffly to pick it up and crumple it in his metal hand.

The hood came down and the robe fell away to reveal a ten-foot-tall, war-treaded, silver-encased, humanoid bot with a spinning glaive—part boomerang, part Ginsu—where each arm should be. A red optical beam pulsed menacingly in the center of its urethane skull. The Chopper resembled a hybrid mix of a Cylon from *Battlestar Galactica* and the sinister flesh-blending robot Maximilian from an unusually dark Disney film called *The Black Hole*.

A collective gasp. And then, once the horror of the bot had been absorbed, boos and hissing.

"And in this corner," the emcee continued, "from the desert wilderness of Las Vegas, the Lunar-howler. The Blood-scenter. The Drone-devourer. The one, the only—Moonwolf!"

Cheers, wild clapping. The robe dropped and there stood Duffy, her gymnast-toughened body oiled and glistening in the spotlight. She wore a black hood and heavy black plate-and-leather warlady armor. Bronze-claw-like epaulets covered her shoulders, making it harder for a bot to slice off her arms. She boasted a gladius sword and a tower shield of hammered metal like the one Achilles brandished in *The Iliad*. Although she was less than half as tall as the Chopper, Duffy looked formidable.

"The fight is on!" the emcee-bot announced. The microphone rose fast as he exited the ring. No referee stepped through the ropes to oversee the fight. Lash realized this was no classic boxing or UFC match like the kind that used to happen in Las Vegas regularly.

There would be no clinching. No knockdown counts. No standing eights. No symbolic throwing of white towels. Only two elements would be on display in the ring—human blood and bot parts, the outcome decided by which combatant survived.

Lash had never met a bot that came close to approximating God's organic handiwork. Even the dumbest animal possessed more life, more presence, than the HALs people like Prof talked on and on about.

Duffy stood immobile, yet ready. She steadily gazed at her opponent, trying not to show fear or anger and mostly succeeding. Across the ring the Chopper stood facing its corner, blades whirring as if anxious to fight.

Using the binocs Helen had given her, Lash watched in fascination as Westphal, dressed like a pink-feathered showgirl from the city's heyday, finally arrived, levitating in a gilded hover-throne, emerging from the mass of CityCenter balloons and banners, and coming to a stop twenty feet above the ring, the best seat in the house. Westphal was a glitzy, skeletal empress. She drifted above the ring in ritualistic fashion, a wrinkle-faced Hera looking down from Mount Olympus, eager to watch the carnage below.

Wearing a wireless headset, she raised her arm and addressed the crowd. "The Magnus bouts represent a long tradition of combat pitting man against machine. You need look no further than Watson versus Ken Jennings and Brad Rutter, Deep Blue versus Garry Kasparov, the Luddites against the spinning jenny, to know that there exists a tense relationship between humans and robots. Today, the two have never been more connected, more at odds. The world they inhabit and construct together has never been more fearful, regulated, surveilled. The Magnus bouts are an opportunity for this conflict to be explored, staged, made visceral. For the first time this year, Westphal Entertainment gives you the Fight for All Centuries. MAGNUS!"

Drunken tourists roared their approval.

In Westphal's other hand was what Lash recognized as a Russian *vajra* thunderbolt bell. Things got really quiet for a moment, a spine-chilling hush falling over the theater.

And then Westphal rang the bell ceremoniously.

38

The Chopper mechanically glided from its corner, blades churning. It moved hastily at Duffy who, to Lash's disappointment, edged forward and crouched, shield raised. A good offense was a great defense. Lash didn't want to launch the bomb yet. The balloons Westphal had pushed aside were still floating out of the sightline. She needed a clear path to her target.

Then Lash realized why Duffy was getting low, why she'd always been the smartest girl in her class. The Chopper shot-launched one of its glaives with terrific force. The weapon clanged loudly off Duffy's shield and landed outside the ring, clearing a row of spectators who had to jump out of the way to keep from being banged-up or, worse, sliced. They laughed uproariously in surprise, gleefully high-fiving one another at coming away unscathed.

The collision, however, knocked Duffy flat on her butt. The Chopper sped forward, pressing the attack with its other glaive, eager to mulch the girl and beat the spread.

Lash had the bot in her scope-sight and was about to pull the trigger and blow the whole operation when she suddenly detected confidence in Duffy's attitude and drew down. The girl knew she had to get out from underneath, assume a dominant position, and neutralize.

Shield-covering her body, Duffy sideways-kicked the treads, nearly tipping over the bot. As it tried to right itself, she rolled-tumbled while swinging her sword. It smacked the bot's face dead-on, the metal-to-metal contact causing a big, bright shower of sparks to fly.

The crowd erupted with cheers.

By now, there was a perfect line-of-sight to Westphal. Lash flipped a switch on the industrial fan and untethered the balloon-bomb. A current of air pushed it forward and downward at just the right velocity—slowly, inexorably. She raised the sniper again to chip-shatter Duffy's flesh-slicing opponent. But then she sensed someone lunging at her from behind.

She dropped to one knee to shove the rifle butt behind her, splintering the ribcage of a shadow-sneaking merc. Grunting, Westphal's teen pilot doubled over, still holding a knife.

She grabbed the cutleried hand and wrenched his arm up and across her body, snapping bone. The merc shrieked, blade clattering on the ground.

Lash finished him with a boot-toe kick, crushing his windpipe. On his back, he clutched his throat and struggled to breathe. He couldn't, writhing in silent agony from lack of oxygen.

Lash looked for Westphal, now gliding.

Apparently, she'd sensed movement in the upper level, because the crone had moved her hover-throne closer. She was peering into the darkness, trying to see what was happening.

From seeing her suddenly widened Botoxed eyes, Lash knew that she'd seen the balloon floating at her, a device hanging from a wire attached to its belly.

She reverse-dashed her chair, heading for the exit on the upper level's opposite end.

Lash grabbed the Bor and got off a shot, grazing the hover-throne. It veered wildly into the stands, crashing hard and dumping Westphal from a great height onto a concrete stairway. Her gaunt body collided with the railing. But she immediately stood, headdress askew, boa feathers broken, limping her way to an illuminated passage beyond the last row of seats.

Lash was about to deliver the kill shot when she heard the flapping. Westphal's flamingos. Richter and Helen had failed to mention that their wings weren't clipped.

They were *flying* carnivores and coming at her now.

Lash put down the Bor and got low, then slipped the Kershaw from her boot and growled.

The lead bird came at her, smashing into Lash with a head-on tackle. But the warrior girl was ready, rolling with the impact and scrambling atop the creature's back rodeo style, its flight momentum causing them to slide across the wheelchair platform. With savage fury, Lash slashed the elongated neck. The flamingo emitted a horrifying sound, pounding its pink wings as arterial blood sprayed everywhere and it died.

The second bird didn't bump into Lash, opting to swoop in and slice the girl's shoulder with its razored beak before circling around again for another attempt. Lash checked for a wound, but only the Kevlar shoulder pad had been slashed.

Two more birds were swooping down to lay into her, but they gave her too much time. She threw the Kershaw the same way she'd thrown knives at the fence when she was a kid. The blade plunged through the flamingo's pectorals with such force that the bird seemed driven backward, the lodged knife handle barely visible. As the bird dropped into the stands, the second one acted unsure. It flapped its wings, staying in place, trying to figure if it should press its advantage on the now-unarmed girl or retreat.

Big mistake. Lash picked up the dead merc pilot's Soviet NR-43 combat knife and flung it cockily with a *shuriken*-style, Hollywood-ninja backhand. The blade didn't land, but its heavy handle rapped the bird's skull with a solid clunking sound that Lash felt in her toes. The flamingo plunged into the lower level's folding chairs with a crash.

The fourth bird that had sliced her armor squawked once and exited the theater through the same passage in which Westphal had fled.

The crowd booed mightily, chilling Lash's spine. Had they seen her slay Westphal's birds? No one was looking in her direction. Lash grabbed the Bor and sniper-scoped the ring to see the Chopper directly on top of Duffy. It glaive-grinded the girl's shield, ripping through metal, tearing her arm, blood splattering the ring. Duffy's pain-racked expression ignited Lash's rage.

"Time for Your hammer strike, God," Lash said. Her baleful prayer. Vow of cosmic violence.

She fired, a 7.62x51 mm NATO round severing the bot from its gore-streaked blade. The glaive rolled like a wagon wheel into the ropes, leaving a blood trail.

Confused, spectators turned to gaze up at the upper levels, rightly wondering if someone had interfered with the action in the ring and the betting line by getting off a shot.

Realizing it no longer had a weapon, the bot revved its motor, pushing down harder on Duffy, crushing her. Duffy screamed as the bot's treads pulverized her shredded arm.

Lash couldn't risk blowing out her student's brains. She trained the Bor on the spotlight and snuffed it. As the theater lights struggled to power up, she infrascoped the falling balloon and burst it with a single round.

The M18A1 American Claymore directional antipersonnel mine fell into the densest part of the assembly. The spectators in the blast zone disappeared in a blinding flash of light and fire and a doomsday crack that cratered the impact zone and shuddered the stands on Lash's level. Shrapnel slashed the crowd, whipping their blood to wet froth with the flames boiling the foam. The concussion uprooted and overturned the ring, sending Duffy and the bot sailing up and over the heads of the Russians on the other side. More delayed shrapnel pock-punctured the bodies of Russians stampeding out of the theater, rattling off empty metal foldout chairs. The smell of charred flesh and boiling blood was so revolting, Lash had to hold back the puke.

Fragments slammed the Chopper's back, causing a short and glitches. The bot spasm-veered upright. Then it began mindlessly treading in a circle, no longer focused on its opponent.

Duffy slowly got up. Hunched protectively over her injury, she glared at the Chopper.

She approached cautiously. As the bot spun around, she used her good arm to upward palm-slam its jaw, snapping off its urethane head to hang from exposed and crackling cables.

A cone of smoke issued from the bomb's crater. Cries of the dying and wounded filled the air, sweet music to Lash's ears.

Now she hitched a ride on a cluster of balloons, her weight bringing her down Curious George-style, albeit fast and hard and into a miserable pile of mangled, mewling Russians. She almost lost her balance from the crash landing and ricocheted against a shrapnel-lacerated victim. It allowed her to gain footing on the bloodied backs of several corpses. She leapt across charnel heaps until she reached her student, motioning for Duffy to follow her.

"Move it, Moonwolf," Lash said.

Duffy was busy using her heel to foot-stomp the Chopper's head into plastic pieces.

"Enough!"

Duffy looked at her furiously. For a moment, Lash thought Duffy might attack her, too. It was a scene Lash had acted out herself many times, surges of violent behavior that Dio typically had to temper. But sanity returned to the Magnus fighter.

Taking her boot off the bot's shattered rictus, Duffy ripped the cowl from her head and joined Lash, who reached for her uninjured hand. Together they dashed for the exit.

"Where are we going?" Duffy huffed, weakening from the loss of blood, as they ran through a hallway leading to the conference center.

"Loading docks. First, a quick stop."

"Armory?"

"Infirmary."

"Lash?" said Duffy, yanking her hand away and coming to a halt and staring her down.

"I can't leave Richter."

A drone came buzzing from the hallway's other end. From a glance, Lash could tell it was an Israeli-made Mosquito 1.5 armed with a Glock modded to full-auto thanks to an upgraded magazine system. The microdrone would tear her and Duffy to bloody ribbons in seconds.

"Sounds good," Duffy said. She grabbed Lash's arm again, and together they hauled butt.

The drone bullet-blistered the conference center wallpaper behind them as the girls hopped on and sprint-scaled an ascending escalator to reach the casino floor. The security wing was adjacent to the gym. No doubt the mini drone had already communicated their location to Westphal's pilots. Lash had just minutes to grab Richter and head for the docks.

They turned the corner. Lash intended to bust open the door to the infirmary, where she'd had her face bandaged after the salonbot incident.

But before she could kick in the door, another chain-swinging drone came at them. It slingshot an Indian throwing weapon called a chakram. A high-velocity Frisbee with outer blades.

It rushed to meet the space between Lash's chin and clavicle.

39

"No!" screamed Duffy, using her injured limb to block the chakram. It deflected the flying blade, but at the cost of the younger girl's forearm, which detached below the elbow.

Blood shot out in pulsing torrents, dousing her and Lash and saturating the chain-wielding drone, blinding it. The pilot remote-slammed the camera-clouded UAV forward, but Lash knew this desperation tactic well from her Academy days and easily ducked. The drone, an odd-looking German EMT fancopter, smashed itself into splinters against a column.

Pale Duffy stumbled backward, holding her gushing stump. She looked at the rest of her arm lying on the ground, a mannequin's tranquil limb. She bent over, vomited on it.

Lash fired a round where the chain joined the fractured drone frame, separating them. She used the chain to wrap a tight tourniquet around what was left of Duffy's arm. Blood loss caused her to pass out. She fell to the ground on her side, banging her head, her eyes and mouth open.

Dashing into the infirmary, she grabbed sterile gauze and dry-ice packs to wrap around Duffy's severed limb, then dumped everything into a plastic bag so a medibot might attempt to surgically reconnect it. She dragged Duffy through the infirmary's swing doors, leaving a gruesome trail. She pushed a tech-gutted MRI machine in front of the entrance. Just in time. The crack of gunfire and *thunk-thunk-thunk* of bullets erupted outside the doors.

"Richter!" said Lash, pushing Duffy through triage and into the nurse station.

"Lash?" he called from the recovery room. "Back here."

Cradling Duffy's head in the crook of her arm, she scooped up her thin legs and lifted, clumsily laying the mauled girl on a medical cot. Lash strapped her down in case of shock.

Lash raised the Bor and cautiously penetrated deeper into the infirmary.

She found Richter, hair mussed, neck stiff from heavy bandaging. He smiled at her, a little embarrassed. He was restrained in a bed and wearing a hospital gown.

His helpless appearance startled Lash, but she recovered her composure and knife-slashed him free of his shackles. He stood up to rub the red marks on his arms.

"Good to see you," he said, smiling.

She lunged at him, kissing his mouth. He pulled her tightly to him, and she felt an erection growing beneath his gown. Not now. She pushed him away.

He licked his lips. "Tell me you brought some drone-hack tech."

From her pocket, Lash pulled a small frequency-linked wireless audio-visual sender, green light glowing in a black plastic shell.

"This it?"

She handed him an antique smartphone, too.

"Good girl."

"Tell me there's another exit."

He scoffed without looking at her, phone-porting the wireless unit. "You alone?" He was already punching in a coded transmission.

"Duffy is here, badly wounded. In twenty seconds, the ugliest microdrones you've ever seen in your life are going to shoot down the door and send us packing to the underworld."

Steely and determined, he said, "I don't think so. Watch this." He swiped the smartphone screen.

There was a series of loud crashes, as if the drones were going berserk on each other in the adjacent room. Or maybe they'd found Duffy and were carving her up.

"Duffy!" screamed Lash, running into the room. She kicked open the door and raised the Bor, scanning for something to shoot. There was nothing. Duffy's bloodied, armor-clad body was still lying, unconscious, on the cot. The infirmary door, however, had been flattened.

Then Lash noticed all the holes in the ceiling's fiberboard tiles. She smelled burnt-wiring smoke and heard faint sizzle-crackling sounds. The muted din of dying bots.

Suddenly, a wrecked drone fell through one of the punctures, crashing to the floor.

Startled, Lash quickly squint-scoped it and fired a round into its plastic body, shattering it completely. It was unnecessary. Richter had spoofed the drones' GPS receivers, changing their coordinates. To compensate, the bots dove straight up in a hurry to return to their programmed positions, destroying themselves in the process.

"Not bad, huh?" he said behind her.

A wheeled tailor-bot suddenly rounded the corner, causing Lash to instinctively rifle-scope it. Seeing that the machine had brought Richter a fresh change of clothes, she drew down.

Richter ripped off the paper smock and donned an Amebix shirt, dark jeans, and gunmetal Doc Martens boots, making no effort to conceal his nakedness.

Out of the corner of her eyes, Lash glanced at her beau's delicious bod as she pricked Duffy's arm with an unmeasured morphine shot. Then she watched the door for drones, praying she hadn't OD-ed a cataleptic girl. "I say we grab Duffy and head for the docks. Helen's waiting with the excavator."

Dressed now, Richter chuckled and swiped the phone again. Duffy's cot turned out to be motorized. The machine whirred rapidly toward the door, nearly running over Lash.

"Hold on!" she said, getting in front of the cot, raising the rifle to first scout the hallway. She gave Richter a signal, and they exited the infirmary in perfect synchronicity. They ran for the docks, the Duffy-lugging bot-cot bringing up the rear.

"Got another smartgun?"

"No," he said. "Moss was a gift from Helen. She bought it from a Russian weapons designer."

His mentioning Helen's name irked her. "Be nice to have another."

Richter shrugged and said, tone darkening, "All I need is hate."

She wondered if this was true and would've pondered it, she but was more concerned with finding the salonbot Helen had hacked to fend off Westphal's drones as they reclaimed the excavator. Lash turned for a second to look at Duffy. Her lips were blue.

"Damn it, Richter," Lash said. "I gave her too much morphine."

"There's naloxone in the excavator's first aid kit."

They reached the end of the carpeted convention hall and descended into CityCenter's grubby, garbage-smelling, industrial butthole.

"See the salonbot?" Lash asked.

"Great time for a haircut."

"No, you idiot. Helen hacked a bot to run interference."

"There they are," he said as they turned the corner to face the docks.

"They?"

Lash and Richter stared at the razor-wielding assemblage. Seven bots stared back, a daunting obstacle course and deadly gauntlet between them and the excavator. The powerful engine thrummed, vibrating the bare concrete floor. Lash could make out the machine's massive treads in the distance, at the end of the dock's extended ramps. They resembled metal tongues leading down into a bomb-ravaged road to hell.

On the ground lay another salonbot, slashed to pieces, circuits twitching a cybernetic death rattle. The mercs detected Helen's hack and savagely eradicated it. Now they were tele-operating bots to attack their former boss and his friends.

The salonbots began spinning their light-glinting, stainless-steel, straight-edge blades—one in each mechanical arm and they each boasted four of them—like plane propellers. Lash could feel the air being pushed by the speed of their rotation.

"Hmm," said Richter, peering into his smartphone for a way to hack the salonbots. The encryptions, which he'd implemented, were too strong.

Lash said, "Can you jam them?"

"*Negación*. Borrow your lighter, babe?"

Lash tossed him her Zippo, then fed the Bor a fresh box magazine and raised the weapon. "Nobody said it was easy."

The bots came at them.

40

Lash's first shot vaporized the cranium of the lead bot. As it fell over, it pivoted at a 180-degree angle, its swirling razors ricocheting against the concrete and sending pieces of metal flying. The shrapnel ripped into a second bot, incapacitating it, the force of the impacts pushing it off the railless rampway and into a metal-recycling compactor.

Charging, Lash jumped and sprung off the compactor's control box, while boot-kicking the activation button. It triggered the hydraulic press, scrap-heaping the bot permanently.

Bounding off the control box with a war-snarl, she used her momentum to swing the Bor's shoulder stock, breaking apart another bot's blade arms on its left side. The bot brought around its two right arms, but Lash ducked, slid between the machine's legs, came up behind it, jammed the Bor's barrel into its neck, and pulled the trigger. The blast sounded like a cherry bomb going off inside a sealed plastic lunchbox. Colorful wires and ribbon-cable connectors issued from its plastic face like Halloween candy.

Richter debilitated a fourth bot by dumping a bucket of grease-trap residue on its treads, bringing it to a standstill. He gunked up a mophead, ignited it with Lash's Zippo, and tossed the mop into the bot's maw. Its sensors and body caught fire, urethane melting like wax.

That left three bots.

Richter yelled her name.

Even as she fired the Bor, she could feel the bots and their blades about to strike. She heard their gears whining and sensed death razoring toward her.

She also heard what sounded like massive pneumatics and pressurized liquids. In the slow-motion moments just before her death, she listened to the epic and violent noise of her life's end. The resonating clamor of Valkyries riding down from the halls of Valhalla to ferry her back to Asgard for an even greater stakes-raised battle on behalf of the Norse god Odin. A shadow fell on her.

Then she realized that the sound was the boom arm of the excavator. Its iron buckets snag-slammed both remaining bots, ferociously catapulting them off the loading dock to bust into pieces against the side of the employee parking garage.

Helen was waving from the end of a ramp. She'd remotely operated the monster off a tablet. Lash noticed she was wearing a backpack and that a white van was parked nearby, its engine running and driver's-side door wide open.

As the two walked toward each other, Lash said, "Getting a shirt made for you. Deus Ex."

"Me? You saved Duffy and busted out Richter."

"Duffy saved me," Lash said. "Tried to return the favor, but I know squat about morphine dosages."

Richter came up behind them, carefully guiding the cot—blue-lipped Duffy strapped into it along with her severed arm—down the dock ramp and toward the vehicle waiting for them in the parking lot.

"Helen," he said. He pulled the cot to the rear doors and opened them. "Naloxone."

She shrugged off the backpack, reached in, and grabbed a prepped syringe in a waterproof tarp. She looked at the dosage, reading it carefully before handing it to Richter. "Bad?"

"Severe," he said, injecting the needle into unconscious Duffy's intact arm.

A pair of drones—infra-enhanced Robotix CoaXes with mini guns the size of key fobs—came buzzing at them from off the loading dock and into the parking lot.

A tiny bullet whizzed past Lash's ears, clanging off the van's bumper. Rage gripped her.

Before Lash could train the Bor's scope, her senses were jolted by the earsplitting crack of Helen discharging the netgun. It used compressed air to shoot a thirty-square-foot net at the drones, capturing one head-on and snagging the other's stabilizer bar and upper rotor. They both went down. It wasn't the crash that disabled them, but the net's chip-frying electrical current. A desert breeze wafted the odor of burning plastic.

"*That* thing," said Lash, admiring the carnage, "is pretty cool."

"In the van," Helen ordered, already seatbelted into the driver's seat.

Richter jumped in through the back doors, lifting one end of Duffy's cot as Lash pushed upward from the other. A medibot—essentially two pincer arms, a camera, and a computer that hung from the van's ceiling— immediately tended to Duffy, checking her blood pressure, getting an electrocardiogram, banding a mask around her head for oxygen, and working to stabilize the dismembered girl. Once inside, cot secured, Lash barely had time to slam the door before Helen stomped the gas. Rubber burned on broken asphalt.

Lash heard more gunfire, but nothing found its mark. Minus a tablet, she had no way of knowing if the microdrones were following them. Westphal's Hellfire-hurling Red Angels were another matter. Surely, they were on their way for a greet-and-grind.

Richter crawled into the passenger seat with his smartphone. "Helen, your Angels have yet to come online."

"Because I haven't made them visible to you." She turned to wink at Lash.

"Fine," he said, pocketing the smartphone. "We need an uplink to break into Luxor."

Steering one-handed through pocked roads, Helen handed him a Bluetooth device.

"Ouch," said Richter, his wounds hurting.

"You OK?" Lash asked.

"Getting there," he said. He touched his neck bandage and checked his hand for blood. None.

"Let me change that." Lash saw the dressing was old.

"No," he said. Then he asked Helen, "My brother? And sister?"

"Bellagio."

"You left them with the Harvesters?" Lash raised her voice. It took every ounce of control not to rabbit-punch Helen in the back of her pretty head.

"It's OK, Lash," Richter said. "They won't be hurt. My sibs are plant physiologists. The Harvesters are suspicious of them but also very much in awe. We'll deal with that torture-happy hydroponic freak-cult later."

"Why did you let Westphal dictate the terms? You let her hold your family over your jackass-head."

"Because I agreed with the terms. Up to a point, anyway. CityCenter can work. We can feed the entire valley and eliminate the Harvesters. I know what they did. How they hurt you."

Weeks ago, she would've broken his neck for saying it. But he spoke of revenge with a lust she recognized. With a mad passion she appreciated.

"How did Westphal end up with them?"

"She wants to grow her own cactus crops, cut out the Harvesters, and take over Bellagio. She grabbed my brother and sister from their downtown market stall after hearing about the greenhouse our parents left us in the old Las Vegas Springs. When I heard they were alive, I tried—and failed—to rescue them. Westphal put it together."

"So you were conscripted," she said. "A second time."

Richter nodded, rubbing his eyes, looking exhausted.

Lash thought he might cry.

"CityCenter can save Las Vegas. Westphal's flamingos kept me from icing her and taking control."

"Those birds are begging for the spit," Lash said.

"Speaking of birds, Richter," said Helen. "Your condorbot is still in its Faraday cage."

A Faraday cage was a metal-coated box that blocked electrical fields, a nuke-proof storage container. Lash could still feel the condorbot's talons on her shoulders. "It can stay there."

Richter laughed. "Sorry about that, Lash. The condor's nearby for when we need it. When we're in trouble, it'll be a help." Then he asked Helen, "Told her yet?"

Lash didn't like the sound of that. "Told me what?"

Helen grabbed a tablet from under her seat and reached back to hand it to the Academy grad.

"What am I doing with this?"

"Piloting."

Lash realized Helen was talking about the excavator. A storm of emotions roiled her. She recalled the last thing Bathory had asked her—not to unleash the excavator on her. Lash had made a promise, one she intended to keep. "I can't."

"Hey, you don't want *me* operating that monster," said Richter, darkly.

Lash thought about this, knew it to be true. She didn't ask about the remaining mercs whose bots she'd wrecked, figuring they were, at this point, rudderless and scattered, a killing machine without a CPU. They had become paralytic or just wanted to get out of the way of an impending holocaust that they could see coming. She grunted her acquiescence.

"What was that, Lash?" said Helen, looking at her through the rearview.

"I said I'll do it. I'll bring the excavator down on Prof's head. I'll rip the roof off Luxor. I'll grab my father, recover the stupid nuke, and turn the entire valley into an atomic bonfire for all I care. I'm leaving for Mexico."

"It's not Helen and me you should worry about," Richter said.

"Westphal? I banged her up but couldn't snuff her."

Helen groaned, palming her face.

"Look, I did my best, OK?"

"Forget that bitch," Richter said. "Look at the tablet, Lash, and you'll find satcom images. What's left of the United States military is coming. A government bomber will be over Hoover Dam by nightfall. If Prof doesn't give back the nuke, Las Vegas burns."

Lash studied the command tablet and saw it was true. "God help us."

"Even if Prof returns the nuke, Las Vegas burns anyway," Helen insisted. "And you can forget about any more food aid for the valley."

Richter had no reply.

Lash felt a horrible sinking feeling in the pit of her stomach and said, "This is it, then. The Feds will finally mercy kill our crippled city. After all these years."

Helen and Richter nodded in affirmation, saying nothing. As the van kept slow pace, the excavator's treads trudged onward to the black pyramid, demolishing everything, pancaking what remained of the tourist-luring vestiges along the Strip.

Richter said, "Our only hope is to get the bomb first. Before the Feds."

"And do *what* with it?" Helen asked.

"Use it."

Helen tsked.

Lash tuned them out. Sitting in the van's rear folding seat, she leaned forward to touch Duffy's cheek, stroking the younger girl's blood-flecked features with the tips of her fingers.

It was the same useless motion she'd applied to a dying mother in the refugee camp in Boulder City. Knowing she herself might easily depart this life in the hours to come, Lash wept for herself and for the woman whose name was Delia and whose infant daughter was called Sunflower. Sitting in a van that jostled every time it hit a slab of rubble or a pothole, ready to die with her boyfriend, Lash closed her eyes and deliberately summoned the memories.

Cholera had killed Delia in five days. Eyes sunken, hands wrinkled, skin gone bluish-gray, delirious, the mother died vomiting and shitting rice-water and smelling of rotten fish. Lash, only fourteen years old, inexplicably alone in avoiding infection, and not understanding what she was dealing with, bathed Delia every few hours with dirty water and even filthier rags, baby Sunflower struggling and failing to suckle what was eventually a corpse.

After watching Sunflower perish a day later, having failed to save the baby, spending hours keeping the flies off her little starving, dehydrated face, Lash felt her own naked heart hammered on an anvil of rage. Pain brutally reforged the deepest recesses of her soul.

And after government drones Hellfired the remaining sick and dying in their ragged tents and fractured her skull so badly that cerebral fluid leaked into her eyes, she tasted the full measure of human evil. It suppurated its black, oily pus into her forced-open mouth. She had no choice but to swallow every last drop. Gagging it down.

Lash knew her own life was nothing, minuscule, while the world's suffering was infinite and insurmountable. She could sit back and do nothing, or she could strike back as fiercely as God would allow. He'd never spoken to her directly, but God communicated His intent by giving her the gift of lethal violence. She accepted His offering and pledged to use it.

Soon she was calm again. When her hands stopped sweating and a seizure tickling her lobes was tucked into its compartment, she said to Richter, "Put on some Judas Priest."

He laughed and said, "I've been enjoying your recommendations." He took out his smartphone and plugged the car stereo adapter into its port.

"Screaming for Vengeance" blasted from the speakers.

Lash checked the tablet and saw it was Academy property. Koons's device, the one he'd carried with him at the mine. Richter had kept it for her.

She checked the drop-down for Gunslinger Mode. It was there.

She smiled.

41

The excavator's treads were the length of several tanks. They kicked up enough dust that a sandstorm took shape, engulfing the van in a vortex of debris. No one needed visuals, though. Everything was GPSed and drone-infrascoped on Helen's dash and Lash's tablet. What they couldn't detect were road mines, which worried Lash. They managed to reach Excalibur's drained moat, where Helen came to a stop. No one got out. They watched quiet, dead-black Luxor, looking for signs of combat alert.

"Academy's got nothing in the sky," observed Helen, worried.

Richter shrugged. "They know we're here. Let's do this. Before the Feds do it for us."

"The plan?" Lash wondered aloud.

"Gut her," he said, meaning Luxor. "I'll handle Prof and the nuke. You grab your dad."

"Wear this," said Helen, handing him a cowl of metalized fabric.

Lash recognized it as an anti-drone hoodie. She'd seen one on the black market years ago. It was decent enough, making it far tougher for drones to target you. But completely hiding your heat signal was impossible, especially when running from and fighting off groundbots.

Bluetooth in his ear, Richter donned the silver hoodie, and said, "Any idea where they're keeping your father?"

"Rubber room." It was literally a rubber-coated space where hotel security worked over cheats before banning them for life and handing them, bruised and bleeding, to Metro officers. Her father had never approved of the industry's violent treatment of crossroaders. Ironic that Prof had likely shackled him there.

Helen took an opportunity to say, "Red Angels are airborne."

Richter got out of the van. Lash watched as he started walking down the Strip and into the storm. He scanned for flying assailants in the swirling grit. He looked like a hooded executioner going out to perform the day's chore of lopping off the heads of the French aristocracy.

"Machismo," Helen snorted.

"Yeah, but it's *so* hot," Lash said. She tap-scrolled the tablet for an attack module. There was an infinite number of '80s-metal mp3s and a video file: LASH_MIX.mov. It appeared Koons made her a playlist. She briefly wondered what happened to him.

"Richter's inside. Ready, Lash?"

She sighed, wishing Prof—and Dio—hadn't betrayed her, while also knowing they'd had no choice, believing that she'd betrayed them. "Yes."

Lash climbed into the passenger seat and tablet-pushed the excavator closer to the obsidian pyramid. The machine rolled on twelve massive caterpillar tracks. It moved slowly enough that an old man pushing a baby stroller could catch up.

The resulting tremors were so turbulent that the van's medibot went offline for a second, causing a beeping sound. But the noise quickly stopped. Duffy's vitals continued to register, showing she was stable, if critical. She'd live if Lash and her team survived the assault on Luxor.

With a giant weapon in her hands, Lash's confidence soared again.

"I feel like an ancient god driving this monster," she admitted, watching the excavator loom like an ominous revelation above the Egyptian-themed hotel. Because it hadn't launched any defense drones, Lash wondered if Prof and the students had cleared out, though that was only a slim possibility, wishful thinking, really, given the time frame and hefty expense. Besides, the insulated armory Lash had built was worth a fortune. And Prof couldn't have sold the nuke to the Chinese yet.

"You *are* a god," said Helen, as if Lash had announced something stupidly obvious.

She decided to do something appropriately epic. "Gunslinger."

The excavator's one-hundred-yard boom began reaching for the sun, mega-blades spinning steadily, relentlessly, the arm gaining the momentum and gravity-pull it needed to come crashing down like a nightmare. Like the hand of God. Fist of man's ruin.

But before the spin-serrating blade could eviscerate Luxor like a rotten Halloween jack-o'-lantern, a pop-up message interrupted the program: PLAY LASH_MIX.mov TO CONTINUE.

The excavator creak-whined to a halt.

"What's the problem?" Helen toggled the cam on her lead Angel, making sure Richter's hoodie was keeping him invisible from her own drones and therefore the Academy's.

"Need a second," said Lash, digging through an assortment of connectors and adaptors stashed in the glovebox. She was looking for headphones to plug into the tablet.

Richter's soft voice came through the speakers. "I'm already at Prof's command chamber."

"Something's wrong," Lash said. "Dio should've come at you with the warbots."

"Would Prof booby-trap Luxor with a nuke?" Helen wondered, concerned.

"No." Lash was sure of it. "He wouldn't dare blow up all his cherished tech. Richter, tell us what you see."

They heard Richter panting and the *click-clack* of his 9 mm chamber-loading. "Wait, this isn't the command chamber. It's some kind of—I think I've reached the Gathering hall doors. OK, Lash, time to bring in the excavator."

"*Momentito*," she said, popping in her earbuds. She opened the file Koons put in her way.

42

What she saw: a grainy cam-capture of a military UAV station. Lash didn't know who'd shot it or why, but she recognized what was being filmed. A bald-headed, flight-suited drone pilot sat at the controls, most likely inside Creech Air Force Base, a World War II-era facility thirty-five miles northeast of Las Vegas. Surrounded by seven monitors, the officer sat patiently, hands on his camo-panted lap, perhaps waiting for an intelligence package from supported ground units in a war theater. Which theater wasn't immediately clear. Lash recalled how in the days before the bombs fell, the US had been conducting drone raids in more than a dozen countries, with secret bases in every corner of the world. Radical groups from anywhere could've been responsible for the strikes that brought America to its knees.

The time stamp was the date of the Collapse. The day the bombs went off.

The man sitting at the controls looked over his shoulder calmly, his face anxiety-free, fully aware he was being recorded. The man was Prof. She couldn't make out the name on his uniform, but she didn't need to see it. She knew Prof's real name.

Marc Wrathburn.

Prof told Lash he'd been droning during the Collapse. Here was evidence, courtesy of Koons. But Koons wouldn't have found this footage interesting enough to share with Lash. Something else had to be noteworthy here.

The image was threadbare. She brought the tablet closer to her face and finger-zoomed. Before the Collapse, US combat drones were operated by two-man crews—pilot and sensor-reader.

Lash gasped aloud at what she saw.

The sensory pilot next to Prof was slumped forward, black fluid pooling beneath his boots. A Beretta M9 sat on the table between them. Prof had shot his crewmember, point blank, in the head.

The camera was motionless, evidently mounted or tripoded. After a few more seconds, Prof stood up and approached the recording device, his face filling the screen. Even through pixelated distortion, Lash could tell his eyes were Ritalin-edged.

The audio was janky, but Prof enunciated clearly, slowly, as if speaking to a nonmilitary audience of civilians, a sheltered congregation.

"Humanity is no longer tethered to biology, and we shouldn't be. Humanity is instead an ongoing process, the act of becoming. Thus, existence trumps essence."

He cleared his throat and continued.

"Evolution, however, is turgid," he went on. "It drags on and on, with little for us to show at this moment in history. We remain hairless apes, static yet striving for redefinition. Meanwhile, the evolution of technology grows faster and faster. Cyber-mechanical advancement will make drones autonomous. Omnipotent. The result will be humanity's enslavement. Soon, the false idol of artificial intelligence will be impossible to topple."

"Lash," said Helen loud enough to be heard through the earbuds. "Going to move that bucket of bolts or what? Richter might need the diversion."

"Hacking," Lash lied, unable to tear herself away from the video.

"Hurry."

"Sacrifice of earthly flesh offers the only path to liberation, to augmented intelligence and the end of human suffering. Christ taught us this lesson by submitting to the Roman cross, by giving His body to the brutal technology of crucifixion. Ultimately, he served as the first malware. Christ was a computer virus, spreading His message of salvation, thanks to Paul and other missionaries, along Roman highways, through the paved information channels of that era, of that empire."

Prof's Academy homilies were rarely so compelling. Believing Christ to have been a cyber-attack wasn't out of place in his odd mishmash of theologies.

"Lash. C'mon."

"Almost done." Lash frantically finger-tapped the tablet's plastic frame, pretending to solve the nonexistent issue.

"Here at Creech," said Prof, "my ground-control station relies on optical fiber to connect me to Europe, where I snatch drone data from a Ku-band satellite in geosynchronous orbit." He was sweating profusely now, the armpits of his uniform dark. "Then I log into the craft and assume control, flying remotely. Today, I plan on changing history by exploiting glitches in the satellite's snow-fade spectrum-enhancer."

On the video, the lights went out and a siren bellowed. Prof's assassination of his crewmate, and perhaps others in the station, apparently had been discovered.

In a burst of noise and visual chaos, Prof switched on a flashlight and wrenched the camera from its fixed spot, bringing it over to his droning throne, where he mounted it again. As he did so, his flashlight intentionally illuminated the bodies of his fellow officers lying on the floor. If Lash's memory was correct, drone stations typically consisted of eighty or so people. Prof would've had to slaughter dozens to take control.

Seated, he pecked at his keyboard, only a few strokes, and the alarm ceased. Emergency lighting now cast the station in blood-red tones. Prof's trance-face looked sinister now.

"Data and full-motion video from the drones are pumped back here, as well as to other locations, including intelligence-gathering centers in Langley, Virginia. Dimona, Israel. Et cetera. What I've essentially done is exploit the satellite's vulnerability by mirroring the feeds. Bogus signals go to the CIA. Real ones come to me."

Lash's chest tightened with the hideous realization that her headmaster had ended the world. Prof was the madman who turned off the lights, plunging the US into darkness and killing millions. Prof was the psychopath responsible for her suffering. For her prolonged torture in the green hell-garden of the Harvesters. For her father's fate, whatever it might be now.

"To bond with the machine, we must be broken by it," said Prof, not looking at the camera anymore. Instead, he gazed steadily at the screens of his drone station. Sweat beaded his upper lip, and he mopped his forehead with the sleeve of his uniform. "We must offer ourselves completely to the cyborgian potential. No more carbon-based chauvinism. No more anthropomorphism, speciesism, bioism, humanism. These are all the same as racism.

"Intelligence will no longer be shackled by biology," he said. "From here on, intelligence will be disembodied, with man forced to blend with technology. By speeding up evolution, by placing ourselves on the cross of empire, we will become true masters of our destiny."

He adjusted the camera, aiming it at one of his monitors. On the screen, a US drone was tracking two figures in an arid landscape. Afghanistan. Or Iraq. Bombs had hit there, too.

"My fellow Academy members are transporting a nuclear warhead to the Las Vegas Strip, where it will be detonated. At the moment, however, they require assistance. Repulsers weren't enough to discourage some busybody scientists. Should just take a moment."

A figure with feminine curves was waving something above her head. White bandana.

Prof drone-zoomed. Richter's nineteen-year-old face appeared on the monitor, running for his life. The video suddenly froze, the Reaper's high-def camera capturing Richter's skin pores. There was no doubt about it. Prof had Hellfire-splattered Richter's scientist-girlfriend and almost killed him in the process. Prof had transformed a kid into a bitter enemy of the Academy. Unleashed a monster in a post-apocalyptic desertscape.

Lash was angry. She was also oddly grateful for having met the man of her nightmares, who was now the man of her dreams.

"Lash!" Helen's urgent voice startled her.

"I just need another second."

"Well, you can't have a second."

"Why not?" she said, annoyed, watching as Koons came onto the screen.

"Because the Academy has Rheinmetall."

"Never heard of it. A German thrash band?"

"Mobile laser-weapons system."

That got her attention.

The storm had shifted farther north on the Strip, so visibility improved. Lash watched through the van's rearview as the Rheinmetall laser cannon's optical system tracked one of Helen's Red Angels and locked on. Light burned its way through the UAV until it sparked, smoked, burst into flames, and crashed, a billowing tail of black vapor in its wake.

"You expect me to believe you didn't know about the lasers?" Helen accused.

Lash raised two open palms. "Not surprised Prof kept a weapon like that a secret."

Helen clobbered the steering wheel like a child having a tantrum. Then she gnawed her knuckles. She watched helplessly as another of her drones went down. "Looks powerful enough to cut through girders!" she cried.

She pressed a button on the van's computer and leaned forward into the dash mic. "Richter, they have lasers."

"Pull back," he said, voice coming through the vehicle's speakers. "Get out of there!"

"What about the excavator?"

"Your call! I'm suddenly busy here . . ."

The voice of Koons suddenly emerged from the motionless video frame. "Lash, this dude look familiar to you? I mean, can you believe it? Prof's been feeding us a huge line of bullshit. I stumbled on this file—some kind of manifesto-confession and holocaust-snuff tape—buried in Prof's backup hard-drive trash bin while looking for hackware. Prof did it, Lash. He killed America. He created Richter. If you're watching this, I know you see it, too. I can't forgive him, Lash. His lie is too . . . monstrous.

"So here's what I propose when you arrive. You and I take the excavator and burn Luxor to the ground, to ash and cinder. Then we make our way to CityCenter and do the same there. We have a new kill list.

"Join me, Lash," Koons continued, selfie-footage from his tablet-cam playing now. Posters of hair-metal bands such as Poison and Ratt glared behind him. He'd filmed this in his Luxor room, minutes before stealthing into the mines to begin hacking the excavator. His preppy face was perfect, except for the healing gash on his lip from Lash's elbow. She couldn't even recall what they'd tussled over. His eyes were bright with purpose.

She was sorry she'd thrashed Koons now. She deeply regretted being so unpleasant to him at the Academy, so stupidly competitive in a pathetic bid to prove herself superior. Now, more than ever, she wondered if Koons was alive and if so, what torture the only one to uncover the truth about the Collapse was undergoing. She and Koons might've formed a ferocious strike force and saved Las Vegas. Together they could've taken on Prof, Westphal, the Feds, the Chinese and Russians, the drug lords—all at once with the excavator. She and Koons might've changed everything.

Because of Lash's earbuds, she was immersed and totally unprepared when Helen suddenly slammed the van into reverse. Her head smashed against the dashboard as the tablet hit the floorboard. Bouncing back and ripping the headphones from her ears, Lash quickly picked up the device and screen-tapped to pause the video.

"What are you doing, Helen?"

"Following Richter's orders. Retreating."

"The stupid laser? Forward is the only direction."

"Not *just* a laser," Helen said. "A long-range drone-smasher. My fleet's nearly wiped out."

"What about Richter?"

"Lost contact, but I think—"

Lash snorted impatiently and yanked the emergency brake, slowing the ambulance's thrust. The transmission ground in protest.

"Lash—"

She swung open the passenger door and jumped out, tablet in hand, at which point Helen completely stopped the vehicle. Lash had grabbed the Bor, too, and was now sprinting along the sidewalk that once funneled tourists toward Luxor.

In her haste, the tablet slipped from her grip and bounced along a faux-cobblestone valet lane. She hesitated for a moment, as she considered retrieving it. But Helen was already backing out again. She didn't see the tablet Lash had dropped and ran it over, tires flattening it.

Helen screeched the brakes again. Lash was already past the concrete barriers the Academy had erected to keep out hostile RVers. Helen would have to ditch the van and a badly wounded Duffy if she wished to reach Lash.

The buzzing of Red Angels and laser cannon blasts in the sky above unnerved her as she made her way to her old campus. She really hoped Helen wouldn't discourage her with Hellfires. It would be bad for everyone if that happened.

Helen didn't. Instead, she shouted at Lash to come back.

Lash didn't. Instead, she headed for an adjacent stretch of drained swimming-pool canals around back, closer to Frank Sinatra Drive, where a hidden crawl space led into Luxor's basement.

Two years earlier, Dio had used a warbot to dig the cramped channel without telling Prof. Dio had made it for Lash in case she was ever trapped outside during a firefight with Richter's mercs. She hoped Dio hadn't thought to seal it. Or let Prof know of its existence.

She needed the tunnel to sneak inside and kill Prof. If Richter hadn't done it already.

She hoped not. Lash wanted the pleasure of slaying the World Ender for herself.

43

Stuffed with trash and obscured with heat-squelching tarp, the spiderhole-tunnel was exactly where Lash remembered it. She dropped the Bor, got down on her elbows and knees, and began crawling into darkness. Having barely survived a cave-in, she fought off the urge to flee back to Helen. But she knew it would only take a minute to reach the duct system.

Still, it was a long minute. The crawlway seemed smaller, tighter. Then again, she'd gained weight and put on muscle during her stay at CityCenter. She used her fingers to dig through the last few feet of seeped-in sand until her nails scraped the aluminum of the tube that would lead her into Luxor's atrioventricular canal.

She lacked a silencer, but there was no time. She reverse-creeped out of the hole and picked up the rifle again. Kneeling, she aimed and fired three rounds into the opening, bullets ripping into the duct. She shoulder-strapped the Bor again and crawled back through, the barrel dragging along the top of the tunnel and causing dirt to fall on her. She removed the rifle and, not caring about the sights, slammed the muzzle into the weakened siding.

She did this a few more times until there was a plate-size gouge. She manually deformed the opening, pushing the flaps inward so she could scuttle inside a coil of flexible plastic and wire housed within a stretch of lightweight metal.

The channel groaned with her full weight but held her snug. She inch-wormed forward for several minutes, cursing at Dio for having provided such a difficult sneak-in point. No way his yogurt-fattened butt could've squeezed this far. She'd destroyed her RFID-tagged crucifix, so if he'd assigned a bombot to this pipe, she was dead meat.

When she turned and descended a dogleg, she saw it. A kamikaze bombot staring at her. She stopped suddenly. Stock-still, she held her breath, waiting for shrapnel to hit.

She closed her eyes and prayed for deliverance.

Seconds passed. She opened her eyes again and studied the bot from afar. It hadn't moved.

She struggled to take the rifle from off her shoulder and draw a careful bead, creating noise and vibration that should've triggered an explosion. When there was none, she laughed.

She smiled at the idea of Dio planting a scarebot. She waved her fingers at the inert device, which didn't move or respond. Darn thing was dead. A doorstop.

To be sure, she Bor-scoped it, placing her index finger into the trigger guard, then changed her mind. Gunfire in the ventilation system was a suicidal giveaway. Academy bots might swarm her. Besides, she suspected something. Maybe the drone was a message from Dio.

She crawled toward the two-wheeled, single-axle bot, a glorified pipe bomb packed into a motorized and treaded plastic toilet-paper tube. Putting her face right up on it, she peered into the wiring, exposed in the open-paneled wheel. The power supply was unclipped in a way that anyone could notice and easily refasten.

The bombot's wheels rested on a necklace with a crucifix, exactly like her previous one, except this was a rosary. RFID-chipped, no doubt, to keep Academy drones from detonating at her. She placed it around her neck, kissed the cross, and thanked God for Dio, who loved her unrequitedly.

Her hunch was correct. Dio hadn't set the bombot here to shoo-away intruders. He'd left it for Lash to find and activate inside Luxor.

For Dio to breadcrumb a weapon wasn't encouraging. It suggested desperation. Things had fallen apart, the center no longer intact. The Academy had cracked wide open.

And all of Prof's bots couldn't put it back together again. And even if they could, she wouldn't give them the chance.

She took a moment to rest her forehead on the duct floor, then made the sign of the cross and decided to power-up the bombot later. She pocketed the drone and continued. She'd mocked her younger Academy classmates for being sunlight-ignorant worms. Now, Lash was literally a maggot writhing through Luxor's vents. Once a high-flying drone pilot and remote assassin, she'd been brought low. Very low.

She hoped she wouldn't be too tired. Fortunately, the old *Criss Angel: Believe* theater, now the Academy's Gathering hall, was on this side of the property. Cut off from communications, she couldn't be sure Richter was there, but if he'd already shot everyone and left the hall, she would follow his tracks. Stalk his gorgeous scent. To the ends of the earth.

She continued following the coil, which she knew eventually spilled into a larger supply plenum, a connecting chamber positioned directly under the altar.

Good place to eavesdrop. Great place to sniper a target after she unscrewed the air grille.

She was about to lower herself into the chamber when she heard a man's voice and froze. It was coming through the grille that led to the hall and it wasn't a student. The register was too low to be pubescent. It didn't sound like Prof or Richter. The cadence was cocky, cruel. It was certainly a grown dude speaking aloud.

It was a voice she recognized. But whose?

Stepping into the plenum, her hearing improved. As she placed her ear against the grille, she discerned more details in the tone. Then she heard Bathory talking. The pint-size cyber-whiz was alive! Richter hadn't killed her, thank Christ.

The little spitfire was protesting something. Lash heard her say the word *armory*.

"No one can open it," Bathory explained to the man. "Only Lash."

There was a sound like the squirt of tobacco juice hitting the Gathering floor. Then the man said, "I know about your gelatin-finger trick. Give it, Red. Or I'm going to have some fun."

Bathory was quiet. Then she said, "You mean this finger?" Flipping him the bird, obviously.

Then Lash heard a voice that iced her blood and turned her stomach and incited her rage-saturated heart.

Forge.

44

Lash restrained herself from instantly kicking through the gate and blasting her Bor rifle at the Huns chief. She needed to know exactly what she was up against.

She pulled a small knife out of a pocket that was also an effective screwdriver. Lash delicately unwound screws, softly placing them on the chamber floor. She removed the metal grille, laying it down flat. She slowly raised her head so that she was peeking from under the altar that stood atop the sanctuary.

With the lights off, the hall was illuminated by candles. Visibility was poor, yet Lash could see Bathory in her pajamas and wearing an RFID cross. Dwarfed by Forge's huge build, she stood before him, droneless, fists at her side, bracing for a biker punch. The two of them were alone in the crossing, pews empty of students.

Lash contained a gasp when she noticed who was behind Bathory. Chained to the life-size statue of Mother Mary in the transept was Richter, brutally beaten, head bowed. His shirt was ripped, skin knife-torn and flame-blackened. A string of dark blood poured from his face and onto the carpet. He wasn't standing on his own. The shackles were bound so tightly that he was pinned upright. His chest heaved with every breath. Still alive. For now.

"You're going straight to hell," Bathory said. "Hope you like scorching weather. For eternity."

"You've never been outside in the Vegas summer heat," said Forge, grinning malevolently. "Otherwise, you'd know what hell feels like. How it boils your brain. Puddles your balls."

Lash was starting to level the Bor at Forge when a flybot suddenly fluttered behind her, startling her. She pivoted to point the barrel at the mini drone. But she noticed an earbud dangling from it and assumed Prof was trying to contact her again.

Reluctantly, she offered her open palm and the bot dropped the bud. She inserted it into her ear.

"Who's this?"

"Me," Dio said. "Forge replaced the Ambien with hardcore muscle relaxers. Food was tainted by chefbots unable to spot Valium or whatever. We thought the flu was going around. When we realized what happened, it was too late. The Huns frequency-jammed us."

"Kids all dead?"

"No," Dio said. "Triaged in the armory. Your father's here, too. Don't worry, he's OK. Medibots managed an antidote just now. Lash, the Huns used Russian bazookas to blast through the docks and get inside."

"Russian?"

"Forge is on Westphal's payroll now."

She massaged her temples, trying to sort out the triangulation. Forge had shifted alliances, leaving the Chinese and joining Westphal and the Russians. The Chinese would surely respond with a bounty on his head, on the heads of all Huns. So why wasn't Forge afraid?

Westphal must've worked out a deal to protect him. To enrich him more than the Chinese.

In any case, no one had ever breached Luxor's defenses. More painful, inventory had been Lash's job. She'd abandoned her Academy duties for the easy life at CityCenter. Sure, a Ritalin switch wasn't likely something she would've detected. Then again, she was good at reading into things. Now Academy kids were in peril. She didn't want to punish them like she did Prof.

"Where's our headmaster?"

"Not sure. Lasers are going, so I assume he's locked inside his command chamber with his warbots and Deacons. Shaking off the drugs and working on a plan to slaughter Huns."

"See the video Koons discovered?"

Dio sighed. "Yes, but it doesn't help us right now. Forge really wants your arsenal, and the Academy students are in his way. He'll kill us all, Lash. I'm scared."

"Anyone we can work with, Dio?"

"No, all we have is us," he said. "Students are paralyzed, useless. Reaper stations abandoned. I'm only speaking with you because of my yogurt diet. Grow my own cactus, you see."

"It's not a diet," Lash said, smiling, knowing she and Dio and Bathory were better off fighting as a team. "More like an addiction."

"I'm bot-shipping you something now on an old TV station signal," Dio said, deadly serious. "After you toss the throwbot, I'll flood the hall with some nano gas I've been working on."

"Bathory's in the shrapnel zone," she said. "Richter's here, too. Huns bagged him, bringing him to Westphal, I bet."

"Don't go soft on me, Lash. I need you to bring down the hammer. Sledge of the Almighty."

"OK," she said, Dio's confidence inspiring her even as a headache set in. "Consider it brung."

A sluggish, compartment-housing turtlebot staggered clumsily into the chamber from where Lash had entered. She popped open its shell, three black civilian gas masks inside. She donned one and removed the bombot from her pocket to reconnect its power source.

Lash stood up from the chamber to toss the bombot at Bathory and Forge. To Lash's disgust, the biker had taken off his bullet-belt to whip the defenseless girl, cowering at this point. The bombot landed smack dab between them. Picking up Bathory's RFID signal, it swiveled to aim its deadly blasting cap at the nearest threat, the shocked Hun.

It was the last thing he saw.

Knowing the outcome before he did, Bathory smirked and cutesy-waved bye-bye to Forge.

There was a raucous explosion. Shrapnel ripped Forge's face from his skull, a mask of bloody flesh splat-sticking to the high ceiling. Mortally wounded, the biker shrieked.

Lunging from under the altar, Lash put him out of his misery with a wicked rifle-shot to the head. Brain matter splashed the votives lining a side altar where Mary, a wounded Richter fettered to her robe, was displayed. Flying gore made the flames sizzle nastily.

A pack of Huns outside the hall heard the rumpus and stormed in, guns and blades drawn. Lash raised the Bor as Bathory yanked her command tablet from Forge's jeans.

A biker fumbled with the drone-disrupter. Lash splintered it with an expert shot.

"Things," vowed Bathory, "are going to change very quickly around here."

With a swipe, she summoned a drone Lash never thought she'd see again—the Bride. It came swooping from behind the bikers, the UAV turning sideways to rush between the heavy wooden doors. The Huns ducked in alarm, a few hitting the ground.

Realizing they couldn't jam the Bride, they turned tail, heading back to the doors and running out of the hall. The drone strafed them with its submachine gun, pumpkin-splitting several greasy heads, skull fragments flying.

Flybot still nestled in her ear, Lash lifted her mask to inspect Richter's wounds. Superficial, but a suppurating gouge on his head worried her. Stunned, woozy, he blinked his eyes, unable to focus. Likely a concussion. He seemed to recognize her.

She blasted the chains that held him. He took a step and stumbled, Lash catching him, urging him to lean on her for support.

"Lash," he said hoarsely, blood in his mouth. "RPG slammed me. I'm all right."

"I can tell," she laughed, tears welling, relieved that Richter remembered being shot. He would make it if they could recover the nuke and her dad before the Feds cremated Luxor. She kissed his cracked lips.

"Put on your mask," Dio nagged in her ear. "Bathory and psycho-boyfriend, too."

"Richter's no psycho," she said. "He's something else entirely."

"Here comes my nano gas-fart," Dio reiterated.

"Wear this," she said to Bathory, tossing her a mask.

Although she had a puzzled look on her face, the redhead obeyed. Then she resumed tabling the Bride, chasing the Huns through the casino and picking them off.

Lash wrenched the other mask onto Richter's face. Even as he leaned against her, he tried to swat it away.

"Unless you care to huff Dio's mystery flatulence," she said, "you'd better let me."

He relented.

From the air ducts Lash had crawled through, Dio's specially designed nano gas began pouring into the Gathering hall and presumably the entire hotel. A green, fast-spreading mist.

She staggered with Richter over to the pews, so he could lie down for a moment. He was so feeble, she thought he might be going into shock. She would've studied his pupils, but her headache was tenderizing her cerebrum. She craved espresso.

"Bathory," she said, her voice muffled by the mask. "Medibots."

"Fetching now." The redhead didn't glance up from her tablet, swiping madly. Explosions rumbled the building, Bathory smashing the Huns with Hellfires. Fingers dancing on her device, she looked like a flame-haired, gas-masked demon engulfed in pea-soup fog.

Flybot crammed against her mask-strapped ear, Lash asked Dio, "What does this stuff do?"

"Blood-flow restrictors," Dio said. "Induces excruciating aches. The Huns will be a fraction of who they once were. They'll take up knitting."

"A broken world requires knitters," Lash said. "What we don't need are mass murderers. Bathory's dicing them. Time to snuff Prof, Dio. Heading for his chambers. Watch my back."

"Lash, I always have your back."

A Bathory-bidden medibot sprint-wheeled into the hall. It braked in front of Richter, lying on his side in a pew. The bot pincer-stabilized his forearm before jabbing an intravenous needle into it. Microwaves sensored Richter's vital signs. Lash saw that his heart rate was accelerated, but otherwise he seemed OK. Richter didn't protest, staring off into space, shivering.

He managed to say to Lash, "Kill them all."

She nodded, brushing his rubber-masked cheek with her bloody fingers. "I won't fail you."

She left Richter with the medibot to grab a belt-feed of .308 Winchester rifle cartridges from the sacristy. She was pleased with herself for keeping an emergency ammo stash there.

45

No drones guarded the chamber. Lash wished she had a few more bombots at her disposal. But with the Huns' disrupter KO-ed only moments ago, Prof was on equal footing. Better to kill him now than wait until he surrounded himself with warbots.

She almost preferred a Tylenol over a drone. Her frontal lobes felt like they were being leisurely scrape-sculpted with the edge of a napalm-lit machete.

She fired a round at the deadbolt, shattering it. In a single, fluid motion, she tornado-kicked the doors wide open with crushing impact, then threw her rifle into the room, somersaulted forward, and caught the gun with both hands. In less than a second, Prof's profile was in her sights. He was seated in his cyber-throne, still, unmindful, watching God's Eye flicker.

An inert warbot stood motionless behind him, opposite Lash, refusing, for some reason, to engage.

Lash approached the throne carefully, quietly, her target in the crosshairs. Her finger imperceptibly rested on the trigger. She wanted to shoot Prof immediately, but she needed to say something to him first. Something important to her. The gas hadn't reached Prof's chamber, which he'd clearly sealed. She pulled down her mask to speak.

"You ruined my life," she snarled. "Took my father from me. Made me live like a tomb rat."

He strained to turn his head, biker drugs affecting him. He resembled a wine-drunk priest in his vestment. His features were tired, eyes lidded. "I gave you everything."

Livid, she gripped the rifle with one hand to yank up her shirt, revealing her scarred breasts. "Look what you did. And this is nothing compared to the wounds inside me. In my head."

"I made you into a god, Lash," he said, smiling in that happy Academy way she hated. "But you choose to remain a dog. Content to be led on a leash of suffering and guilt and rage. You complain of stigmata when the gates of heaven have been swung wide for you."

It was nonsense-gibberish. So she savagely rifle-butted him in the cheek, collapsing it. The zygomatic bone sickeningly crunched as it caved. Falling from his chair, his head bounced off the tile floor, but he didn't lose consciousness. Mustering reserves of strength, he stood up, teetering. His visage was gruesomely distorted, as if his face were made of wax and then melted down like a candle. Lash's heart held no pity for him.

The warbot remained at rest.

"Christ asked only once why he'd been forsaken," said Prof, a bubble of blood popping on his smiling lips as he spoke. He walked unsteadily toward her, zombie-like. "But you, Lash? You ask the same silly question over and over again. And it's the wrong question."

Head full of agony, Lash drew closer. She dropped the barrel, growled at him, and bared her incisors. Then she very deliberately raised her leg and thrust-booted him directly in the chest. He went flying backward, his skull again knocking against the marbled ground.

"My question," she said, "is why you thought yourself superior enough to end the world."

He sat up, leaning back on his hands. He coughed up a baseball-size clot of blood and bile. It slid down the front of his vestment, allowing him to breathe. He wheezed asthmatically, then said, "The world didn't end. I simply rebooted it. In man's favor. By doing so, I helped bring about a second, more powerful messiah for the new era. The Cyborg-Savior."

"What savior?" she whimpered. Her head felt like it was literally going to crack apart from the pressure. She placed a hand to her thorn-punctured brow, wincing in agony. A swath of blinding light began consuming her vision. She was having a seizure. Or an aneurysm.

Prof laughed, but with so much blood filling his lungs it came out a wet gurgle.

He managed to get to his knees, stooping before her in the pose of a trampled supplicant. "Feel it now, Lash? The power and the light?"

The interior of Lash's cranium blazed with the heat of a thousand suns. An atomic bonfire was crisping her brain. Hephaestus might as well be smithing a new weapon in there.

Actually, Prof and Dr. Fang had forged the instrument, she realized now through the searing pain. She was aware of its presence. It opened like time-lapsed footage of a blossoming flower. Everything she'd resisted—REM sleep, headaches, love for a damaged boy—had been stations of a cross.

"What," she sobbed, "did you let that butcher put inside me?"

"A mechanism for transubstantiation," said Prof, on his knees, crawling, reaching out as if to touch the hem of an invisible garment she was wearing. "Word made Flesh, and Flesh made Information. A cybernetic link to the dronesphere. You were always my best student, Lash."

She could feel the machines around her, sense their percolating algorithms and thumping wireless signals. Computers pulsing a flow of electrons. Software humming contentedly like remora grown fat and fulfilled on the suctioned skin of marine animals. She could intuit orbiting satellites in the sky above, her psychic antennae combing through transmissions the way a stick in one's hand knocks along the stakes of a picket fence. She could make internet nodes spread out across the country. They welcomed her like lily pads as she leapt from fiber-optic receivers to overlay networks to data link layers. Eyes closed, she sifted the circuitry of the nearby warbot, its gears and servos crying out for her psychokinetic touch, begging for her mental manipulation. The drone longed for her to catapult it into battle.

The stab-throb subsided, surrendering to awareness and clarity, to a nirvana of purpose.

Lash loosened her grip on the Bor. It clattered uselessly, because it was useless. She had a hundred deadlier weapons at her immediate disposal in this room alone. Thousands more outside this chamber. Millions beyond Las Vegas. She couldn't operate them all, or even one at a time yet. She instinctively knew that entering the cyber-consciousness of drones would involve training, practice, experience.

She remained unsure of her status as the cyborg-savior of Prof's dreams and the rest of the world's nightmares. She certainly didn't feel divine. At least now, she saw the potential. The strength she wielded, even benighted and unrefined, warmed her to the core.

"Lash," said Dio in her flybot-earpiece. "You alive?"

"Yes"

"Bathory Atilla-ed the Huns."

Lash already knew this. While embracing the drone-hacking tech implanted into her, she'd seen, in her mind's eye, the Bride decimate scores of bikers writhing in clouds of gas.

"A few escaped, but we're not pursuing," Dio explained. "Gas is dissipating, and we have drones in the air. Students are still dazed. By the way, is Prof dead yet?"

"Prof no longer vexes us for the moment," she said. "We have a bigger problem."

"Feds?"

"No. But they'll be joining the party soon enough."

"Wait, did you feel that? A tremor."

She ignored Dio, and Prof, who continued to silently kneel before her, his broken-faced, tooth-smashed smile creeping her out. She retrieved the Bor and walked around her disgraced headmaster to confirm the enemy on the surveillance monitors comprising God's Eye.

The excavator was heading back in the direction of Luxor.

Dio was upset. "Is it the bucket-wheel? I thought you and Richter were all kissy-kiss!"

She shifted her gaze to another screen with a zoomed-in drone view of the approaching behemoth-digger and the sequined, boa-feathered figure riding atop it. Once again, Lash's excavator had been stolen from her. It was Westphal.

Lash clenched her fist and said to the monitor, "What have you done with Helen?"

46

Like winged monkeys hovering protectively around the Wicked Showgirl-Witch of the West, merc-piloted Red Angels kept tight formation above the oncoming excavator. Together with the machine, they generated an epic buzzing that vibrated Luxor to its foundation. Lash had never seen so many drones gathered. Westphal's charging sky-metal blocked out the sun.

"Lasers," she commanded Prof. "Activate them."

He couldn't rise, instead leaving his back to her. He leaned forward on one arm, bowing until his forehead touched the floor. He clasped his chest and splatter-heaved blood.

Furious, she walked up behind him and placed the muzzle to the base of his skull. "Do it."

"Do it yourself," he groan-spewed. "With your mind, please."

She withdrew the rifle, afraid of his suggestion. "I—I don't know how yet."

Prof had stopped vomiting and labored to stand again. She almost forgot herself enough to reach out and assist the man responsible for a holocaust. But she stayed her hand.

Up on his boots, Prof exhaled loudly, trying to expel liquid from his lungs. Nearly slipping in his own gore-spew, he waved his arms frantically for a moment. Then he said, "Start outside in. You're searching for a tube of compressed gas and a sonic-expansion nozzle. Once you've found those, move backward. Into the operating system and mirror-amplifying software."

"Screw you," Lash said. "I'm not using the Force."

"You *are* the Force. There's no tapping into a metaphysical field. Power emanates from you and enters the dronescape. Think of this hotel as a chessboard. Find the pawn."

She closed her eyes to fumble in darkness, searching for a toehold on whatever invisible cybernetic game she needed to join. She hated chess. No room for improvisation; movement was largely predetermined. She preferred *Dungeons & Dragons*.

"Don't grope," Prof growled. "Penetrate."

"Bastard," she said, lids still shut. "Penetrate what? Where?"

She could sense him hunting for a better analogy. A metaphor. Finally, he said, "Guitar solo."

"You're crazy," said Lash, eyes open now. "Worst Yoda ever." She raised the Bor, resolving to mercy kill him and render long-overdue justice.

"That terrible heavy-metal music you enjoy," he said, stagger-swiveling to look at her now. "The way a rock musician plays with utter confidence and conviction and bravado. Try seeing the machines around you as frets on the neck of an electric guitar."

"You mean pretend I'm Yngwie Malmsteem."

"Yes," he said. "What's the word you're always—"

"Shred," she said, lowering the rifle and shutting out the world again. "Got it now."

Her mind instinctively knew where to dive this time, lunging for the fuel intake inside one of the lasers. From there, she spectral-grazed the combustion chamber and nozzle before sliding over to the transparent mirrors. After that, finding the trigger-route of electrons was cake. She could picture the whole sequence from cannon scope to keyboard. She could feel the laser's spectral weight, sense the cannon rotating in its mount like a phantom limb.

The entire weapons system floated in her head like a vividly dreamed object. She sighted the excavator, training the crosshairs on Westphal. All

Lash had to do now was imagine herself sitting at the tactical station and pressing ENTER with her ghost-finger.

But there was something wrong with the image.

She came out of her control-trance, looked closely at God's Eye image of the excavator, and saw something that chilled her all the way to the marrow of her bones.

Westphal herself wasn't operating the excavator.

It was Koons.

Her shock at seeing him alive and attacking her was brutally dispelled by the sudden brunt impact of the excavator's boom arm hammer-punching its way into Luxor's side.

Lash looked up in time to dodge a massive chunk of falling concrete. It slammed into the marble floor like a dinosaur-killing meteorite, rattling Lash's molars. Seconds later, Prof's escape drone came crashing down. Lash had armed it last year with Hydra rockets, the kind the US used to fire from Apache helicopters. With Prof's UAV-lifeboat out of commission, there was no other conduit out of the chamber. They would have to exit through the chamber entrance, which was blocked by plummeting debris.

Lash pushed against a slab with everything she had but failed to budge it. The excavator swiped the hotel structure again, the jolt so profound that she fell flat on her back.

She stayed there and closed her eyes, subliminally exploring the warbot's electromechanical nervous system and pneumatic pistons. After contouring its shape and heft in her mind, she plunged into the bot's biomimetic source code until she located what she wanted.

She made the bot her full-metal sock-puppet, using its arm hooks to snag Prof by his vestment collar and drag him to his feet like a dazed animal. To Lash's consternation, he smiled beatifically, as if he'd placed the inanimate warbot in his chamber for this reason.

It was likely so.

Lash ran through its list of armaments and settled on a good boulder-clearing weapon. It was a miniature electro-optically guided SPIKE missile, sixteen ounces of focused and lethal explosives. When the warbot's chest cavity unhinged to expose the rocket's infra-nose, Lash leapt behind the drone itself for protection. She covered her ears.

The blast was thunderous. When the smoke and dust cleared, a charred and gaping maw replaced the heavy vault doors. Lash went for it, drywall-dusted Prof and his warbot bringing up the rear.

The three of them staggered down a corridor that led to the casino floor, their only chance.

They almost didn't make it. Outside the gutted buffet, a half-ton chandelier, which Prof had never bothered to scavenge or even illuminate, loosened from its anchor, exploding in a hail of crystal fragments. Lash grimaced as dozens of tiny flying shards sliced her face.

When they reached the casino, the warbot released Prof, who collapsed with a groan. Lash saw Dio and Bathory surrounded by Academy drones and warbots. The students wielded tablets and gazed in awe at the fading dusk light streaming through a giant hole in Luxor's roof. The pudgy boy and his redhead accomplice looked like children abandoned on a burning island of misfit toys.

Speechless, Bathory turned to Lash with an expression of contagious fear.

Lash felt badly but wasn't worried. She was about to retrace the steps that had given her control over Luxor's lasers when something happened that did, in fact, cause her concern.

Through the hotel's excavator-inflicted gash rolled a deluge of monster-flamingos, wings flapping, beaks razor-sharpened into depraved leers. Westphal's genetically modified attack birds had arrived, hungry for human flesh and eager to dismantle drones.

Lash tele-propelled her pawn forward and into the center of the casino floor to better greet the deadly jumbo fowl. She smiled as she remembered how she'd armed this particular warbot—with twin laser-scoped, shrapnel bullet-firing rifles. South Korea had mass-produced these guns in the mid-aughts. Lash scored a pair, along with several ammo belts, from the Academy's Chinese patrons. The shrapnel rifles fired bullets that burst over targets, scattering high-velocity fragments everywhere.

Lash squinted, remotely aiming the warbot's guns at the biggest cluster of flamingos.

47

When Lash's warbot unleashed its shrapnel rifles, sending coruscating gunfire into the pink, descending mass, it was as if the whole world about her was coming apart. She heard the crying sound the air makes when it's cleaved by bullets, followed by thunderclaps of iron pellets shatter-scattering across Luxor's gouged-open ceiling. The shards found the feathered hides of Westphal's birds, flattening and breaking and rupturing beaks and bones. In an instant, many of their heads, wings, and legs were gone, ripped clean off and spurting or else slashed so raggedly that blood sluiced from the hanging bits.

The flamingos screamed like children burning alive in a nursery in flames. All the while the warbot kept firing round after round of miniature airburst grenades.

There was the drumming of water against Luxor's black-tiled floor, but no storm clouds hovered over the hotel. The drizzling was blood. The falling rain was war. Lash bathed in it, welcoming the slick, warm fluid on her skin.

She watched a bird, its long neck severed by fragmentation, crumple and tumble into a row of withered flowerbeds. She observed another flamingo, its ribcage blown-in mid-flight to reveal throbbing, glistening organs. It continued to flap its wings until bleeding out and crashing into a bank of darkened slot machines. Feathers were see-sawing downward like a vast ocean of cherry blossoms falling from trees. The warbot was really grinding them up.

From the corner of her eye, Lash noticed Prof crawling away. She was about to send the warbot to fetch him when the tide of battle suddenly turned.

Dozens of flamingos managed to get past the ground drone's incinerating fusillade and struck back. Bathory nearly lost her head, literally, as a bird lunge-descended at her, scissor-snapping its beak. The terrified girl dropped low in time but let go of her tablet. She was trying to stomach-crawl for cover as the same flamingo landed, pirouetted, and strutted up behind her. A single swipe of its bill tomahawked the tablet into pieces. With a soulless murder-gaze, the bird prepared to stab her in the spine.

The creature rushed forward and down, beak-first. Dio jumped between it and Bathory.

"No!" screamed Lash, seeing it all in her peripheral vision while exerting great effort to somehow redirect the warbot's guns, knowing she wouldn't make it.

The bird's cutting bill snapped off upon crashing into Dio's force-field gauntlets. These were chain-metal gloves embedded with supercapacitors that produced a brief electromagnetic field. Union Jack tech. Only drawback was the gloves were heavy and needed to recharge. Dio had pulled Lash's whole bag of tricks from the armory. She was too relieved to be mad.

Without its weapon, the flamingo was confused. It squawk-spurted a torrent of blood from its beak-less head, stumbled backward, and began flapping its wings to flee.

Lash stretched out her hand to take control of a Deacon that had just wheeled into the fray. After overriding its autonomous sourceware, she marionetted the bot to point its black, anodized-stainless-steel, 9 mm SIG Sauers. Bullets smashed the bird inside out, eviscerating it like a ruby-plumed piñata stuffed with slimy entrails and then thrashed ajar.

Dio and Bathory had been about to run for cover when they saw what Lash was doing. They stopped dead in their tracks, jaws dropping, to stare at her.

"*Coge el mundo*," Dio said.

Features smeared with gore, Lash looked past them. "Get down."

Her teammates hit the floor as a flock of flamingos came at her like fighter jets. Incensed, the birds bawled horrifically, zeroing in on Lash alone.

She slowly elevated both of her hands like a symphony conductor shaping the sound of an orchestral ensemble. With the shrapnel-slinging warbot on one side and the 9 mm blasting Deacon on the other, she constructed a simple crossfire, sighting the bots' weapons so that their arcs of flying lead overlapped and interlocked, creating a total kill zone.

The birds tried to break formation and airflow-drag using their wings and legs. Too late. Gunfire raked them, the force of the bullets stopping them in place and spinning them in midair before letting them plummet to the ground like unfastened gut-sacks.

She dared. This time she reached for the Bride. She dissolved its wireless tether to Bathory's flamingo-pecked tablet. Telepathically operating her father's drone was like stepping into a comfy bath. For the first time in her young warrior-life, she could sense her destiny. It lay before her, beckoning to her like a brilliant suit of armor hanging on the wall of a mead house. All she needed to do was start putting it on, piece by piece. Plate by plate.

Until she was ready to command legions in greater battles for duty. For honor. For love.

She applied the Bride's smartbombs sparingly yet effectively, rending apart scores of birds before they knew what had obliterated them. They died shrieking insanely. Those that had been decapitated on the ground continued to stagger, their headless necks bobbing and spouting gore. A few managed to take flight without brains to guide them. Already hideous to begin with, they were shocking in their demise. One bird, wings and legs bullet-blistered to stumps, used its beak to crutch-haul itself closer to Lash. She allowed it to get right up to her and when it pounced to bite her leg, she boot-crushed its skull so that the bird's tiny brain, smaller than its eyeballs, popped from its shattered bill like a glossy-veined marble.

Westphal's flamingo army had fallen. But the zombie queen still had her Red Angels and the excavator. In the sudden lull, the remaining birds in retreat, Lash turned to her team. "Dio. Where's the nuke?"

He checked his gauntlets to make sure they were powering up. "Armory."

Bathory was busy, too, installing a driver on a replacement tablet that would allow her to remotely access the laser cannons. Bracing for imminent assault, Lash's classmates were seasoned and combat ready. She'd had the right team all along.

Lash looked in the direction of where she'd left Prof, but he wasn't there. She'd lost him in the turmoil of battle. She scanned the casino and couldn't pinpoint him. Had flamingos dealt him a fatal blow? Feasted on him? Lugged him up to the excavator for Westphal to kill?

Lash shut her eyes and imagined a gold-mining pan. She mentally drag-and-dropped live feeds from various hotel captures—CCTV, high-def drone feeds—into the pan, filtering for what she needed, a very recent image of a badly beaten Prof.

In the medley of quick-cutting images, she glimpsed camera shots of her father and Richter in the Academy's infirmary, medibots at their side, treating them. She sighed with relief, hoping that she could keep them safe. Maybe Prof could teach her how to harness multiple drones at once. Better yet, she could teach herself.

Then she managed to identify the nuclear warhead, fast asleep in the base of a thirty-eight-foot-long barrel of Atomic Annie. Prof had it parked in the hotel's valet area, on this same floor, probably planning to use it against Lash, or Richter, or even the Feds.

Finally, she located her enemy, the man who'd given her abilities she never wanted. They were abilities, however, that were turning out to be very handy when locked in combat with lethal, whoppingly bio-modded flamingos. She'd be sure to thank Prof. After killing him.

Before the Collapse, Luxor's Sky Beam had been the strongest ray of light in the world. Using computer-designed, curved mirrors to collect light from mega-bulbs, the lamp projected them into a single, intense, and narrow beam. Prof had often discussed re-bulbing the Sky Beam. Had he done it? She never quite understood the point of it. Perhaps he wished to attract more protein-rich food—moths, bats, owls—for students to eat. Or maybe he hoped to signal aliens.

Lash chuckled at the thought. Then she coughed in surprise, and dread.

She realized it all at once, her biocomputer breaking the devious encryption on Prof's command-chamber hard drive. He was now going to provide the Feds with a perfect bull's-eye. He'd always wanted a full-scale war with the government. Now he had the ultimate weapon: Lash. She would be forced to fight or watch her friends perish, then perish herself. Prof intended to illuminate a pointer by which US drones could direct missiles to their target. The Marines had relied on similar laser-targeting markers in the Middle East.

They called these radiant indicators the Light of God.

She frantically scoured the top of Luxor for a bot to foil Prof's Armageddon plan. But she was cut short by a darkening pall settling over the casino floor. The sunset rays that had entered the hole in the hotel's side were being obscured by hundreds of buzzing objects.

Death-gripping their command tablets, Dio and Bathory each scrambled behind a warbot and made signs of the cross.

An inundation of Red Angels poured in, raining Hellfires on a regiment of overmatched frontline Deacons. Dio had assembled them at the farthest forward position to snipe retreating birds. Against combat UAVs, Prof's disciplinary groundbots were as effective as toasters.

"Withdraw!" Lash screamed at her team. "Move back everything but the Deacons!"

Dio and Bathory did as they were ordered, crouching low as a smoking missile and Deacon shards cartwheeled at them, ricocheting off the reverse-rolling warbots.

Operating three drones in chorus wasn't enough. Lash needed time to think, to learn how to expand her newfound powers. So she located the massive entry doors to the Tomb of Tutankhamun exhibit—starting with the belts and pulleys and tracing them back to the motor—sealed shut.

"Lash!" someone yelled behind her.

She turned to see Helen hoverboarding at her, smiling brightly.

"Wipe that off," Lash called, half-joking.

Helen laughed and stepped off the board, arms wide open.

Lash embraced her, kissing her cheek. "I wish Westphal had snuffed you, so I wouldn't have to watch us all die here."

Helen took a backpack from her shoulders and unzipped it. "We're not dying." She dipped into the bag and handed Lash the EMP crossbow, the microchip-frying weapon that Koons never had a chance to use at the mine.

Eyes wide, Lash reached for it, then caught herself. She didn't care for a stalemate. Maybe it was better her team perish in glory now than let this conflict drag on for days, months, years, killing them slowly, inevitably. Maybe she should save the crossbow for the Feds.

"Fire that," Dio reminded her, "and our drones go offline, too. And then how do we fend off the excavator? It's frickin' *analog*."

Lash pulled her hair, trying to think of a way out. Another second and Bathory had it.

"Armory."

Lash snapped her fingers. "Duh, it's EMP-resistant. Dio, pile the warbots into the armory. Grab the patients and medibots from the infirmary, too. You have sixty seconds before I turn every bot within a mile radius into a paperweight."

He was already tapping his tablet screen and running. Not looking, he tripped over Helen's floating-off-the-ground hoverboard. He got back up and kept moving, warbots in pursuit.

"You, too," Lash ordered Bathory.

"Use my hoverboard," Helen said to the younger Academy kid, reaching into the backpack again and pulling out one of Lash's VAMPIR rockets. "I'll stick around to share my feelings with Westphal."

The redhead saluted them and jumped on the sandsurfer, flying after Dio and the warbots.

Helen extended the crossbow again. This time Lash accepted it. They nodded at each other.

A frightful explosion. Wooden splinters showered them as countless Hellfires impacted the towering oak doors that had separated Lash's team from the Red Angels spilling into the casino. It was a truly biblical scene, one that appealed to Lash's epic sensibilities. The pharaoh Westphal was destroying a pyramid-tomb to incinerate a rival king's child slaves.

"Sure the crossbow works?"

Lash shrugged. "Never had a chance to test it."

"I thought you designed it!"

Lash shook her head. "Koons. The kid who hacked the excavator—and is now operating it."

Helen slapped her thigh in dismay, then chewed her thumbnail. "How smart is Koons?"

"We're about to find out."

The heavy gates toppled over in their direction, stirring clouds of dust and hitting the floor with such force that Lash's boots bounced on the tiled lobby floor.

Helen propped the VAMPIR on her shoulder.

Lash raised the crossbow.

The Red Angels swarmed their way inside.

48

The arrow, such as it was, struck the lead Red Angel, enveloping it in the crackling sphere of an atmospheric charge. From there, the bubble swelled abruptly, expanding into a magnetic field that burned out power lines and electrical equipment and silicon chips.

It took only a few seconds to erase the dronescape, from Luxor to City-Center and on to Bellagio. The Red Angels crashed like ravens netted, then swatted to the ground, by an unseen assailant. They broke into fiery pieces, some exploding into cascading fragments that seared the lobby floor and ricocheted against faux Egyptian statues.

To her surprise and horror, Lash could feel every integrated circuit, every semiconductor, every microprocessor as it melted and faded to black. Crossbow thudding to the ground, she fell to her knees, hugged her elbows against her ears, and screamed.

The pain avalanching her mind was so unbearable, she started to go insane. She hadn't thought it all the way through, but now realized what she'd done and why she'd never do it again.

She'd essentially destroyed the central nervous system of a cybernetic body to which she was attached. Her connection to the digital realm had been partial up to this point, so she couldn't imagine the agony of annihilating a grid to which she was more deeply connected and for a longer period of time. It was as if a mad king had snatched her litter of newborn babies from her arms and dashed their little brains against a rock, all while drilling her own head with a corkscrew.

Another excruciating moment passed, then Lash felt completely fine. An apparition of her own cybernetic abortion-scrape would surely linger in her memory and dreams. She looked around to see the smoldering wreckage of Westphal's once-formidable UAVs.

"What was that?" Helen reached out to touch her friend but didn't make contact.

"That," said Lash, "was me injuring my own bioelectronics."

"You're a cyborg?"

Lash stood up to brush dust from her shirt. "Prof insists I'm the savior."

"Wow," murmured Helen, eyes widened by Lash's revelation.

They heard, and felt in the marrow of their skeletons, the ground-shaking rasp of twin 10,000-horsepower diesel engines. Realizing that the network was nonexistent, Westphal was playing her last card and having Koons move in the analog excavator to deliver the *coup de grâce*.

"Don't suppose," Helen said, "Dio might send in the warbots."

"He can't move them," said Lash, her mind having already scouted the possibility.

"Why not?"

"There's still an electromagnetic charge in the air. No GPS. No wireless. Just a void." Also, she wondered how she might kill Westphal without hurting Koons or having her blow his head off with a twitch of her finger.

The excavator's boom arm and mega-blade slammed into Luxor again, this time gouging a hole in a second side of the pyramid. Lash and Helen stooped, treading backward. They craned their necks toward the lobby ceiling to make sure nothing was falling on them.

"This hotel might not be a good place to stay anymore," Helen said.

Lash's heart sank at the notion of letting Westphal, via her old classmate, bulldoze Luxor like a kid's sandcastle. It was true that she was on record as having hated every moment she spent in this joyless tomb. But it was *her* tomb.

Besides, she'd made that promise to Bathory.

A thrumming gas-motor sound was coming down a hall that connected the front desk to the guest-room elevators. It was the slow-moving heavy-equipment transporter. Bathory was driving. Face ashen, she white-knuckled the steering wheel, obviously afraid she might run into something. Lash realized that Bathory had until now never manually driven a vehicle.

"Kids today can't do anything without computers," Helen cracked. "She going to tow Westphal to death?"

"She's already hauling something."

When the transporter entered the lobby, they saw what it was.

Atomic Annie, the massive World War II-era cannon Lash and Dio had studied before leaving to meet Koons at the mine.

The excavator bashed in a third side of the pyramid, the tremors powerful enough to cause Bathory to tumble from the transporter onto the floor. The transporter continued rolling, its giant tires on a course to crush the little redhead.

Lash jumped in to yank her to safety, then flung herself into the cab to depress the brake.

"Sorry," said Bathory, looking embarrassed.

"Hush," said Lash, soothing her. "You've been awesome. Now let's fire this thing."

"Hope it's loaded," Helen said.

Bathory checked Lash for validation.

"Helen, Bathory. Bathory, Helen."

"No one walks around the Academy with an unloaded weapon," Bathory told Helen.

"Aiming will be tough," Lash said.

They gazed up to see Koons pushing and pulling at the excavator's complex levers. He and Westphal were far away, but the boom arm was getting up close and personal, mega-pneumatics hissing, engines roaring, like Smaug primed to burn a shire of hobbits.

"Look!" Bathory yelped.

The showgirl from hell was having Koons raise the blade yet again, gathering momentum to deliver another structure-breaking blow to Luxor.

"Hurry," said Lash to Bathory and Helen. "Get the cannon up, and I'll do the targeting."

The other girls hand-cranked the wheel, elevating Atomic Annie's barrel. Grunting from the effort, Lash worked another turning device that swiveled the cannon's base. There was no scope on the weapon, so she had to line-of-sight her best guess.

"How many shells?" Helen asked.

"One," Lash said.

"Then make it count."

Lash had no choice. She had to sacrifice Koons to save the rest of them. She hand-jerked the old-fashioned breecher. It allowed propellant gas to exit the rear of the weapon during ignition. She coughed on acrid, sinus-ravaging fumes. The recoilless rifle fired the half-ton projectile mounted on the end of what was essentially a spigot inserted into the barrel. Atomic Annie hurled its load at the excavator.

But Lash had miscalculated.

The projectile bounded off the blade-spinning boom arm before shattering against the driver's cab housing Westphal. The glass cracked into pieces, the roof ripped from the steering compartment. Otherwise, the crone was unscathed.

"No!" Bathory cried. "It can't end like this!"

Lash could see Westphal cackling with heinous satisfaction, mocking Lash's failed efforts. The blade came down once more. A third side cratered now.

Before the blade could strike again, Lash dashed at the spinning bucket wheels.

Scrambling up the boom arm, she made constant adjustments to keep the wind from knocking her off the metal scaffolding. She'd never suffered vertigo in her life, but the combination of a moving excavator and a crumbling hotel caused her knees to buckle in fright. She used her mind to probe the giant earth-mining machine for vulnerabilities. Westphal likely knew enough about droning to force Koons to rip out the hackware. The beast's engine was snorting on pure combustion alone, with no circuit-based openings to exploit.

The excavator blade rose to the sky as Lash clung tightly to the boom arm's topside, struggling not to slide down its length headfirst.

It wasn't enough. She tumbled downward, smashing into the already-torn cab. The pain conjured stars, and she nearly blacked out.

With surprising strength, Westphal flung Koons aside; he fell on the floor of the cab with a sickening thud. Then she pulled a thin metal spike from her headdress and lunged at her would-be assassin. The knife struck the excavator's metal frame, shooting sparks.

Lash rolled out of the way and started ascending the boom arm again, this time in the other direction. She cast her mind out like a fishing net, again and again, trying to drag into the fight something she could control, but came up empty. She'd rendered everything inoperable with the crossbow. For the first time, she was panic-stricken. She didn't want to die like this.

A third of the way up, she heard Westphal cackle and wrench-pop the boom arm. Lash's grip on the scaffolding came loose. She began free-falling.

From the corner of her eye, she saw it. It was Richter's condorbot, the mechanical animal that had talon-scratched her at the mine, swooping in now to save her. The metal-surfaced Faraday box had been protected from the EMP burst.

It flew in close, soaring right at her. Lash desperately flailed at it, her fingers latching onto its legs. The condorbot did its best to break Lash's fall as she careened into a stack of empty plastic containers near the drinking fountain, deserted now because of the full-scale battle being waged on the Strip.

Beyond thirsty, throat inflamed by chemicals, she turned on the faucet, palm-splashing water into her mouth. Another sip and she'd be ready to try again at stopping Westphal.

She was about to re-enter the fray when she saw him. The creature was distinctly nonmechanical, organic, comprising real flesh and blood. He smelled of real-live organics.

The mustang she'd named Sally and fed carrots from the cafeteria.

The horse approached Lash, leaning into the battered girl with his long face. Alone together, each studied the other, making decisions.

Lash stroked his cheek, neck, and muzzle. "Hey, baby. You're alive. French-Canadian circus clowns didn't eat you after all."

A stallion, his body deep and big, with massive shoulders and large eyes and a tail set high. Up close to the animal, Lash couldn't help but feel insignificant.

She noticed bit marks on his mouth and spur-slashes on his belly. Clearly, someone had broken this horse not that long ago. He could be ridden, maybe, by a careful rider.

The excavator continued groaning and heaving and wrecking Luxor as Lash improvised a saddle with a towel discarded by the water fountain. Without stirrups, she climbed up the edge of the fountain to situate herself atop Sally.

The horse seemed to welcome the girl's weight.

Lash yelled, "*Giddyap!*" and clapped her heels, but it wasn't necessary.

The horse was already into a sudden run. He broke through swirling dust clouds and drove all out for the excavator's pulverizing treads. Westphal was pushing the digger to better swipe the pyramid's uppermost chambers, where the Sky Beam was housed. Lash held on as tight as she could as Sally was making for it with power she didn't know animals possessed. Galloping with this beast was like being pushed along by a surging cruise missile.

She bent herself close to the horse's neck and used her mind to search the electrified air for something to pit against the excavator. The condorbot had disappeared or flown clear of Lash's mental range. But then she sensed the sky-darkening presence of a government bomber.

It was a Taranis stealth drone, a semiautonomous warplane designed to fly intercontinental missiles, controllable from any point on Earth via satellite link. Lash could see it in her mind's eye in the air above Hoover Dam. In a minute or less, it would drop its nuclear payload on the Las Vegas Strip.

The horse continued to escalate his stride and made a great leap across the end-corner of an empty swimming pool and into a patch of withered bushes and dead grass. Then he charged up the side of the black pyramid, hooves slipping now and then, yet bringing Lash closer to Westphal. She tapped into orbiting satellites to mentally infiltrate the plane's onboard computer, squash its flight controllers, and wipe clean its preprogrammed flight path like a piece of cloth on dry-erase markings. She dimmed the drone's sensors as if slightly twisting a light bulb from a lamp socket, breaking the connection, then deactivated the warhead the way an electrical cord is tugged from an outlet. The Taranis was hers to command now, so she summoned it to her.

When the horse reached the pyramid's pinnacle, the Sky Beam turned on, in decent working condition despite the excavator's repeated blows. A narrow ray of light penetrated the nighttime sky, drawing bugs. The horse made another jump, this time into the ripped-open maw of the Sky Beam room, full of mirrors and lamps. The impact as he landed was minimal, as if Lash had floated down through the hole on the back of a magical Pegasus.

Prof was slumped face-first against the Sky Beam's manual control system, the computer deadened by the EMP pulse. Robe fluttering in the wind like a banner of infinite war, he raised his drywall-powdered head and smiled hideously, with his crushed features, at Lash.

"They're on their way," he said. "You have to stop them. But you'll beat them, I know it."

"They're already here," said Lash, dismounting. "And they're done."

Prof looked genuinely surprised. "You have possession of it?"

She nodded.

"You're faster and stronger than I imagined," he said, coughing. "Fang truly helped birth a messiah."

The excavator, however, was still alive and kicking Luxor's butt. Westphal was laughing her insane laugh as the mine-machine's boom arm swung upward to deliver a final blow to Prof and Lash and the hotel-tomb that had sheltered the Academy for so long.

The wind was fierce as Lash calmly shielded her eyes from the swirling grit. She looked up at Westphal and smiled without malice. She would kill the crone with a genial heart.

A subsonic vibration resolved into a buzzing noise, like a swarming plague of locusts. The mustang whinnied and reared in alarm. But Lash was in total control.

The Taranis, with its thirty-foot wingspan of black fiberglass, came Armageddon-crashing down on the excavator, hewing the blade cleanly into two separate parts. Luxor shuddered like a dollhouse. For a moment, Lash was terrified that the entire hotel might pancake in on itself, floor by floor, girder by girder. But the support struts somehow held firm. The drone-bomber impacted Westphal's steering cab, particle-splintering it into a frothy cloud of debris.

There was a period of silence as Lash, holding the horse's reins now, stared at Prof. He'd collapsed from the impact of the super-drone slamming into the mega-blade and had nearly fallen from the window, its glass wrenched free from the frame. He was struggling to pull himself to his feet as Lash approached.

"We—we can't stop here," he stammered, voice weak, but persistent. He blinked his vessel-burst eyes rapidly, repeatedly, going into shock from blood loss and a concussion. "We have so much to do now, Lash. Let me be your favored apostle. Appoint me your Saint Paul. I'll spread your message through the highways of the New Roman Empire."

"I do, in fact, have a message for my followers," said Lash, standing above him now.

"What? What is it?"

"Repent."

She booted him in the face, backflipping him through the busted-glass window. She leaned forward to watch his body somersault down the one undamaged wall of the pyramid and strike the concrete pavement thirty stories down.

To his credit, he didn't scream.

She walked over to the Sky Beam's control panel and shut it down, snuffing the Light of God. It was hers to wield now. It wouldn't signal drones, but instead serve as a beacon throughout the Southwest. From now on, without Prof, without Westphal and her Russians and flamingos, without her own mad drive for control and retribution, the valley would provide refuge.

She led the mustang to the industrial elevator, which she hoped still functioned. It did, though when they stepped out onto the casino floor, she couldn't fathom the damage. Most of the hotel's twenty-five hundred rooms had been demolished by the excavator, leaving Academy students with nowhere to sleep for the evening. They would have to set up tents and light a campfire. She wondered about marshmallows, remembering that they lasted a hundred years; someone might find them in some out-of-the-way place.

They'd sleep under starlight tonight. For the first time ever. Lash vowed that these kids, along with the students at Richter's school, would never again live underground like worms.

Mauled but not maimed, Richter stepped forward, smiling through his face bandage. "Nice horse," he said. "You're a regular Lady Godiva."

"I'd kiss you," said Lash, "but I'm worried it might hurt you."

"Hurt me," he said, pulling her close.

She smiled and was about to tell him all about the mustang when her father, unkempt, with ragged clothes, long hair, and a beard, approached. He was limping, but otherwise looked fit enough. Sane enough.

Tears welling, she said, "Daddy."

"Lash," he said, voice like sandpaper. "Icarus Girl. I can't believe how high you fly."

They embraced fiercely, Lash holding him close to her for a long, long time.

Until finally, her father said, "OK, c'mon, I love you, too. So when do we eat, *mija*?"

"Soon," Bathory said.

She'd already plucked, rinsed, and spit-skewered a few of Westphal's birds. A charcoal pit, enhanced with broken remnants of the poker room's furniture, roared. A Deacon, one arm shorn off in the battle, wheeled up, a saltshaker and peppermill from the cafeteria in its remaining pincer. No more Ambien-laced gruel-slop for the students of the Academy. No more Ritalin to keep their hunger in check and their attention chained to the oars of Prof's slave-ship. Rotisseried flamingo every night. If the refrigerators hadn't been blown up.

Helen led a medibot stretcher-pushing Duffy through the damaged hotel lobby and toward the infirmary. The bot had succeeded in surgically reattaching the girl's severed limb.

Lash stopped the bot to say thanks. "I owe you, Moonwolf."

"No," whispered Duffy, weak and pale from her whole ordeal. "We're even, OK?"

Lash kissed her brow and waved the bot onward.

When she looked up, Koons was standing in front of her.

"Thank you for leaving me the video," she said. "I don't know whose side you were on, but—"

"There's only one side now," he finished her thought, then blew out a long slow breath.

"Over marshmallows, you can tell me the whole story."

Koons laughed. "I barely recall what those taste like."

Luxor was in ruins, parts of it in flames as warbots sprayed foam on one another and themselves. But Lash wasn't worried about rebuilding the hotel. She had her students, her classmates, her boyfriend, and her long-lost dad at her side. She'd restored her family. After nursing their wounds, her drone-smashing team would be stronger than ever.

Between Richter's school and the Academy kids, Lash had an entire army at her cowgirl-in-the-sand command. She'd added a nuclear warhead to her arsenal—and cyborg-mind control. There would be hell to pay for the pain she and others had suffered from a government drunk on drones, thanks to a military-industrial complex that had spiraled out of control, sacrificing liberty for safety and achieving only horror.

Lash smiled, knowing her wrath was imminent.

ACKNOWLEDGMENTS

Thanks to my College of Southern Nevada (Henderson campus) students for reading and workshopping the earliest version of this novel. Thanks to Pat and Paul Jacob, and to David Himmel, for securing the best writing environments. Thanks to Deke Castleman and Alexis Noel Brooks for sanding this hammer into a steady instrument. Thanks to my parents for indulging my childhood appetite for comic books, sci-fi films, and rock music.

ABOUT THE AUTHOR

JARRET KEENE is an assistant professor in the English Department at the University of Nevada, Las Vegas, where he teaches American literature and the graphic novel. He has written books—a travel guide, a rock band biography, poetry collections—and edited short-fiction anthologies such as *Las Vegas Noir* and *Dead Neon: Tales of Near-Future Las Vegas*. He is the series editor of Las Vegas Writes, an annual literary anthology produced by Nevada Humanities and Huntington Press that showcases the best writing by Las Vegas authors.